———————————— ★ ————————————

Williams had his eyes on me and he leaned over to unlock the passenger door for me to slip in beside him. I was almost even with the front fender when the windshield exploded in a shower of glass.

I hit the ground unevenly, scuffing my palms on the curb. I crabbed my way on all fours to the driver's side of the car. I used the car bumper, then its hood, to pull myself to my feet. Crystalline chunks of windshield littered the hood's surface. Inside, Jim Williams sat strapped into the driver's seat with his shoulder harness in place.

The bullet had taken out the driver's window, half his face, and a good part of the front windshield. Assuming it was only one bullet. There could have been several, I supposed, with a silencer—I hadn't heard any of them. But then, everything happened so fast I realized now that I hadn't absorbed much of anything.

———————————— ★ ————————————

"...memorable details...and an edgy, paranoid atmosphere."

—*Booklist*

Forthcoming from Worldwide Mystery by
CONNIE SHELTON

HONEYMOONS CAN BE MURDER

MEMORIES
CAN BE
MURDER

CONNIE SHELTON

W✦RLDWIDE.

TORONTO • NEW YORK • LONDON
AMSTERDAM • PARIS • SYDNEY • HAMBURG
STOCKHOLM • ATHENS • TOKYO • MILAN
MADRID • WARSAW • BUDAPEST • AUCKLAND

For Grandma. I miss you so much.

MEMORIES CAN BE MURDER

A Worldwide Mystery/March 2002

First published by Intrigue Press.

ISBN 0-373-26414-3

Printed in U.S.A.

Acknowledgment

Special thanks and appreciation to those without whom this book would not have happened: Dan Shelton for his steady support and strong shoulders; Susan Slater for careful editing and fixes to the plot; and finally to the members of the Moreno Valley Writers Guild, the gang who have always encouraged me to do all this.

ONE

WE COME TO certain crossroads in our lives. It is inevitable. Some are planned—marriage, career changes, cross-country moves. At other times we come to these crossroads quite suddenly, with no warning. I was orphaned in such a way over fifteen years ago and managed to get on with my life anyway. But within the past few days the discovery of some boxes of old papers dumped my preconceived ideas about my own life suddenly and completely upside down.

Last Tuesday started out as an ordinary enough day. After a month-long jaunt to Kauai in September to help my fiancé close up house and make ready to move to New Mexico, I'd arrived back in Albuquerque to our characteristically perfect October weather. Several days of confinement in the office followed, my penalty for taking a month off. So it came to be that Tuesday was the day I spent a couple of hours visiting with my eighty-six year old neighbor Elsa Higgins, and Tuesday was the day she dropped the bombshell on me, the fact that the circumstances of my parents' death were not at all the way I'd always believed.

From the day I'd received that fateful news, delivered by my best friend Stacy's mother while I was sleeping over at their house, I'd been of the belief that my parents' flight had been a vacation trip to Denver on a big steady commercial aircraft. Now Elsa was informing me that theirs was a small private craft, chartered by Sandia Corporation, my father's employer. That the plane had gone down in the northern New Mexico mountains under suspicious circumstances. In my self-centered state at sixteen, I'd only absorbed the fact that my parents were gone, that I'd be moving in with Elsa Higgins, Gram as we'd always called her, until I could legally be on my own, and that I'd be missing the Spring Break dance that Saturday night. In my ultimate selfishness these things were important but not necessarily in their true order.

I'd locked myself away in my room to alternately pout and grieve. I'd watched little of the television news coverage, read no newspapers, and no one had ever thought later to explain it to me.

Gram made tamales last Tuesday afternoon and I'd simmered a pot of pinto beans all day. Sometime between this filling main course and the pecan pie that followed was when the conversation turned to the past. I left her house feeling a bit queasy—from the tamales, the pie, or the news, I wasn't sure.

In the intervening days, I've been rearranging my house and my style to accommodate the crates of Drake's household goods which will arrive in a few weeks time. He'll be here Monday.

This morning I decided that there was no way everything from two entirely full households would fit into my place. So I started in on the closets, discarding, rearranging, sorting through junk I haven't even looked at in years. By noon a decent sized pile awaited transfer to the attic. An even larger pile is going to the Goodwill, and three trash bags will get hauled off on Monday. I felt pretty good about my progress.

The pull-down stairs creaked in protest as I tugged the rope to bring them down. At least two cupfuls of dust sifted down into my hair and onto the floor in the hall. I tried to remember the last time I'd been into the attic, but couldn't. Certainly not within the past ten years, and maybe not the last fifteen.

I tested the ladder-like stairs with my weight then crab-crawled my way up, figuring I'd better check out the situation above before hauling any boxes up. The dust and cobwebs were incredible. Literally measurable in places, no dustcloth would have an effect on this stuff. I'd have to see if I could drag the vacuum cleaner up here.

Rusty, my ever-present red-brown canine helper, waited expectantly at the bottom of the stairs, his head cocked to one side. He probably wondered how on earth I'd opened a hole in the ceiling. I stood on the next-to-the-top step and surveyed the space, feeling my throat tighten as dust motes worked their way into my nostrils.

The attic was a large rectangular space high enough to stand up only in the center of the house. Where I stood now, above the hallway between the bedrooms, I would have to bend at the waist to enter. My father, at over six feet, must not have wanted to bother because about a dozen file boxes with his angular writing on the ends circled the opening. They'd been pushed about an arm's length away from the edge, with no attempt to stack or organize them. Beyond them, I could see evidence that my mother had, at one time, tried to institute some order.

Trunks and boxes lined the far walls. A baby crib, high chair, and folded wooden playpen stood against a far wall, unused for nearly thirty years, as I was the last kid. I wondered if they had planned any more after me. Maybe she'd kept the furniture in hopes that grandchildren would use them one day. Both my brothers had produced offspring, but Mother had not lived long enough to meet them.

Enough. I had work to do.

Rusty sniffed at my jeans and sneezed mightily as I descended the steps.

"Fool," I told him. "Teach you to stick your nose right into the dust."

He wagged and sneezed two more times.

I pulled the vacuum cleaner out of the hall closet. It's not one of those lightweight plastic jobs and I battled with it until I got it up the ladder and resting safely on the attic floor. Hauling myself up after it, I brushed my hands on my jeans and looked around for a place to plug it in.

A bare light bulb overhead with a string hanging from it provided the only light source. I pulled the string and scanned the sloping walls. The only electrical outlet I could find was an attachment the light bulb was screwed into, so I used that one and connected the hose attachment to the vacuum. Thirty minutes later I'd cut through some of the dust on the floors and scooted my father's file boxes to one area against the north wall.

I stacked the last box, attempting to make them take up less space, then turned and spotted a small rubber-banded group of papers lying on the floor. The age-rotten rubber band snapped when I picked them up, revealing a small notebook folded within the papers.

A memory from my childhood flashed into my consciousness like an electric shock. My father always carried this little leather notebook in his shirt pocket. A scientist always, he pulled it out at the oddest times and jotted notes about whatever idea or theory crossed his mind. I stroked the worn smooth cover. It was designed as a case to hold a small spiral notepad. I wondered what he did with the spirals once he filled them. Over the years he must have surely filled dozens.

I flipped open the cover. Every page began with the date written in his neat slanted writing in the upper right corner.

On the off chance that he might one day make a significant scientific discovery, I guess he wanted documentation.

The spiral I held must have been a fairly new one because only a few pages contained writing. The first entry was dated less than a month before his death. I flipped to the last written page. The notes were dated April 23, the day he died. Odd. Why would he write in the notebook that morning, then stash it in the attic before leaving for their trip? Why didn't he take the notebook with him? I couldn't remember a time when he hadn't had that little book somewhere on his person. I'd even seen him make notes while watching television in the evenings.

Something about my conversation with Gram three days ago clicked in. I'd always been under the impression that my parents were on their way to Denver for a weekend getaway. She'd told me that they were actually bound for Colorado Springs in a plane chartered by Sandia Corporation. If the trip was business, I *know* my father would have taken this little notebook with him. I flipped to the last page.

Heat really on, he'd written. *Call WA first thing Monday/ get protection.*

Get protection? What was that all about?

TWO

I STRAINED MY memory banks but could recall very little detail about my father's professional life. As a scientist at Sandia Labs during the cold war years, he'd been sworn to secrecy to such a degree that it was probably a wonder that he dared to keep any kind of written journal. He'd certainly never carried stories home, and I couldn't even remember him mentioning names of fellow workers very often.

The late afternoon sun poked dustily through a vent at the far end of the attic. Characteristically for October, the temperature had dipped into the thirties overnight, but climbed to something over seventy this afternoon. In sweatshirt, jeans, and heavy socks, I realized I was becoming sticky. I gathered the small group of loose papers with the little notebook and jammed them into my back pocket. Unplugged the vacuum cleaner and pulled the light cord before heading shakily down the ladder.

Rusty danced little circles around me when I finally descended, glad to see me back on familiar ground again. I let him out to romp in the back yard while I put my cleaning stuff away and carried the boxes I'd originally planned to store back up the ladder. Thirty minutes later I realized my back was aching and I was stickier than ever.

I stripped off the jeans and sweatshirt and spent fifteen luxurious minutes under the shower. The outside temperature had begun to drop back to evening levels by the time

I wrapped myself in a terry robe and let Rusty back in. He shot me a winsome look while I fixed myself a plate of crackers and cheese and poured a glass of wine. I filled his bowl with yummy nuggets and carried my feast into the living room where I could watch the news and look back through Dad's papers while I ate.

Have Hannah cancel dentist. Hannah—his secretary. What was her last name? I sipped at my wine. I could picture her in my mind. Shirtwaist dresses, dark hair in a bun, sensible shoes. She'd probably been in her fifties at the time I'd met her as a young kid tagging along on errands with my mother. She'd have to be seventy or more today. I wondered if she was still in Albuquerque or even still living.

Hannah, Hannah...what was her last name?

I flipped through the loose papers that had been rubber banded together with the notebook. Several of them were pink telephone message slips, faded now to pale salmon. *Jack Cudahy X243* was the only thing written on one of them. Jack Cudahy, our Congressman? I didn't realize he'd ever been affiliated with Sandia. 243 must have been his phone extension. No number was given because it was an internal call. The slip was dated April 10 and the initials at the bottom were HS. Hannah Simmons. The name clicked into place easily.

My feet were getting cold so I went into my bedroom for a pair of socks, then carried my empty dinner plate to the kitchen. I pulled the phone book from the cupboard beside the kitchen phone and looked up Simmons. There were probably twenty of them, but only two beginning with H, Harold and H.B. I vaguely remembered that Hannah had not been married so I took a chance that she was H.B.

"Ms. Simmons? I hope I have the right number," I apologized. "Did you work at Sandia Labs years ago?"

The voice sounded elderly and hesitant.

"The reason I asked is that my father was a scientist there and I'm trying to locate his secretary."

"Are you Bill Parker's girl?" she asked.

I acknowledged that I was.

"Well, Charlie, for goodness sakes! You know I often wondered about you kids after Bill and Arlene died."

"We're all doing fine, thanks." I explained briefly that I'd just come across some reminders of Dad and told her I'd like to get together with someone who knew him well.

"Why don't you come over tomorrow," she invited. "I just got a sack of apples from Dixon. My neighbor drove me up there this morning, and I was planning on baking a pie. I'll do it in the morning and we can have us a cup of tea and a nice visit."

She gave me directions and I told her I'd be there around two o'clock. I hung up the phone feeling a mixture of anticipation and dread.

The next morning I puttered around the house, carrying the remaining boxes of junk up to the attic. The dust had settled a bit today, making the atmosphere less oppressive. I stashed my stuff against one wall, thinking that one day I really should get up here and clean out the old things my parents had stored all those years ago. After all, what use could I possibly ever have for baby furniture or scientific notes?

By noon, I was coated with dust again. I took a quick shower and made a sandwich for lunch. At one-thirty I told Rusty to guard the house while I was gone and I headed across town to the address in the northeast heights that Hannah Simmons had given me.

Her all-brick home was located near the fairgrounds, at one time on the very outskirts of the city but now smack in the middle of town. The white bricks had aged to a golden blond and the yard was neat with precise arbor vitae flanking the front door and pyracantha bushes hiding their deadly spikes behind thick clusters of orange berries. The Bermuda grass lawn was now tawny gold for fall, so the only highlights of color aside from the orange berries came from several fat bunches of chrysanthemums in bright purple, orange, and yellow. A ten-year-old blue midsize car sat in the driveway. I parked at the curb.

Hannah Simmons greeted me with frank curiosity. I got the feeling that she was scanning my face for physical traces of my father's genes. She had changed vastly from my childhood memory of her. I'd remembered her as tall, dark, and somewhat intimidating. Now she'd shrunk to just around five feet, with rounded shoulders, gray skin and white hair. Her blue eyes, once piercing, had become narrow slits behind her glasses, like it was painful for her to open them very wide. We both seemed at a loss for words for a couple of minutes.

Finally, she pushed the screen door open toward me. "Well, Charlie," she smiled, "it's so good to see you. You're not a little girl any more."

Yeah, twenty-some years will do that. "No, I guess I'm not," I assured her. "And how are you doing these days?"

She led me into a living room crowded with heavy old-fashioned furniture and carpeted with a gold sculptured weave that had long ago lost its sculpture. Paintings of ranchland and open prairies decorated the walls, while shelves at one end of the rectangular room were filled with memorabilia from a decade or two of retirement travel. The air was heavy with the scent of apples and cinnamon, reminding me of the promise that dessert awaited.

"Just set your purse there if you want, dear," Hannah said. "I'm going to put a kettle on for some tea."

I browsed the knick-knacks on the shelves while she ducked into the kitchen. Pictures in metal dime store frames filled a couple of the shelves—Hannah on a camel in front of the Great Pyramids, Hannah looking tiny and lost in front of the Taj Mahal, a group shot of thirty or forty people by the Eiffel Tower, Hannah standing before an indistinguishable plaque somewhere with high mountains in the background. Hannah looked timid and uncertain in each shot; none of them evoked joy or fun.

"I see you found my travel collection," she chuckled behind me. "See these little elephants? They came from Kenya." She pointed to a graduated set of carvings, the largest elephant being about three inches tall and the smallest around a half-inch.

I made some polite exclamations over each item she pointed out. When the tea kettle whistle interrupted, just before she was about to name all the people in the group photo, I quickly offered to help slice the pie.

We carried plates and cups to the kitchen table and settled in.

"Hannah, I wanted to ask about he plane crash," I told her. "You see, I only recently found out that Dad was on business and that it was a Sandia plane. I also found that little notebook he used to carry all the time."

She nodded, remembering his lifelong habit.

"One of the last notes in the book said something like 'The heat is on.' What would that mean?"

She finished chewing and took a swallow of tea before answering. "Well, Charlie, I really don't know, dear. It's been so many years, you know."

"What about the plane crash? I'm embarrassed that I didn't pay much attention to the news coverage when it happened, but a friend recently told me there were some suspicious circumstances. What happened?"

"Oh, yes, my goodness. It was quite a big deal at the time. You know, top scientist and wife killed. Not to mention a couple of other people from our office who were to attend the meeting too. Actually, I was supposed to go along to take notes for Mr. Parker, but I caught a cold that week and had stayed home the previous day. He told me to stay home again because the trip would probably make it worse. Actually, I thought he just didn't want to catch my germs, confined in the airplane like that. I would have gone down too, if only I hadn't been sick." She shivered, remembering.

"What about the suspicious circumstances? I always thought it happened because of weather or something."

She offered more tea but I declined. "Well, the weather certainly didn't help. It was spring, you know, which can mean unpredictable weather at best. Anyway, they were up in those high mountains in the northern part of the state, around Cimarron or Red River, or someplace like that. And one of those spring storms came through—dumped over a foot of snow on the plane before the rescuers could get in and find them.

"But the suspicious thing didn't have anything to do with weather. Of course they called in the National Transportation Safety Board to investigate—that's standard. When all was said and done, they found evidence of an explosion on board."

My heart thudded to the bottom of my stomach.

THREE

AN EXPLOSION. My head reeled with the implications. Coupled with Dad's cryptic note "the heat is on," I tried to imagine what might have been going on. Could the "heat" have been someone high up in the company? The law? The Soviets?

"Of course, we had so much top secret work going on at the Labs during those years," Hannah continued, "no one wanted to speculate very much."

"What did the investigation turn up?"

"As I recall, they only said there was an explosion. Any questions that were raised, you know by the news people or anyone like that, were shoved aside by hinting that national security could be at risk. You know the cold war was still very much alive and well back then. Russia, China, and half of Eastern Europe were our enemies. We couldn't chance any sensitive information getting out to them.

"Even the news coverage was purposely kept brief. I don't even remember if they told about the explosion. Hold on a minute," she said, "I might just have a copy of the clipping." She stood up and started toward the living room.

I followed to find her rummaging through a built-in cupboard below the knick-knack shelves. She pulled out a scrapbook bound in red vinyl and carried it to the sofa. I sat beside her as she opened the cover and began to page through it.

Without a husband or children to fill the pages, Hannah's scrapbook consisted of her work and retirement lives. The work recollections were necessarily brief because of the secret nature of the company. Most of the memorabilia consisted of newspaper clippings and occasional company party and picnic shots. No letters or personal notes were evident. It made me wonder all the more about my father's possession of a notebook. Wouldn't that have been viewed as highly suspicious by the upper echelons?

Hannah soon found what she was looking for. Two short news clippings, quite yellow and crisp now, covered the story. One headline read "Prominent Scientist Feared Lost." Apparently written before the downed plane was located. The other started: "Aircraft Located—No Survivors." It recapped the location of the place, the fact that new snow had covered the scene, and listed the names of those on board—my mother and father among them. Dad was described as "A prominent scientist with Sandia Corporation," nothing more and certainly nothing about his work.

"Was this all?" I asked.

"Everything that made it into print," she said. "They never even gave the cause of the crash to the media people. By the time the NTSB had done their investigation, the story had cooled in the public eye and they were able to keep that part of it pretty hush-hush.

"Course at the office, we knew about the explosion, but even there, no one asked many questions. It was just part of the job. You knew when to keep your mouth shut and when not to ask. Everyone went through numerous clearance checks before getting work there, so that was one thing we all knew, not to talk about anything we heard or saw on the job."

"Was there any speculation? I mean, even people in top

secret jobs get together for a beer after work, and maybe there was a little talk?''

"If there was, I never heard it," she said emphatically. "Course, I wasn't one of the bunch that went out for beer. I just never got into doing that." She looked pensive for a minute. "Maybe I'd know more now if I had."

"Can you give me some names? Maybe some people that Dad worked with? Some of those who did go out together now and then?" I asked.

"Well, let me think. It's been so many years now." She paused and gazed at the ceiling. "Jack Cudahy. That one pops to mind right away."

"Jack Cudahy, the Congressman? Really? He worked out there?"

"Sure did. He wasn't a scientist, you know. Had some political connections even then. Something back in Washington."

I pulled a small pad from my purse and wrote it down, although I doubted I'd forget that name. As she talked, Hannah remembered several more names and I put them down too, along with bits of other information she came up with.

By the time an hour had passed, she was degenerating into stories about the neighbor's children. Figuring that the useful information had run out, I began to make exit noises so I could make a graceful escape.

Realizing that it was well into Saturday afternoon and knowing that Drake would be arriving Monday, I stopped at the grocery store to stock up on his favorites before going home.

Rusty greeted me, in true dog fashion, like we'd been separated a month. He bounded out into the back yard to romp and rub his back on the grass. The temperature hovered over seventy, with a deep blue October sky and no wind.

This time next month we'd be facing bare trees, gray days, and my thirty-first birthday. And Drake would be here, living with me full-time, and trying to make me decide on a wedding date. I glanced at the diamond on my left hand.

It was incredibly beautiful, but I didn't want to think about marriage that way. I wanted to be sure we knew each other well enough. It had only been six months since we met and out of all that time, we'd only been in touching range maybe two months. I keep putting him off about a wedding date until we have a little more time under our belts.

Rusty continued to luxuriate in the joy of rubbing his nose in the green lawn, while I stretched out in a lounge chair to take advantage of the last few hours of those last few precious autumn days. I tried to put my father's note-book and Hannah's revelations out of my head, but it didn't work. Fifteen minutes later I went back inside.

Still satisfied with the apple pie and tea I'd had at Hannah's, dinner consisted of a bag of popcorn done in the microwave and shared with Rusty as I flipped back through the scraps of messages and notes I'd begun to accumulate. By eight o'clock I'd compiled a master list of names I'd like to contact, with addresses as nearly as I could get them from the phone book.

Top secret or not, I had a nagging need to know more about the crash and its cause. I fell into an uneasy sleep sometime after midnight with my mind awhirl.

By seven a.m. I could no longer pretend at sleep. As the sun crossed my bed in rose-gold stripes, I dragged myself from under the warm covers and pulled on the jeans and sweater I wore yesterday.

Rusty watched curiously as I brushed my teeth and pulled my hair into a ponytail. I rummaged through the refrigerator while he made a trip outside. Knowing that Drake would arrive within twenty-four hours made me conscious of my waistline, so I sensibly chose cereal with lowfat milk over the more enticing cinnamon rolls. Like one day's dieting would really matter.

I decided that waffling around the house all day, with my mind jumping from thoughts of the plane crash to thoughts of Drake moving in, would be counterproductive so I decided to spend a Sunday in the office so I could comfortably take Drake's first few days here to be with him. Although he would eventually have to get used to the fact that I do have a job and the honeymoon can't last forever.

Rusty bounded out to the Jeep with me as soon as I mentioned the word "go." Within ten minutes, we were pulling into the parking lot behind the old Victorian that houses our offices in a semi-commercial, semi-residential part of town. I noted briefly that the yard service had not yet cleared the flower beds or given the lawn and hedges a final trim for the year. I'd have to call them this week if they didn't come Monday or Tuesday.

The office was quiet and cool. We'd soon have to get the heating system fired up for winter too. I started the coffee-maker for a half-pot and put the sack lunch I'd made myself into the refrigerator. Rusty made his rounds of the rooms, checking to see whether Sally or Ron were around. He returned unsatisfied a couple minutes later.

"Sorry, kid," I told him, "I don't think anyone else is coming in today."

I walked up to the reception area to see if Sally had left any messages for me. Her desk appeared neat and uncluttered, as usual. Ron's desk was the very opposite, a disaster area that never changed. Neither Sally nor I will touch it. She had tossed a couple of pink message slips on top of the mess.

My own office brightened considerably when I opened

the blinds on the south-facing bay window. The autumn sun should do a lot toward warming the room within a few minutes. I'd left things in pretty good order but a pile of new mail stood in a small heap in the center of the polished wood surface. Warm coffee scent drifted up the stairs from the kitchen so I went back down to fill a mug before sitting down to tackle the mail with letter opener in hand.

Ten minutes later I had separated out Ron's mail and delivered it to his chair. Anything left on the desk top was subject to being lost forever. My own work was sorted into stacks of billing to do, bills to pay, and letters to answer. Luckily, I was able to funnel some of the correspondence over to Ron. He's really the private investigator here—I'm supposed to be the financial wizard.

I put my wizardry to work once the computer booted up. Entered payables first, then consulted Ron's time sheets to produce billing for several clients. One was an aviation company that was having Ron do background checks on some new employees. The plane crash situation came rushing back into my consciousness.

Maybe I should ask Ron if he had a contact person within the NTSB. If I could get my hands on the accident report it might help clarify some things that Hannah hadn't been able to fill in. Maybe Ron would be up for some of Pedro's green chile chicken enchiladas tonight. He and I really should talk about the whole situation. After all, they were his parents too. He should know about the notebook and papers I'd found.

I picked up the phone and dialed his number. Got the machine—he was probably out with his kids on a Sunday like this, throwing a ball around in a park somewhere. I suggested to the answering machine that he might give me a call and we could make some dinner plans.

By noon, I'd pretty well taken care of my financial duties

so I stopped for a lunch break before redirecting my energies toward cleaning the offices. Rusty dutifully waited for sandwich crusts and caught a few stray potato chips that managed to leap toward the floor. I switched off the coffeemaker, scoured out the sink, and wiped off counter tops and refrigerator. Picked up a dust cloth and headed toward Sally's office and the conference room. I was well into spraying furniture polish and rubbing it around on the desktops when I heard a noise in the kitchen.

FOUR

MY MUSCLES FROZE. Hadn't I locked the back door?

Rusty dashed down the hall, toenails scrabbling on the hardwood floor, hair raised on his neck.

"Hey, there," a male voice soothed, followed by high pitched kid sounds. Ron and his boys.

I lowered the spray can I'd automatically aimed toward the doorway. Rusty zipped toward me, tail lowered, headed for the crawl space under Sally's desk. Three munchkins in stair-step order dashed after him.

"Rusty! Come here!" their pint-sized voices command-ed.

"Whoa, whoa," I intervened. "Give him some time and don't all of you chase him down at once."

I reached out an arm to capture the lead kid. Justin, Jason, and Joey. What had Ron and Bernadette been thinking when they assigned these confusing names to three kids only fours years apart in age? How did they think I'd ever keep them straight? Especially when they each grew two sizes every time I saw them.

Ron idled into the room. "Anything happening here?" he asked.

"Not much. There might be a couple of new phone mes-sages on your desk, but I can't really tell. The new mail is on your chair. I left a message on your machine. Any chance we might have dinner tonight? I have something important to talk about."

He glanced at the kids, then at me. I shook my head slightly

"They have to be back at Bernadette's by seven. I could come over after that. Or I could meet you somewhere?"

I thought about it. "Well, this is kind of sensitive. How about picking up some enchiladas at Pedro's and bringing them over? I think we need to talk about this privately."

He gave me a quizzical look but was interrupted by a kid pulling at his shirt tail.

"It's not about Drake moving here, is it?" he asked.

"Oh no, I'm ready and eager for that."

He relaxed visibly. He and Drake had hit it off so well when they met this past summer that Ron would have probably been the most disappointed if things didn't work out for me and my pilot.

"He gets here tomorrow, right?"

"Yeah. That's why I thought we should go over this other stuff tonight. I may get busy…"

He grinned in a way that made me blush.

I tossed the dust cloth at him. "Just shut up and bring enchiladas when you come."

The kids trailed behind him, whining to be allowed to get a soda from the kitchen. He told Justin to get one can and they could all three share it. This met with some groans but hey, life is tough.

I continued to work my way with the dustcloth around the reception and conference rooms, then on to my office, saving Ron's office and the bathroom for last. At some point Ron and the boys left, with a vague "See ya later" in my direction. I ran the vacuum cleaner over the hardwood floors and Oriental rugs and made an ineffectual stab at Ron's office before deciding to call it a day.

The sun was a large ball of fire over the western volcanoes as I drove down Central Avenue toward my own quiet neighborhood. The tall trees in this older part of town were well into turning shades of brilliant gold and rich amber. The late sun intensified the colors, making them just short of painful to the eyes. In another couple of weeks, we'd be raking all that color off the lawns.

The air cooled considerably as the earth swallowed up the bottom of the fire ball in little increments. Smoke drifted in little tendrils from chimneys along the block as I approached my house. We'd soon lose that too, as the city declared "red" air alert days when the winter inversion set in.

By the time Ron arrived with two Styrofoam containers emitting green chile fumes, I was more than ready. I blended up some margaritas and, although they lacked something that Pedro managed to accomplish, they were passable. We set to work on the enchiladas before they could cool off.

"I was clearing out some stuff from the attic the other day," I told Ron, "when I came across a lot of Dad's old papers. Did you know he stored notes up there?"

"Well, he always carried that little leather notebook."

"Yeah, and apparently a lot more. I found file boxes full of stuff. I haven't had time to look through much of it, and it's probably so scientific that I wouldn't know what I was reading anyway. But I did find something interesting."

I cut through another bite of tortilla, chicken and cheese before describing the notes I'd seen. "That one notation 'the heat is on' really bothered me. Especially since he wrote it the morning of the day he died."

I told him about visiting Hannah Simmons and showed him the list of names I'd compiled.

"Do you remember any of these people?" I asked. Ron

is six years older than I and he was probably a lot more conscious of everything that was happening at the time of the crash.

He scanned the list while chewing slowly.

"Hmm, George Myers, Wendel Patterson...those names ring a bell. And didn't Harvey Taylor and Larry Sanchez bowl in a league together or something?"

"I don't know. I was a high school kid then, Ron. So wrapped up in dances, clothes, boys—I just wasn't interested in Dad's work life. Guess I only cared that he brought home enough money for a new prom dress."

"Don't be so hard on yourself," he said, patting me on the hand. "Kids are always like that." I wondered for a second whether he really was referring to me or if he was losing touch with his own kids.

His attention was already back to the list. "I think you have the wrong address for George Myers. Seems like I remember something about him moving up to the Holiday Park area."

"Okay. If I can get a phone number for him, I can still see about talking to him."

"What do you plan to talk about anyway, Charlie? These guys will have all retired ten years ago. They don't know anything that's going on out there any more."

"But that's just the point. I need to know what was going on *then*. Why Dad was keeping these notes. What he meant about the heat being on. Why his plane exploded and why that fact wasn't brought out."

"It was all top secret government work, Charlie. The cold war and all that. Remember, Dad wouldn't even talk about work to us? Every time Mother asked how his day went, the most she'd get out of him was, 'Fine'."

"I know. But a lot of this stuff has to be declassified by now. The cold war is long over, so what harm can it do to ask around. I'd just like to know that if Dad died for his country, it really was something worth dying for. And if that plane exploded needlessly, then someone is responsible and someone is running around out there free while our parents are dead."

I took a large swig of margarita and nearly choked.

"You're right about that part," he agreed. "I'd never really considered it, but there could be someone out there who got away with murdering five people."

"Do you have any contacts at the NTSB, Ron? Could we somehow get hold of a copy of their findings. Hannah told me they did conclude that there was an explosion, but then everything was hushed up. She never heard that the investigation went any further. I want to know why."

"I'll see what I can do." He twisted at a non-existent mustache. "We investigators haf our vays, you know."

I cleaned up the food remains after he left, feeling like we might start to move forward with some answers. I'd like to get back up into the attic and start going through the rest of those boxes. Maybe after Drake had been here a few days and we'd had a chance to settle in a little.

That night I dreamed that Drake and I were in a small plane over the mountains. I woke up sweating and shaking just before a fireball consumed me.

FIVE

THE 767 ROLLED UP to the jetway as I pasted myself to the terminal windows in hopes of catching sight of Drake. Tiny dark silhouettes moved behind the little square windows but none were recognizable. I edged toward the open door where the passengers would emerge.

He was among the first dozen or so to walk out and he agilely dodged around a wide woman to grab me up in a huge hug.

"God, that was the world's longest flight," he said. "I was so eager to be here."

We kissed unabashedly while the crowd flowed around us.

"How many bags do you have?" I asked, once we'd walked down the long tiled corridor and taken the two escalators to the baggage claim area.

"Just one. The movers are bringing everything but my immediate wardrobe. In fact, I've been in Hawaii so long I don't even own many winter clothes. I'll probably need to buy a bunch of new things. You can lend your expertise on that."

Like I'm a real clothing expert. My own jeans and T-shirt wardrobe is, of course, completely up to date in the fashion world.

I stood back as Drake joined the crowd at the carousel. His trim body and dark hair with just a touch of gray at the temples were still enormously attractive to me. I glanced again at the ring on my left hand. A few months ago I couldn't imagine sharing my home and my life with anyone. Now I couldn't imagine my life without him.

We walked out into the cool autumn evening to grab lungfuls of bus and taxi exhaust. I pointed the direction to the parking garage and we located the Jeep without hassle. Ten minutes later we were cruising I-25, making the transition onto I-40. Traffic slugged along, coming to a clog then miraculously thinning out again with no visible reason for the slowdown.

Rusty leaped at Drake the minute we entered the house, twisting and leaning into Drake's legs in hopes of getting his back scratched.

"Hey, boy, how are you?" Drake made growling noises as he obliged the dog's wishes.

"Are you hungry?" I asked, heading toward the kitchen. I circled the living and dining rooms, pulling drapes and switching on additional lights. Figured by staying busy, I might avoid that awkward moment where we would stand in the hall shrugging our shoulders at each other and wondering what to say next. Moving in together was a different experience for both of us.

"Do we have anything to make a sandwich with? And maybe a beer?" He'd set his bag down behind the sofa and headed toward the kitchen. We nearly collided at the door.

"I can get it," he assured me. "Please? I don't want us to fall into some kind of pattern where you think you ought to wait on me."

That was fine with me. I didn't want to get into a pattern of waiting on *anyone*. I reached out to put my arms around him and received a kiss that weakened my knees in return.

"You know where everything is here; help yourself." When he'd spent a week here this past summer, I'd found

Drake to be extremely capable in the kitchen. And when I'd spent a month at his place, we worked together well, although his culinary expertise far outshines mine. I pride myself on being able to come up with acceptable fare from cans and boxes, with slight help from the microwave. Drake actually uses recipes. I even saw him use the oven a couple of times.

I left the kitchen to his expertise and I took his bag to the bedroom. Rusty opted to stay with Drake since that seemed like the better bet for tidbits that might fall his way. I returned to the kitchen to find Drake pulling something out of the oven. He took the split submarine roll topped with shaved ham, sliced tomatoes, and melted cheese and deftly sliced it into several sections and placed the sections on two plates.

"I thought you might be hungry by now, too," he offered. "What would you like to drink?"

I rummaged through the fridge and came up with a Coke. We took our seats at the kitchen table—I had a brief flash forward to the two of us in these same chairs thirty years from now. The vision felt reassuring and comfortable.

"Here's to us," he said, raising his beer glass. I touched it with the rim of mine.

"To us."

His smile went straight to my heart.

"You'll never guess what happened when I went up to the attic to store some old stuff away," I said.

His cheek bulged with sandwich so he merely shrugged his shoulders.

"I found some old papers that belonged to my father." I filled him in briefly on everything I'd learned from Elsa Higgins and from Hannah Simmons.

"I thought the plane was commercial," he said.

"I always did, too. This all came as a complete surprise."

"So, what are you going to do about it?"

"Ron's going to see if he can get a copy of the NTSB report. Normally, I would think they'd follow through but this time it appears that someone hushed up the investigation. Drake, can you imagine? There was an explosion on board and nobody bothered to follow it up and find out what happened?"

He reached out and ran his index finger along my jawline. "What else is bothering you, sweetheart?"

Tears welled up. "I don't know. I feel so guilty. I should have asked more questions at the time. I was so damned concerned with myself then. I mean, I was more worried about missing a stupid *dance* that weekend than about finding out what really happened. Now the trail's probably completely cold. How many clues can possibly exist after all these years?"

"I'll help if I can," he said gently. "And stop that guilty stuff. There was nothing you could have done that would have changed the outcome, now is there?"

I shook my head mutely.

"And I defy you to find a teenager anywhere that isn't more full of themselves than any other subject on earth. Right?"

He picked up a napkin and dabbed at my cheeks for me.

"Now, you want to hear some really good news?" he asked. "I think I've found a ship."

"Drake, that's great! Your own helicopter. So…what's the plan? What kind is it? What kind of work will you get? Come on…"

He pushed his plate back and interlaced his fingers. "Well, I was talking to one of the tour operators on Kauai a couple of days ago and he mentioned that a mutual friend of ours in Colorado was getting two new machines and might be looking to sell one of his used ones. So, I called the guy. Hadn't seen him in years. We worked together about twenty years ago in South America, and he remembered me right away."

I sipped at my Coke, listening to the growing enthusiasm in his voice.

"Anyway, it's true, he does have an aircraft he'd like to sell and he's willing to make me a deal on it. He'll carry the financing and provide maintenance if I want him to."

"What kind of money is he talking about?"

"We didn't get down to anything specific yet. I'll need to go up there and take a look at the records, find out what kind of time is left on the components, all that stuff."

"Do you think it's a good move?"

"Well, I'm gonna have to work my butt off to line up some work for the machine. I'll have to put some numbers to it, but obviously I'll have to fly some minimum number of hours a month to make it pay. I have some government contacts in Arizona, since I grew up in Flagstaff, but not too much here. I'll just have to get out and hustle to find out what I need to do."

"Ask Ron about that kind of stuff too. He knows lots of people around here. I'm always amazed at where he comes up with contacts."

He grinned like a little kid. "This could be my chance, Charlie. I've always wanted to have my own operation, maybe in some little out-of-the-way place."

"Albuquerque isn't a major hub, you know, but I wouldn't exactly call it out of the way."

"We'll see. Maybe there's work to be had around here too, but I'm thinking that some of the rural areas that don't already have any helicopter service might be good bets. Remember that little town we went to this summer?"

Valle Escondido. Sally's hometown where we'd discovered dirty goings-on. It really was a beautiful area though.

"Anyway," he continued, "I thought I might buzz up to Pueblo to check out this aircraft in the next week or two. Want to come?"

"Sure, that sounds like fun." I told him how I'd asked Ron to check out the NTSB report on the plane crash and that I'd like to see if I could find out more about that before going out of town.

I caught him staring at me with that certain tender look in his eyes. The next thing I knew we were in the shower together, leaving Rusty to worry about cleaning up the kitchen.

We awoke early Tuesday morning, with our legs entwined, my face buried against Drake's chest. I raked my nails lightly down his back, causing him to stretch and pull me closer.

"Mfmph!" I struggled.

He backed away. "What?"

"That means I love you but I can't breathe."

"Sorry." He stroked my hair. "I guess I just don't want you to get away."

"You don't have to worry about that," I assured him. "I have no desire to get away. Except maybe to go to the bathroom?"

He released me to attend to immediate needs. Rusty raised his head, watching me from his rug at the foot of the bed. By the time I emerged, he was standing at the door wagging anxiously to go out. I slipped on a robe and let him lead me to the back door. When I returned, Drake had made the bed and was brushing his teeth.

"Can I take you out to breakfast?" I asked. "Then maybe we can go by the office—Ron and Sally will be eager to know whether you made it home."

"And you might be just a little eager to know whether Ron got any leads on that accident report?"

He read me so easily. He wiggled his eyebrows at me as he plugged in his electric razor.

"Okay, okay, you're right."

An hour later, we'd stuffed down a couple of Egg McMuffins and were pulling into the rear parking lot at the office. Both Ron's convertible and Sally's four-wheel drive waited there. Rusty bounded out as soon as I opened the car door for him and raced to the porch.

Sally stood at the kitchen sink, rinsing the coffeepot. Now in her fifth month of pregnancy, she had begun wearing loose shirts to cover her growing tummy. At least she'd gotten past the green-faced mornings.

"Hi, Drake," she exclaimed, pulling him into a big hug. "It's good to see you again."

He blushed and made some greeting noises.

"So, are you all moved in?"

"My household stuff won't arrive for awhile yet," he said, "but Charlie has everything rearranged at the house so it will all fit when it gets here. So far, the only thing I really need is my truck. I have the feeling Charlie will get tired of chauffering me around by the time it gets here."

I squeezed his hand to reassure him that I wasn't about to get tired of his company.

"I'm going up to check my mail while you two visit," I told him.

Sally was reciting their list of possible baby names by the time I reached the stairs.

Ron sat tipped back in his office chair when I peeked into his room.

"Hey, did you find out who we should contact at the NTSB?" I asked.

"Better than that," he grinned. He held up several pages of fax paper. "I've got the entire report here. And the name of a contact person."

"Wow, you *are* good."

"I haven't talked to the investigator yet, but he's still with the agency, still here in Albuquerque, so it shouldn't be too hard to reach him."

"And the report? What does it say?"

"I'm just getting into that. Come here and read over my shoulder." He beckoned, sliding his chair forward so I could squeeze in behind him.

I read quickly, through lots of technical terminology and paragraph upon paragraph describing the location of the crash and the scene. By the third page, my eyes were glazing over and I knew I'd have to reread this carefully when I could analyze and fully absorb it. Ron was reading slowly, word for word, while I was eager to get to the bottom line.

When he turned to page four, I jumped to the bottom of the sheet. There were a couple of paragraphs describing the composition of the explosive material in great technical detail, none of it making sense to me. But the words that did stand out were there. Conclusion: explosion on board, most probably originating in the pilot's carry-on bag.

SIX

THE PILOT? Why on earth would the pilot have carried the explosive material on with him? A suicide motive? Blackmail, a threat, or had he brought the death vehicle aboard without knowing it?

That seemed the most likely scenario to me.

I turned to watch Ron's face. His concentration was total. About two-thirds of the way down the page, as he reached the final section, his eyes began to scan faster. As he read the final paragraphs I watched his face register shock, then disbelief. He turned to me, his eyebrows pulled tightly together in a deep V.

"Hey, Ron, how's it going?" Drake's appearance broke the intense moment.

Ron stood to shake hands and I stepped aside.

"Still got that nine-millimeter Beretta?" Drake asked.

"I sure do. When do you want to go out to the range again?"

I stepped across the hall to my own office, leaving them to talk guns. When Drake had visited this past summer, Ron and I had been in the middle of an on-going argument about gun control. Breaking down my longstanding distrust of guns, Ron and Drake had taken me to the gun range on the west side of town, where I'd actually begun to enjoy target shooting. I hadn't gone in a couple of months now and kind of missed it. I found myself half listening to their conversation as I sat at my desk.

"I'd sure like to shop for a new pistol myself," Drake was saying. "Where do you recommend I look?"

I pulled out my letter opener and slit the few envelopes that had arrived. Nothing appeared too pressing.

"I'd like to get Charlie a little gun of her own, too," he continued. "Something she can practice with until she's thoroughly familiar with it."

Ron chuckled. "You should have heard her talk about gun control a few months ago," he said. "The idea of getting her own gun would have been out of the question."

I tossed a Kleenex box toward his office so it hit the doorjamb.

"See? Women—I tell you Drake, you never can tell about 'em."

"You two better quit talking about me," I warned.

Drake leaned into my office and tossed a kiss my way.

I filed the incoming mail according to whatever I'd have to do with it next, then turned my attention back to the fax. It had been sent from Washington but there was a name, Jim Williams, with an Albuquerque phone number. His name had been mentioned often in the report, apparently as the chief investigator on the case.

I dialed the number and got Williams on the line almost immediately. I identified myself and read him the case number from the top of the fax.

"Would it be possible for me to meet with you in the next day or two?" I asked.

His voice sounded hesitant. "I don't know what I could tell you, Ms. Parker. I mean, besides what's in the report."

"You were on the scene," I said. "These are my parents we're talking about. I guess I just want to…" My voice petered out as I failed to come up with a valid sounding reason.

He sighed. "I've got fifteen minutes between two other meetings this afternoon. It's supposed to be my coffee break, but I'll give you a little time if you can be here at two-fifteen."

He gave me an address in the downtown Federal Building. I hung up the phone wondering what exactly I would ask him.

"Want to go downtown with me this afternoon?" I directed the question toward both men.

"I can't," Ron said, "I've got a deposition to give at Haworth's office at two o'clock."

The lawyer was one of our better clients and there was no way Ron could stand him up.

"I'll go," Drake offered. "I can either attend your meeting with you or I can scout around among the government offices for some helicopter work."

"That's right! You might make some valuable contacts for yourself. Let's do that. I'll meet with Mr. Williams and you can do some prospecting."

At two-ten I walked into Jim Williams's office in the local branch office of the Department of Transportation. I'd let Drake out at the door so he could get a head start while I parked the Jeep in a lot down the block. Now I faced a long Formica counter with a bureaucratic looking woman behind it.

"I have an appointment with Jim Williams at two-fifteen," I volunteered after she ignored me for a full two minutes.

"He's in a meeting, ma'am."

"I know, but he told me to be here when they take their coffee break."

She looked at me like she couldn't believe any sane person would give up a coffee break.

"Really, he did. Can you let him know I'm here?"

"He's still in the meeting, ma'am."

"Yes. I meant when he comes out of the meeting."

I went ahead and sat down in a vinyl-seated metal chair against the wall despite the fact that she hadn't made a move on my behalf. My eyes kept straying to my watch. At precisely two-fifteen, I heard a door open somewhere down a hall and voices drifted toward me.

A large red-faced man with thin sandy hair stuck his head around the corner.

"Marge, is there..." He caught sight of me in mid sentence. "Charlie Parker?"

"Yes, you must be Mr. Williams?" I stood, ready to follow him.

"Let's go into my office."

I followed him down a tiled corridor past a series of identical wooden doors. Williams was about six feet tall, barrel shaped body, narrow hips and legs, fifty-some years old. The redness in his face extended to the back of his neck and to the bald spot at his crown. He stopped and opened the fourth door on the left, stepped aside and motioned me to precede him.

"Sit down, Ms. Parker," he invited, indicating a chair like the one I'd just vacated. He grunted as he took his seat behind the metal desk. The desk top was clear except for a telephone and computer terminal. One battered file folder lay in the in-basket behind him and he picked it up. Inside was a thin sheaf of papers.

He opened the folder and rubbed his eyebrows with thumb and index finger as he glanced over the first couple of pages.

"I received a copy of the final report from Washington,"

I began. "The conclusion that an explosive device was carried aboard in the pilot's bag naturally surprised me. I was wondering what ever came of that. Did they think the pilot intended to sabotage the flight? Or did someone plant the device aboard, and if so, who did it?"

Williams continued to flip through pages as I asked my questions.

"I remember this case now," he said, looking up at me with sharp blue eyes. "It's been a long time."

I waited, hoping he'd remember enough to be of help.

"It was a pretty hairy location," he said. "Way at the top of Baldy Mountain up north of Eagle Nest. We had one of those spring snows, dumped about a foot or more on the wreckage before we could get up there. At first, the assumption was that the weather probably caused the crash."

"How did you learn about the explosive?"

"Oh, as soon as we saw the airplane, it was obvious," he assured me. "I don't know why anybody ever thinks they can disguise an explosion. A gaping hole in a fuselage doesn't happen because of a snow storm."

"So, what ever came of it? Was anyone arrested?"

"Nope. The whole thing was snatched out of our hands as soon as we said the word explosion."

"Snatched? By whom?"

"Someone pretty high up at Sandia Corporation, I assume. They don't tell me stuff like that. All I knew was, one day we were working on the case, the next day I was told 'Wrap up your findings, do up a short conclusive report, and file the thing away.' Usually at that point, some law enforcement authority will take over, you know, the FBI or somebody, and follow it through to make arrests and see it through. I don't think that ever happened here."

"Did you ask about that?"

"Tried to. I got called in to the administrator's office,

stood there on the carpet, and was told to forget the whole business."

I leaned forward conspiratorily. "What do you *think* happened?"

"I don't get paid to think." A touch of sarcasm in his voice. "I *surmised* that maybe someone on board was carrying top secret documents and the corporation wanted to have their own people retrieve them. That was laughable because everything from that crash was scattered for miles."

Including bodies. He seemed to read my thoughts and he covered quickly. "There were papers all over the place, and with the wind up on those mountain tops, that stuff would have been carried for miles."

"So, even though you were chief investigator on the case, no one would let you follow through."

He nodded, the sharp blue eyes staying firmly with mine.

"Who would make that kind of call?" I mused, thinking aloud.

"Sandia Corporation was a major government contractor in those years," he hinted. "Major enough to call a lot of shots."

"So I guess I need to figure out who wanted to be rid of someone aboard that plane. And I have to assume that the person on board who knew the most, who was most important in the scheme of things at Sandia, was my father."

Voices out in the hall reminded Williams of his second meeting.

"All I can say is, this file was about two inches thick with my reports and findings." He held up the few sheets of paper. "Now look at it. Everything else was taken away so the official report would never hold more than this."

"Can you remember much of the detail that's missing now?" I asked. "Would you be able to reconstruct some of it, some of the pertinent facts that might tell me where this leads?''

He rose, moving toward the door. ''I can try. It's been so long, I'd hate to promise how much I can come up with.''

''Can I call you next week?''

''Yeah, do that. I'll let you know.'' Already his attention had fast-forwarded to the meeting he was supposed to attend. I left, feeling unsure whether he'd even remember my request by five o'clock that afternoon.

I rode the elevator to the lobby and found a padded bench where I could wait for Drake. I jotted a few notes in my spiral while Williams's conversation was relatively fresh. The Federal Building lobby was a constant traffic area and I ignored most of it until I heard someone call out, ''Congressman Cudahy!''

An entourage crowded past me with Cudahy somewhere in the middle of the group. His familiar face with the publicly practiced smile beamed above the heads of those surrounding him, eyes scanning constantly, deciding where to bestow politically correct acknowledgements. I, being nondisabled, non-challenged, and of no particular color other than plain vanilla, did not receive such acknowledgement. I stood up and quietly followed the select few who apparently followed the Congressman's every move.

Someone near the front of the group pushed an elevator button. They all paused, as one, waiting and staring up at the spot where a green ''up'' arrow should appear. I snuggled in close enough to be assured of a spot on the car.

The elevator deposited us at the top floor and I exited along with the rest of the fan club. The Congressman was no longer quite as concerned with his smile as we entered his suite of offices. He began barking orders to one aide after the other until he and I were the only ones left standing in the reception area. It was almost comical to see the nonplussed look that crossed his face just before he remembered that I could be a voter.

"Yes, ma'am, and what can I do for you today?" The smile was slick as ever.

I felt as though people were aging me prematurely today, as this was the second man in the last thirty minutes that had called me ma'am. "I'm Bill Parker's daughter," was all I said.

"Yes, ma'am." His smile stayed fixed, but I could see him struggling internally to place me in some context.

"You worked with my father years ago at Sandia Corporation. Bill Parker? He was one of their top scientists."

"Oh yes, I remember Bill quite well."

Liar.

"Could I talk with you for just a few minutes, Congressman?"

He glanced around, trying vainly to find some way to tell me no, but his receptionist had disappeared and none of the other underlings came along to rescue him.

"Uh, sure. Certainly. Come right on into my office." The invitation wasn't quite sincere, but it would at least give me a shot at asking a few questions. Whether or not I liked the man personally, he might be able to use his influence to get me some answers. He had connections in both Washington and at Sandia Corporation.

He led the way into a large corner office. The spartan government look was entirely missing here. Plush green carpet stretched out before me like a lawn made of currency. A heavy, cherry desk with matching credenza and side chairs gleamed in front of the windows that somehow, despite the other high rise buildings downtown, managed to showcase a spectacular view of the Sandia mountains to the east.

"Sit down," he invited. "Would you care for some coffee? I'm sorry, I didn't catch your name." His three piece suit perfectly matched his salt-and-pepper hair with the hundred dollar haircut.

He was attempting to be a good host while still trying to figure out who I was. I declined the coffee.

"Charlie Parker. I'll try not to take too much of your time, Congressman. I'd just like to see if I can find some answers about my father's death. I just recently learned that the plane crash that killed him was chartered by Sandia and that it doesn't look like the crash was an accident."

His lips pursed in a concentrated pose of deliberation as he made a few notes on a yellow pad. I told him the date of the crash and the location. He acknowledged occasionally with a nod or an "Um-hmm."

The phone rang at just the same time that an aide tapped at the door then entered. Cudahy raised an index finger while he picked up the phone. He um-hmm'd a couple of times into the receiver. As soon as he hung up, the aide spoke up.

"Your finance committee is waiting in the conference room, sir," the young man in the perfectly tailored three-piece suit told him.

"Fine, Brad, tell them I'll be right there." He stood, holding his hand out to me and making firm eye contact. "Charlie, I'm so sorry to hear this news about Bill. Of course, at the time we were all stunned by the crash, but I never realized there were still unanswered questions." He circled the desk with my hand still clasped in his.

"Charlie, I'll certainly look into this for you, and I'll do my best to get some answers for you and your brothers. Now, if you don't hear from me within a couple of weeks, you be sure to call this office. I may be back in Washington by then but my secretary will have the information for you."

He had placed an almost imperceptible hand on my back as he steered me out the door and down the hall.

"Now Charlie, again, I'm so sorry about your loss and you just rest assured that I'm here to help." Again the suave smile as he turned away.

I wiped my right hand against my pants leg and wondered how long it would be before I got onto his campaign mailing list. Would he *really* try to help me? I supposed anything was possible in an election year. Maybe I needed to be more politically savvy and learn how to use these guys when I needed them.

The elevator took forever to make it up to this floor and I belatedly remembered that Drake would probably be waiting downstairs, worried that my initial fifteen minute appointment with Jim Williams had now taken close to an hour.

I tucked the business card I'd taken from Cudahy's secretary's desk into my purse and pressed the button for the lobby. Drake sat on the same padded bench I'd occupied earlier. He didn't see me approach because he was looking at something in his hand.

"Hi, handsome, wanna take a pretty girl home with you?"

"Sure baby, what'd you have in mind?" he replied without even looking up.

"You! What if that hadn't been me making that offer?"

He reached out and wrapped his arm around my waist. "I knew it was you, baby. Felt your vibes from the minute you got off that elevator."

I flopped down beside him on the bench. "What'cha got there?" I nodded toward his hand.

"A good start," he replied, revealing several business cards. "Talked to a couple of people that would be real interested in using a helicopter based in the northern part of the state. I was just making a couple of notes of things I'd have to do first.''

I was pleased to see his enthusiasm.

''I'll have to get on the state bid list. Here's the phone number I have to call to get the paperwork. And the guy with the Forest Service told me what equipment they require for most of their work.''

''Can I buy you a beer?'' I asked. ''Let's walk down the street and find a comfortable place to sit.''

A crisp breeze funneled between the buildings. With no sunshine reaching the street, it sent a chill through my light jacket. Drake slipped his arm around my shoulders and pulled me close to him. I matched my stride to his and drew warmth from his body.

''So, what did you find out from that investigator?'' he asked, once we were seated in a corner booth in a dark little bar. ''He must have been interested; he gave you a lot more than your allotted fifteen minutes.''

I filled him in on the visit with Williams and my chance encounter with Congressman Jack Cudahy.

''Cudahy promises to help track down some information for me, but we'll see. He's really your typical politician.''

The waitress set our drinks down and Drake squeezed my hand across the table.

''You'll find out what you need to know,'' he assured me. ''I know you. Charlie The Undaunted always gets her man.''

''I got you, didn't I?''

''See what I mean?''

He sipped from his beer, then licked the foam off his upper lip.

''So tell me more about your helicopter plans,'' I invited. ''What kinds of work will you plan on doing?''

''The guy I talked to at the Forest Service was really

encouraging. He said they have quite a bit of work they can hire me for if I get a machine equipped according to OAS standards.''

"OAS?"

"Office of Aircraft Services. They certify private aircraft for government use—everything from the seat belts to the radio systems. It can be pretty expensive to equip a machine the way they want, so I'm hoping to find one with most everything in place already.''

"And once you get all that equipment?"

"Well, then I can fight fires, do wildlife counts, maybe move some heavy equipment... I'll get a water bucket and a couple of long lines for sling work. I love doing that kind of work, the variety is so much greater than I ever had by flying tours.''

I chuckled at the childlike enthusiasm in his voice.

"So, you want to come with me to Pueblo later this week? We can take a look at that machine, test fly it...''

Ooh, yes. I agreed without a second thought.

SEVEN

THURSDAY MORNING we got up early, piled the three of us into the Jeep and headed north on I-25. Clouds had moved in during the night and hovered now, low across the face of the Sandia Mountains. Drake had switched on the weather report about six o'clock and was convinced that it wasn't a long lasting storm. It should move through by this afternoon. We'd stay over in Pueblo tonight and have a nice clear day tomorrow for test flying the helicopter.

Rusty settled into the back seat, using my duffle bag for a pillow. I leaned back in the passenger seat and let Drake do the driving.

"Do you know how long it's been since I could just hop in a car and drive all day and be in a different city by nighttime?" he asked.

"I guess island life does have its limits, huh?"

He breathed deeply, taking in the wide open spaces as we left Albuquerque behind. I poured coffee from the thermos I'd brought and handed him a styrofoam cup. I felt like we were honeymooners, taking off together in the middle of the week.

Traffic was light and the miles peeled away. By noon we'd reached Raton and decided to stop for a quick lunch. Rusty helped finish off the last of the fries. We ordered him his own cup of water, which he gulped eagerly, crunching down the ice cubes like candy.

When we reached Pueblo about mid-afternoon, Drake pulled a small note from his pocket.

"Here, read me the instructions on how to get to this place," he told me.

I looked at the scrap, turned it around, squinted again. "I think you're going to have to decipher this," I laughed.

"Are you saying I have messy writing?"

"Okay. '234 2L, blue bl R planes red truck.' Does that make sense to you?" I handed the note over to him.

"Sure. Take exit 234, turn at the second left, watch for a blue building, turn right, look for airplanes on a ramp. They have a red fuel truck parked out in front of their place."

"Oh. Wow, you are good at this."

"Years of navigational experience, my dear."

I stuck my tongue out at him.

He followed the cryptic note's instructions and sure enough, within about ten minutes we'd arrived at High Mountain Helicopter Service. Drake's energy level visibly picked up.

"This flying really is in your blood, isn't it?" I teased.

"Irrevocably. Old pilots never quit."

He took my hand as we walked toward the metal building. "I hope you don't mind," he said.

"I think it's great," I replied, kissing his earlobe.

He pushed aside a metal door that groaned like an old man doing pushups. Inside, a large room served as customer lounge, radio center, and flight planning room. A scarred metal desk served as the reception area. Four or five pieces of radio equipment were stacked across one end of it. Static crackled from them relentlessly. Two sagging couches draped with grimy Mexican blankets stood against one wall. Above them, a three-dimensional topographic map filled the entire wall. Pins and red ribbons decorated it with flight routes and job sites. I took all this in within a couple of minutes, noticing the absence of people.

A man's voice drifted from a back room. From the pauses and increasing volume of his voice, he was apparently on a phone call in which a dispute was not being resolved. I glanced at Drake.

"Should we wait outside?" I mouthed.

He shook his head and cleared his throat loudly. "If that creaky door didn't alert him, maybe this will."

He wandered over to the wall map and studied it intently. I followed, not sure what we were looking at, but curiosity is one of my virtues. The map covered southern Colorado and northern New Mexico. I found my eyes wandering down to the area where Jim Williams had pinpointed my parents' plane crash.

Baldy Peak stood near Eagle Nest, New Mexico, with an elevation of 12,441 feet. My eyes followed a straight line from Pueblo to the top of Baldy. It didn't look very far in air miles. Hmm...

"Hi, folks, can I help you?" The voice was the one we'd heard on the phone. The man was tall, thin, fortyish. He wore a red plaid shirt, jeans, work boots and a black down vest. His dark hair was mostly covered by a black ball cap that sported his company's logo on the front.

"Bill Whitaker?"

The man nodded with a sideways tilt to his head as if his neck hurt.

"Drake Langston. Remember me?"

"Hey, Drake—hell yes, how are ya?" He extended a hand with black-rimmed nails.

"And this is my fiancée, Charlie Parker."

My hands were in my jacket pockets and I settled for a nod and smile in lieu of one of those grimy handshakes.

"Well, I guess you want to see the machine," Bill offered.

He led the way through another metal door at the far end of the reception room into a cavernous hangar. Three helicopters stood side by side like soldiers in their ranks.

"It's the B-3," Whitaker said.

Drake headed for the machine at the far end of the row. I tagged along, wondering how on earth he knew which one Bill had referred to. I'm still dumb enough about these things I need someone to say "the blue one" or "the green one."

I wanted to comment on how beautiful the ship was, but I noticed Drake eyeing it critically. I'd better keep my mouth shut and become a cagey buyer. He climbed up on the skid and opened a panel, exposing the mechanics beneath.

"You go ahead and look her over," Bill called up to Drake. "I gotta return some phone calls. Holler if you have any questions."

"Okay, Bill." Drake's concentration on the innards of the machine was so total that he didn't notice Whitaker leaving. He didn't notice me either and I quickly ran out of things to check on the aircraft, being that I had no clue as to what I was looking at.

I wandered around the hangar, glancing at what I perceived as unbelievable clutter. The back wall was lined with a long work bench, piled high with boxes, metal parts, tools, and wadded up grease encrusted rags. In one corner stood two large conical gadgets held up by black metal frames. Each had a small motor attached at the side and coils of cable and wire draped around it. I tried to come up with a guess as to what their purpose was, but was completely at a loss.

I glanced back up at Drake. He'd removed a side panel

from the blue and white helicopter and was peering inside intently, occasionally wiggling one little part or another. I kicked a dirty rag aside and continued my inspection of the room.

One of the other helicopters was in the midst of maintenance. The rotor blades and doors were off and a red tool chest stood beside it, the tools haphazardly dumped into the drawers. The third machine looked ready to go. Presumably, if Bill got a call he could crank this one up and be on the job right away.

"That one's a beauty, isn't it?" Drake called to me.

"This one?" I pointed to the one I'd just been looking at. "Yeah it sure is." I was admiring the sleek silver and burgundy paint job, but I felt sure that wasn't what he was talking about.

"Bill said it's brand new. He just took delivery on it last week. That's why he's selling this one."

"What about this other one? Does he fly them both or does he have other pilots?"

"I'm not sure. Probably has at least one other backup pilot. It'd sure be nice if I could afford that. I'd really like to have an operation like this some day." He gazed around the hangar, apparently seeing something beyond the piles of junk and greasy rags that I'd noticed.

"What do you think about that aircraft?" I asked, indicating the one he was standing on.

"Looks real clean," he said. "I'll have to check the maintenance records before I can decide anything."

He climbed down from his perch and opened the door, taking his place in the pilot's seat. "Come on and try it out," he invited. I opened the left hand door and stepped up to the front passenger seat.

"This remind you of anything?" I asked, glancing sideways at him.

He leaned over and kissed me. "Six months ago now, wasn't it? The heliport on Kauai, circling the island, taking you to all my favorite places there…wasn't there some family in the back seat. I felt like they were watching me size you up."

I laughed. "You were sizing me up?"

"Well," he blushed, "sure. Isn't that what guys always do when they meet a woman they're interested in?"

I squeezed his hand.

"Let's take a look at the log book." He pulled a small hardbound book from a pocket at the base of his seat.

I watched while he umm'd over the various entries.

"Looks like everything's in order here," he commented. "Of course, I'll have to get the full maintenance records before I can really see the whole picture. Bill should have those here somewhere and maybe he'll let me take them to the hotel with us tonight."

"How's it going, folks?" Whitaker called out. He walked up to Drake's open door. "You want to take her out for a spin?"

Drake looked at his watch. "Yeah, definitely. But I think at this point I'll wait until tomorrow morning. Getting kind of late now. It'll be dark pretty soon."

"Sure, sure, any time."

"I would like to get the maintenance file with the component tags and look those over tonight if I could," Drake told Bill.

"Yeah, let's get those for you," Whitaker said. "And somewhere around here I've got a listing of the remaining times on the major components. That oughta be helpful."

We stepped down from our seats and followed Bill into his office off the main reception room. He rummaged through a file cabinet whose manila folders sagged against each other weakly. His desk was covered with thick volumes of helicopter maintenance books, files, and faxes, topped with a layer of small telephone message slips. Three styrofoam coffee cups stood in precarious positions among the clutter. I clasped my hands together to resist the strong urge to straighten it up.

"Now here's the maintenance folder for that machine," Whitaker was telling Drake.

"And the log book? Can I take that too?"

"Yeah, we'll get it out of the ship before you go," Bill said. "What else? Let's think what you might need."

I tapped Drake on the shoulder. "I think I'll go let Rusty out for a couple of minutes."

He nodded, flashing me a quick smile.

The dog wagged his entire red-brown body as I approached the Jeep.

"Poor thing," I consoled. "You missed us, didn't you? Come on, let's take a little walk." I clipped a leash onto his collar.

He immediately pulled toward the ramp in front of the hangar, but I steered him toward the road. We kept up a brisk pace for a couple of blocks, then turned around and headed back at a good clip. Drake was waiting at the Jeep when we returned.

"All set?" he asked.

"Yep, I think we both feel better after a little stretch."

We checked into a nearby motel and left Rusty in the room gobbling at his dinner while we went out to locate a decent steak. We returned to the room an hour later, full but happy.

Drake pulled out the folders and log books and spread them out on the table. I stretched out on the bed and watched him at work. Having him around was still so new to me that I enjoyed seeing him in action.

"I had a thought today, Drake."

"Hmm, what's that?" His eyes didn't leave the computer printout he was working over.

"Well, tomorrow you're going to have a chance to fly the new ship. Could we take it anywhere we want to?"

"Within reason," he said absently.

"I looked on the map and it doesn't look that far to Baldy Mountain."

"What are you suggesting?" He looked sideways at me through slitted eyes.

"That maybe we could check out my parent's crash site?" I tried my best flirty manner, but wasn't sure I pulled it off. "I'd pay for the extra fuel."

He paused. "Let's see the map," he said.

He pulled a sectional chart out of the briefcase he'd brought with him, spreading it out on the bed beside me. I scanned it quickly and pointed to the spot. He brought out a little measuring device and checked the distance.

"I think we could manage it," he grinned.

"Will Whitaker care? I mean I don't want to cause a problem with him."

"I'll just ask. Tell him I need to take it out long enough to see how it performs at altitude."

"Did I ever happen to tell you that I think you're one terrific guy?"

"You might have mentioned it. But you could tell me again."

I crawled onto his lap and showed him instead.

EIGHT

AT OVER 11,000 FEET, I felt like I was standing on top of the world. Literally. I turned in a full circle and breathed deeply of the thin, cold air. Drake came up behind me, running his arm around my waist after shutting down the helicopter's engine. Neither of us said a word until I began to giggle.

"This is just so incredible," I laughed.

Below us, the mountain fell away in graduated sloping steps. Each compass point showed a different panorama, the blue-gray hills to the east, the dark green mountains to the north and south, majestic Wheeler Peak crowned in white to the west. Tiny towns dotted the lower elevations, most discernible only as a bunch of dots with a thread of a road running through the middle. Gray clouds hung above our heads. Drake kept looking up at them.

"We aren't going to have much time here," he said. "This weather could close in any time."

I pulled a small note from my pocket. "Here are the coordinates I got from the NTSB report," I said.

He pulled the portable GPS from his jacket as he glanced at the note.

"Okay, it looks like we're really close." He looked around for a trail. "Let's try this one."

I followed him toward a dip that led downward between

two large boulders. A trail, in reasonably good shape, snaked its way up the mountain in a series of switchbacks.

"Probably another hundred feet or so," Drake called back over his shoulder.

My eyes were glued to the path, my legs a little unsteady on the loose pebbly surface. Drake stopped and I bumped into his back.

"Look over there," he said, pointing down and to our right. "See the two broken trees?"

We left the path and sidestepped our way across the steep surface.

"See how they're broken, up high? They've put on a few new branches but the tops won't grow back. The plane probably took off those tree tops as it came in."

I stopped short. We were directly uphill from the broken trees and I realized that I was probably standing almost exactly on the spot where my parents and the others had lost their lives. A heavy feeling settled in the middle of me. Oddly, no tears came, only that rock—somewhere between my heart and my stomach.

Drake bent down, scratching at the dirt at the base of a rock. He picked up a small metal object and brushed the dirt off it. I crabbed my way down the hill to him.

"Looks like an aircraft bolt," he said, holding it up. It looked like just any old bolt to me.

"Specially hardened steel, tested to meet aircraft specs," he said. "They don't look any different, do they? Cost about fifteen times more than any hardware store bolt though."

"How can you tell that's what it is?"

He scrubbed the head of the bolt against his jeans, then held it up to me. "See that little number stamped into the head? Every part on an aircraft has a part number. The FAA catches you using some unapproved part on your aircraft, your ass is grass."

My eyes traveled to the ground, looking for further evidence. I don't know what I thought I'd find—obviously, anything crucial to the investigation would have been removed by the NTSB, or whoever came along after...

A tiny white grain floated across my field of view. I looked over at Drake. He'd apparently just noticed them too.

"We better get going," he said, gazing up at the sky. "This is going to close in fast."

We turned around and limped our way back to the trail. Climbing up was a bit trickier than coming down had been, but I let Drake take the lead and I imitated his moves up the tenuous path. By the time we'd buckled into our seats, adjusted our headsets and waited for the turbine engine to whine into motion, the snowflakes had thickened considerably.

"You comfy?" Drake asked.

I looked nervously at the sky and nodded.

"Don't worry, the ceiling's still up there. We're just going to get below it and head lower. Once we're below 8,000 or so, it should clear up."

He broadcast a call to any air traffic over the radio and maneuvered the aircraft into the air and we nosed downward into the valley toward Cimarron. As he'd predicted, the snowflakes became tinier until they were soon non-existent. By the time we circled the heliport in Pueblo, blue sky was peeking out of the clouds in large patches.

Again, I excused myself to tend to Rusty, who'd waited in the car while we took our flight, while Drake went inside to talk deal with Whitaker.

"Well?" I asked when he got back into the car thirty minutes later.

"Well, it looks good," he said, starting the Jeep and backing out. "I'm real pleased with the machine and all the records look clean. Now I just have to figure out a way to afford it.''

"And what would that be?'' We'd not really entered the sacred realm of finances yet. Drake had left a good paying job in Hawaii, and I assumed he'd socked away savings toward this dream of his. For my part, I'd only hinted that I do have a nest egg stashed from my inheritance. The money I draw from Ron's and my business partnership is minimal, but then, so are my expenses.

"If I can get a contract lined up for some government work, I should be able to work out financing for the aircraft. Once I sell the property in Hawaii, that can help assure my ongoing operating expenses, a facility, and a way to help you out with household costs too."

"Do you think you might be close to a contract?'' We'd joined the southbound traffic on I-25.

"It'll take some time to get anything firm, but I'm hopeful about the contacts I made in Albuquerque.''

"How soon do you have to commit to Whitaker?''

"I gave him some earnest money and asked him to hold it for me for thirty days. If I can't get something put together by then and if another buyer comes along, I'll just find something else. This isn't the only helicopter in the world, you know.''

He reached over and squeezed my hand. "We could have such a good time with this, hon. This has been my dream for so long.''

The excitement showed clearly in his eyes. I smiled back at him, sharing the feeling.

"I'm so glad to have you in my life,'' he said. He lifted my fingers to his mouth and placed a tender kiss there.

The drive home seemed longer than the trip north. We stopped in Santa Fe for dinner and rolled into Albuquerque late with me snuggled asleep in the passenger seat.

NINE

"SO WHEN'S THE wedding going to be?"

I was sitting in Elsa Higgins's over-warm kitchen, stuffing bites of cinnamon toast into my mouth, passing a morning while Drake went downtown to meet again with some of his contacts in the Federal Building. Although Elsa had been my life-long neighbor and had taken me in to live with her for my last two years of high school, the question rankled.

"I don't know," I answered, a little sharper than I'd planned. I regretted it immediately. "Gram, don't worry, Drake and I are getting married. I just haven't felt ready to set a date."

I walked to the stove and poured hot water from the kettle into my tea cup.

"It's just that, well, I've watched so many of my friends get divorced. I mean, look at Ron and Bernadette. That got so ugly."

Her fluffy white hair nodded.

"I just don't want that to happen to us. I want to be very sure. We haven't known each other that long." I carried the cup back to the table and reached for another slice of toast. "How long did you and Mr. Higgins know each other before you got married."

"Two weeks," she answered promptly.

"You're not helping my case here. How on earth did you know it would work out?"

She looked puzzled. "Splitting up wasn't an option. We vowed to stay together. Better or worse and all that stuff." She wagged her finger toward me. "We went through some of those 'worse' times, let me tell you missy, but we rode them out. Everyone did. People today just look for the easy way out whenever things don't go to suit them."

I licked sugar off my fingers.

"Did Mother or Dad ever talk about his work?"

She chuckled. "Well, that sure was a neat way to dodge the subject."

"Enough said. I'm working on it. What about Dad's work?"

"Not really. I don't mean this to sound tacky, but your mother was awfully wrapped up in her social life and I don't think she ever once mentioned Bill's work."

I knew what she meant. My mother's family had money and social standing. They'd always considered that she married beneath her when she picked a working slob—even one with a PhD. Mother had spent her time, as nearly as I could remember, involved in Junior League and the country club life.

"Bill, of course, couldn't really talk about his work. Just about everything Sandia Corporation worked on in those days was classified."

"I know. I feel like the plane crash must have been connected to something he was working on. Why else would someone have planted an explosive on a company plane? But I'm just not getting anywhere with my questions."

She rubbed at a water spot on a spoon with her gnarled fingers. "You might look through your attic," she said. "I know we packed up a lot of papers and files from your father's desk and stored them up there."

"I found a lot of that stuff," I told her. "With Drake moving in and all, I haven't had time to look through it. And now that his household stuff will be here in a while, I don't know if I have room to bring all that attic junk down."

"Well, bring it over here if you want," she suggested. "You know your old room is sitting there empty. You can spread out in there if it'll help."

"We'll see. I guess I should get it out though and see what's there. Although I can't really imagine that he'd have anything very secret at home."

"Maybe not secret, maybe incriminating."

From the mouths of babes.

Why on *earth* hadn't I put that little bit of logic together?

"You are a darling," I told her with a hug. "I'm going to get right on this."

It took me nearly two hours to haul the boxes down from the attic, having to stop and check briefly in each one to be sure I wasn't simply moving old family junk around. It quickly became obvious that the dining room table would not contain it all and I decided to take Gram up on her offer to spread it all out in her spare bedroom. Taking it over there used up another thirty minutes, by which time Drake had come home and we stopped to make a sandwich for lunch.

He'd brought home a stack of forms to fill out so I set him up in my home office, formerly my brothers' bedroom, with the portable typewriter. I cleared out a drawer and gave him a stack of file folders where he could locate his new business venture. I left him muttering over bid lists and punching numbers into the calculator.

Gram was wiping dish suds off her hands when I got back to her place.

"You go ahead and do whatever you need to," she said. "I usually set down after lunch and watch my shows."

I trailed her into the dim living room that always smelled of moth balls and lavender. She switched on the television set, adjusted it to her preferred channel and settled into her rocker across the room. I headed down the hall toward the spare bedroom, where I'd stacked the file boxes. There were probably a dozen of them. I took a deep breath.

Within thirty minutes, I wished I'd looked through them a little more carefully before going to all the trouble of carrying them down from the attic and over here. The first four boxes had proved to contain Dad's notebooks and papers from college. Two more, at least, were graduate school work. I flipped briefly through each notebook, occasionally coming across a personal letter or photo. I put these aside, wondering if there would be enough of them to make up a scrapbook or album. Mostly the notebooks contained lecture notes, research notes, and pages and pages of formulas and equations. None of it made any sense to me, and I couldn't see any possible connection with his later years at Sandia Labs.

A fifth box contained the pages from his leatherbound notebook, banded in several stacks with the dates neatly penned on top of each bundle. I laid them out on the floor chronologically and pulled the rubber bands from the most current one. The pages in this stack had been completed more than six months before the beginning of the first notebook I'd found, and a reading of the entries going back nearly a year revealed no further mentions of clandestine activities or threats. I sighed and put them all back into the box.

The light in the room began to fade so I got up to switch on the overhead light. My hands were dusty, which somehow made my mouth feel extra dry, so I decided to find something to drink in the kitchen. Elsa dozed quietly in her rocker, head tilted to one side, her mouth hanging open. Dramatic organ music announced the end of one soap opera. I tiptoed through the room, found a glass in the same kitchen cupboard where they'd always been, and drank a full glass of water in a couple of long swigs.

When I walked back through the living room, Elsa was still dozing and a new show was starting. I glanced at my watch. Three o'clock.

I stacked the boxes I'd already checked into one corner of the room, intending to carry them back home soon to keep them out of Elsa's way. My back felt achey and Drake was probably wondering by now what had happened to me. I'd just about decided to give up for the day, but glanced into the next box, which didn't have a top. One of the folders was labeled SANDIA. I picked it up along with the photos and some personal letters I'd found earlier and decided to carry them home with me.

Elsa stirred when I walked into the living room and I asked gently, "How was your show?"

"Oh, it was good today," she assured me. "I always watch those same two. Been watching them for years."

I smiled. She'd probably been dozing through them for years, but I'd bet she could tell me exactly what the plots were.

Drake was still at the desk when I got home. He had several neat stacks of papers clipped together, with envelopes addressed to the recipients on top of each stack.

"I'll need to get to a copy shop tomorrow," he said. "I want copies of these bids to keep on file."

"We can take them to the office and do it there, if you'd like." I started to put my arms around his shoulders, but realized how dusty I was.

"I thought I'd make beef stroganoff for dinner," he

called out, as I headed toward the bathroom to wash up. "Is that okay with you?"

"It sounds wonderful," I assured him. "But you better watch out, I could get really spoiled to this."

"I'd love to spoil you rotten," he said, nuzzling my neck from behind as I dried my hands and arms.

The kisses trailed down my neck, while his hands worked their way around my waist. I started to pull away and protest that we had work to do, but didn't. Wouldn't it be better if we were always like this?

We allowed ourselves a few more moments of closeness before we both drew back.

"Guess what I found in those boxes?" I led him to the dining room where I'd laid the folder and other papers I'd brought home.

"Bring them in the kitchen and tell me about them while I start dinner," he suggested.

I parked myself at the kitchen table, flipping through the envelopes in the small stack.

"Looks like a few letters from my mother that Dad received when he was in college. She must have been away one summer...let's see, 1950. They're mailed from Newport."

Drake took a package of steak from the freezer and set the microwave to partially defrost it.

"Gosh, I knew her family were society people, but Newport? You suppose she hobnobbed with those wealthy types?"

Mother's parents had died before I was born. I was never really clear on when. Mother had talked about her childhood and growing up years as though it was a magic time, and as a kid, I imagined castles and princesses. Maybe that was closer to the truth than I thought.

"Got any sour cream?" Drake asked, staring into the fridge.

"Yeah, somewhere in there."

I opened the first envelope, a fragile cream paper with two sheets of fine linen-weave paper inside. Between the folds of the letter was a small photo. Mother, looking very young and glamorous, with a Grace Kelly hairstyle, wearing a single strand of pearls against her slim bare neck. The letter was from a typical college girl to the boy back home. She missed him. The parties were nice, the people lovely, but she wished he could be there. She dropped a few names that you'd probably find in *Town and Country.*

The smell of browning meat and onions reached me. Drake was stirring a skillet at the stove, humming an old Beatles tune. I thought of the hours we'd spent on the telephone during our weeks apart, a luxury even the rich didn't often indulge in during my parents' time. We'd probably become closer in a shorter time than they might have, but we'd never have perfume scented letters and black-and-white photos to remember our courtship by either. Somehow, a two-hundred dollar phone bill doesn't carry the same feeling.

I opened the next letter. Apparently, they'd had a tiff of some sort. She'd wanted him to fly out for a ball at somebody's "cottage." He'd evidently not dropped his studies to go and she was miffed. The letter recounted the gala evening in detail so he'd know what he missed. A long-forgotten conversation came back at me like a flash.

It had taken place in this very kitchen. I'd probably been six or seven. Mother stood at the stove, where Drake stood now. Dad had just come in from work, his tie loosened, his jacket hanging over his arm. The back door stood open, letting in a faint breeze from the back yard. I was at the table, coloring a picture. It was so hot, I remembered how the backs of my legs stuck to the vinyl chair seat.

Mother was angrily stirring something on the stove. Dad was apologizing that he just wasn't up for a party tonight. He'd put in a long week and just wanted to put his feet up and watch the baseball game on television. But this was a personal invitation from Mrs. VanCliff, Mother said. Didn't he know what an honor it was to be invited to one of her summer soirées? I watched both their faces, each intent on its own purpose, neither of which I could fathom. I ducked out the open back door and ran all the way to the park and back.

"Hon?" Drake's voice snapped me back to the present.

"Huh—I'm sorry, what were you saying?"

"Where were you? I just asked whether you wanted some iced tea."

I let out a pent-up breath. "Yeah, that would really hit the spot." I set the letters aside. Maybe this could wait.

Drake set the tall frosty glass in front of me. "I'm just going to let that simmer awhile," he said. "Are you okay?"

"Oh, yeah. It's just amazing what kind of memories this kind of stuff can bring back. Let's do something else. I'll come back to this later."

We spent a quiet evening watching television and acting like old married people. I worked hard to suppress the pictures of my parents, whose life had very much resembled this but always with an undercurrent.

TEN

I AWOKE SUNDAY MORNING to find Drake's side of the bed empty. Rusty wasn't in the room either. I stretched and felt a tingle shoot through my muscles. We'd watched an old Ingrid Bergman movie on television last night, which somehow put Drake in a romantic mood. I preferred to think it was because she'd worn her hair dark in that particular picture and it reminded him of me, but I didn't ask. After a glass of wine, we'd retired to the bedroom but hadn't fallen asleep for close to two more hours. I glanced at the clock.

After nine. Even for a weekend, this was an indulgence for me. I stretched again, enjoying the decadent feeling for another moment before slinking out from under the covers and pulling on a terry robe.

Coffee smell wafted from the kitchen. Drake was at the table with the *Sunday Journal* spread out before him. I poured myself a mug of vanilla macadamia Kona blend and spotted Rusty out in the back yard, intent on some small critter in the far corner.

''Morning,'' I mumbled into Drake's hair.

He pulled open the front of my robe and planted his good morning kiss there. I slid into the chair beside him.

''Ron called a while ago,'' he said.

''Really? I didn't hear the phone.''

''You were sleeping the sleep of the satiated,'' he grinned.

"Umm. I guess so."

"He asked if we wanted to go out to the shooting range later. I told him probably so. I'll go anyway, even if you don't want to."

The sweet hot coffee coursed down my throat. I didn't want to do anything as strenuous as planning an activity yet.

"How about if I whip us up some cinnamon rolls?" I suggested. "They're the canned ones."

"Better yet, how about if I whip us up some waffles. With strawberries?"

I glanced toward the counter top. He'd mixed the ingredients in a stainless bowl, just waiting to add the milk. The waffle iron stood there, its indicator light showing it already preheated.

"You better watch out," I warned. "I'm really not one of those women who will get mad if you take over her kitchen. I'll get so spoiled to this that you'll never get me to cook again."

"Oh, I won't let you get *that* spoiled. This is temporary, while I'm waiting for some work to come in." He said it like he felt an obligation to be doing something—without a job to go to, he'd feel better if he pitched in around the house.

Actually, when I'd stayed with him in Hawaii, we'd shared the housework about equally. I expected we'd do the same here.

I watched him whisk the liquid into the dry ingredients in the bowl and test the waffle iron by shaking a few drops of cold water onto it. When they danced to his satisfaction, he poured in the first ladle of batter. While the steam rose from the iron, he pulled butter, syrup, and sliced strawberries from the refrigerator. Shuffling the newspapers aside, he quickly set the table. I sat back like a queen, sipping my coffee and letting him do the work.

"I put your father's folder and letters up here," Drake said, indicating the top of the refrigerator. "I was afraid they might get mixed in with the Sunday section."

"Um, I may take a look at those later when you and Ron go to the gun range," I said.

"Don't you want to go?"

"Next time," I assured him. "For now, you and Ron get better acquainted. It'll give you a chance to do 'man stuff' without me around. You don't want to risk becoming joined at the hip with me, do you?"

He pulled me to a standing position. "Joined there or anywhere else is fine with me," he said, opening my robe and pulling my hips tightly to his.

"You better check those waffles before you start something else," I reminded.

"Oh, shit," he exclaimed.

The first waffle was golden brown. We shared it while the second one cooked. By the time we'd shared a third one, we were stuffed and could no longer ignore Rusty's signal to come in. He was allowed to lick the syrup from the plates.

I rinsed the dishes and put them in the dishwasher while Drake located his boots and a light jacket. Counter wiped and hands dried, I kissed him goodbye just as Ron's horn cheeped outside.

"You guys can take the Jeep if you want," I told him.

"Nah, Ron's already here with his car. And you might need yours."

"Well, I plan to be over at Elsa's going through the rest of those boxes, but if I go anywhere, I'll leave you a note," I said.

I waved at Ron from the front door as Drake hopped into

he sporty Mustang convertible. The house felt empty and ver-quiet without Drake in it. I locked the front door and vent out the back, through the break in the hedge to Elsa's. Vhat I really wanted was a break in my research.

Elsa was out in her garden, pulling the last of the carrots nd potatoes from the ground. A plastic tub stood near her eet, filled with dirt encrusted blobs. Her thin arms worked t thrusting the spade into the loosely packed earth. A wide-rimmed straw hat perched at an angle on her head, held in place by an orange paisley scarf.

I waved and commented on what a hard worker she was, but could tell by the empty look in her smile that she hadn't heard me. I pointed toward her back door and she nodded.

Inside, the house was cool with that early autumn crisp-ness that makes you want to pull out your winter sweaters and bake apple pies. Elsa's breakfast dishes, a cereal bowl, spoon, and coffee mug, stood upturned in the dish drainer. I walked on through to the back bedroom where my cartons awaited. Today, I should probably haul the ones I'd finished back to my own attic.

Two more boxes revealed a variety of stuff, from office memos and telephone messages to personal items and pho-tos. There was one, framed, of my brothers and me. It was a studio portrait, three teenagers with freckles and a few zits, posing stiffly together. Ron's dark hair looked strange to me, now that most of it on top is missing. Paul, a high school senior at the time, smiled with a bit of a swagger. One glance at the dress I wore brought back the day with clarity.

I'd been in the ninth grade at the time, a freshman in a new high school. Mother had tried so hard to make me class up my act, wanting to transform me from the spiky-haired blue-jeaned little tomboy I'd always been into some sem-blance of a young lady. I wore a pastel flowered dress with a scooped neckline rimmed by a wide lace collar. Around my neck hung a single strand of pearls, borrowed from Mother's jewel box. Could they be the same strand she wore in that long-ago photo I'd just found yesterday?

In this photo, a tight smile was pasted onto my face. I'd been belligerent and cranky all morning, wanting nothing in the world less than to be in a photographer's studio, decked out in uncomfortable clothes and my mother's pearls, and being told that I had to smile. The only way they'd gotten me to break loose with any smile at all was by reminding me that the photo was to be Daddy's birthday gift. My throat tightened a little, remembering.

The box apparently held the contents of my father's desk, cleared out after his death by someone at Sandia. Obviously, everything had been scoured by security, because there was nothing here pertaining to his work, only personal mementos. I finished flipping through them but found not so much as a friend's phone number or a notation of a lunch appointment.

I thought again of his little leather-bound notebook. A miracle it had survived. What had possessed him to store it in the attic before the fateful plane crash? If he'd had it with him or left it at the office, it surely would have been confiscated by the Lab and gone whatever way secret documents go—probably to that big warehouse where Indiana Jones's lost ark ended up.

By eleven o'clock, I felt brain-dead. A few boxes remained unexplored, but I didn't hold a lot of hope. There was still the manila file labeled SANDIA that I'd taken home last night, and I decided the leather notebook and that file might end up being all I'd get.

I waved again to Gram as I trekked back through the hedge to my back door. Rusty stood guard on the back porch, wagging happily at my return.

The manila folder was still on the refrigerator. I washed my hands of their collected attic dust, made a cup of tea, and sat down with it. Peeling back the pages one at a time, I found a few company memos, some letters confirming appointments and meetings, and a roster of company employees' home addresses and phone numbers. None of it seemed significant, but this didn't look like the kind of information the security department would want floating around. I wondered if he had smuggled it out.

There were informal memos about company picnics and a few group snapshots of people sitting around concrete picnic tables in mountain settings, holding fried chicken drumsticks and ears of corn. One of the photos was posed, five men wearing plaid shirts and Levi's with their arms looped over each other's shoulders. One was Dad, looking exactly as I remembered him. I turned the photo over. In Dad's bold slanted writing, was a date—the September before he died—and names of the four other men: George Myers, Wendel Patterson, Harvey Taylor, and Larry Sanchez.

It didn't take a lot of detective work to find each of the names on the company roster and come up with phone numbers. Usually when I want to question someone, I prefer to just show up at the door rather than give warning, but I couldn't imagine what any of these men would have to hide at this point, and some of these numbers could be nearly twenty years out of date. I dialed the first number.

"You've reached the Myers residence," an older female's recorded voice said. "Please leave a message after the beep and we'll get back to you."

One for one, so far. I didn't leave a message, but checked off the name as being a valid one.

The Sanchez number was answered by a young child who wouldn't talk. When I asked if its mommy or daddy were home, I got a lot of shuffling noises before a young woman took over.

"Is this Larry Sanchez's home?" I asked uncertainly.

"He's my father," the woman answered with that wariness that means you-better-not-be-a-telemarketer.

"My name's Charlie Parker and I think my father used to work with Larry at Sandia Labs," I rushed to explain before she could click off. "I'd like a chance to visit with your father sometime if it's convenient."

"What about?"

I stammered a little. "Well...about their work, I guess."

"He never talks about his work out there."

"Look, I don't want to grill him about top secret projects," I said, even though I probably did. "My father died fifteen years ago, and I didn't get much information about it at the time. I'd just like to talk to his friends. Will he be home this afternoon?"

"Um, I don't know if this is such a good idea," she muttered.

"Please? Is your address still on Alvarado?"

She grumbled a bit but confirmed that it was.

"I'll come out in about an hour, okay?"

"If you can be here before one o'clock, you can have about fifteen minutes," she informed me, then hung up.

Well, thank you very much. I couldn't imagine a grown man letting his daughter regulate his time that closely, but I'd play along until I found out whether he even remembered my father.

A glance at my watch told me it was already nearing twelve-thirty, and I'd need to allow at least twenty minutes to get up to the northeast heights. I pulled off my dusty sweatshirt and exchanged it for a light cotton chambray shirt. I let my hair out of its stretchy ponytail band and brushed it out straight around my shoulders. Applied a touch of lipstick for good measure.

"You stay here, kid," I told Rusty. His tail drooped in reply, but hey life is tough sometimes. I scribbled a quick note to Drake that I'd be home by three and grabbed the manila folder with the addresses and pictures in it.

Albuquerque traffic patterns get totally messed up on weekends. Monday through Friday, you can count on where the clog-ups will take place, and at what times of day. Saturday I would have easily predicted a tangled mess around the two major shopping centers, which were so wisely built about two blocks from each other. But how would I know that today, Sunday, I'd get caught in the surge of after-churchgoers flocking in droves to Furrs Cafeteria and every similar all-you-can-eat place? It was one o'clock on the dot when I pulled up in front of the Sanchez home.

It was in one of those neat neighborhoods where the homes have probably belonged to their original owners for all of their thirty years. Box-like stucco flat-tops sit among towering deciduous trees that were planted as twigs in the beginning and now, in places, create branch-arches over the streets. Now, in October, the arches are gold and yellow, with a few greens and oranges thrown in.

The Sanchez yard was neatly trimmed, the lawn just beginning to turn winter tan. Lines of pyracantha espeliered themselves up the front of the house with fat gobs of orange berries clustered on their branches. A circular drive filled much of the front yard, curving up to the low porch. Two planters of chysanthemums flanked the front door, their brilliant orange adding a glow to the adobe brown stucco.

I pressed the doorbell and was greeted almost instantly by a child who tugged to get the door open, then ducked behind it when he realized I was a stranger. Same as his phone technique.

"You must be Charlie," the voice I'd spoken to on the phone said. She didn't look any happier than she'd sounded. "I'm Rebecca," she said, holding the screen door open for me. She was about twenty-four or -five with long dark hair reaching to the middle of her back. Her black jeans and cropped purple sweater hugged her trim figure perfectly.

"Thanks for letting me come by. You really have a lovely place," I said, hoping to find some way to warm her up.

"Look, I don't mean to be unfriendly, it's just that my father's health isn't good. I don't want you to upset him." Her eyes and mouth showed a tiredness I hadn't noticed at first.

I mumbled something about how I was sorry to hear it and I'd try not to stay long. I wondered what his health problems were. Judging by her age, and from the group photo I'd found, I estimated her father must be in his late forties or early fifties—hardly ready for senility.

Rebecca turned and led me down a hallway to our right. We passed the open doors to the little boy's room, a bathroom, and a neat feminine room with white French provencial furniture. She opened the last door on the left and preceded me in.

"Dad, are you awake?"

The room's decor might have been taken from any modern metropolitan hospital—complete with mechanized bed, monitors of all sorts, a table on wheels that would roll into place over the bed, and a wheelchair in the corner.

The man in the bed fluttered his eyes toward Rebecca. A thin smile pushed upward, dominating his narrow face.

Rebecca backed out of the room and closed the door behind her, leaving me alone with him and speechless.

ELEVEN

"LARRY? I HOPE I'm not bothering you," I offered tentatively.

"Well, young lady, I sure don't have anything else to do right now," he teased in a raspy voice. He grinned a skeletal smile, but his dark eyes were sharp and clear.

"I'm Charlie Parker. Bill Parker—you used to work with him at Sandia Labs—was my father."

"Oh yes," he answered. "Bill Parker...how's Bill doing?"

I pulled a straight chair from the corner of the room. "Mind if sit by you for a minute?" I asked. I took a deep breath.

"My father was killed in a plane crash, over fifteen years ago. I was a teenager at the time, and I guess I didn't ask enough questions then. I just found out that it was a Sandia plane and he was on a business trip."

His mouth formed a straight line and his eyes darted back and forth. "Plane crash?" he muttered suspiciously.

"Do you remember it?" I asked.

"Plane crash." His dark brows pulled together and his lips formed a tight little knot. "Right before my accident... I...haven't thought about it in years."

"What happened to you?" I asked, wondering whether I should.

"I fell. Fell off a platform—inside the plant."

"At Sandia?"

"Yes. Can't remember now—exactly what we were doing up there. I was an inspector. Had to monitor equipment...well, different things."

I got the feeling his old security consciousness had kicked in again.

"What caused the fall? Did the platform collapse?"

"Don't remember. Woke up in the hospital."

"Were you good friends with my father? I found a picture of you together at a company picnic."

His eyebrows relaxed a little and a tiny smile played at his mouth. "Yeah, Bill Parker was a good guy. You know, not some snob—some of those scientists were."

"Larry, do you have any idea what he was working on when he died?"

His eyes did that darting around thing again.

"I know you're not supposed to talk about work," I assured him, "but that's been a long time ago. Things have changed, and the same secrets wouldn't matter anymore."

His mouth twitched but no sound came out.

"I won't tell anyone," I promised.

"I...I...just don't know," he rasped.

I reached out and took his hand. His eyes closed and I realized the effort had tired him. Within a minute, he was breathing the soft even breaths of sleep.

I gently removed my hand from his and pulled his blanket up to his chin. After replacing the chair where I'd found it, I backed out of the room.

Rebecca was waiting for me in the living room.

"I'm so sorry," I told her. "I had no idea this had happened."

She shrugged. "He was a lot better than this—used to be able to get out some. We'd go to the mall with the wheelchair, or I'd take him to a ball game. This last year has been tough. He had a minor stroke in December, one that most anyone else would have easily recovered from, but it really sapped him.

"The accident left him paralyzed from the chest down and he lost his right arm."

I hadn't even noticed that; it had been tucked away under the blankets.

"Are you the only one here to care for him?" I asked.

"This was my destiny," she replied. "I was nine years old when he fell. I watched my mother care for him until it killed her. I knew it would be my responsibility someday. So I went to nursing school so I'd be ready to take over."

"That's such an unselfish thing to do," I told her. I had a hard time grasping the amount of dedication it would take.

"There's no way we could afford private nurses all these years," she answered simply. "He gets a disability check each month. At least that keeps me from having to find another job outside."

The child had come back into the room, ducking behind Rebecca's legs. She sensed the question in my eyes.

"J.J., go look on the kitchen table," she told him. "I left you a banana peeled and cut up just the way you like it. Sit at the table to eat it."

"His father's not in the picture," she explained, as she must have hundreds of times. "We were engaged when I got pregnant. My mother died the next month and Jerry got a real look at what our lives were going to be like. He ran. Last I heard he might have gone to California. No one seems to know."

She shrugged again. I felt like crying.

"Hey, it's not so bad," she assured me. "J.J.'s the most wonderful little kid—he's my ray of sunshine, you know? Dad won't last much longer, I have to be realistic about that. His life insurance policy will support us until J.J. is old enough for school. Then I'll get a nursing job some-where.''

I wished her luck and walked out to my car. She certainly seemed to have things figured out—one of the only twenty-somethings I'd met recently who did. I started my Jeep but had only driven a block or so before I needed to pull over. It took three or four minutes of deep steady breathing before I felt ready to drive on. I pulled the manila folder from the map pocket where I'd tucked it and reviewed my list of Dad's co-workers.

George Myers's phone number had answered earlier with an answering machine and it was across town anyway. I'd save it for another day. Harvey Taylor's address fifteen years ago had been on Carlisle, about a mile out of my way home, but I figured what the heck. It was a gorgeous after-noon with a deep blue cloudless sky and that crystal clear light that artists love so much.

I took Lomas west to Carlisle and turned north. Trying to catch addresses and drive at a reasonable pace to keep from being run down, gunned down, or both, was a trick. The two lane thoroughfare barely accommodated its traffic as it was, without one Sunday driver holding up the show.

Horns expressed their driver's sentiments as the road wid-ened to four lanes and a dozen or so cars zipped past me. I'd still not found the address I was looking for but was getting closer. Two blocks later, I realized that address was an apartment building.

This would be a dead end. Renters in Albuquerque do not stay long in one place. I pulled into the parking lot and took a half-space that included a generous slice of sidewalk. Everyone seemed to be home on a Sunday afternoon and I'd be willing to bet that one of them wasn't Harvey Taylor. Well, I'd come this far.

The manager snatched open the door, expecting to snarl

at a tenant with a stupid complaint, and looked totally surprised to find me standing there. He made a quick attempt to smooth the few threads of hair that covered his shiny head and to tuck in the T-shirt that boasted a large dollop of salsa at the point where his round belly jutted out. A football announcer screamed from the TV set across the room.

"Sorry to interrupt," I said. "I'm just wondering about one of your tenants."

He set his beer can on an unseen table behind the door as an oily smile slicked its way across his features.

"Sure thing, honey. Come on in."

My teeth began to grind. "No thanks." I bit back a smart remark and backed a couple more feet away from the door. "I just wondered if Harvey Taylor still lives here."

"Who? Taylor, you say?"

"You don't know any Harvey Taylor?"

He was about to shake his head in denial, but decided he could keep me there a bit longer if he checked his records.

"That's okay," I assured him. "If he was here, you'd know it. He would have been a tenant for at least fifteen years."

He chuckled, trying to make it sexy but missing by a mile. "Babe, ain't nobody been here fifteen years. Not even me. I been here about five, and that's only because they give me my rent real cheap for managin' the place. Wanna see the apartment? They're real nice."

"Could I ask you just one more teeny little thing," I said, wiggling my eyebrows and stepping closer again.

He met me at the doorjamb. "Sure, babe."

"Please do not *ever* call me babe—or honey—or sweetie. *Ever.*"

"What...?"

I was halfway to my car before I heard that part and was

backing out of my halfassed parking spot before I noticed that his mouth was still moving. Luckily my windows were up.

I darted into traffic, realizing after the fact that he'd have an easy time getting my license plate number if he wanted to. Stupid, Charlie, stupid. Why do I always feel I have to make a point about pointless things? Well, that guy might think twice before using his routine on someone else.

I watched my rearview mirror for a few blocks but didn't see anyone behind me. He was probably back in his easy chair with a fresh beer, the ball game blasting away as he rubbed his sore ego.

The other two addresses on my list were across town and I was feeling drained and suddenly famished. Drake and Ron were probably back from the shooting range by now and I could probably talk them into going to Pedro's for a comfort dinner. Sour cream chicken enchiladas would go a long way toward curing my ills. Seeing Drake again and having him hold me would help the rest of them.

Ron's convertible was parked in front of the house, facing against traffic as usual, although traffic on my street is virtually nonexistent. He just can't seem to be bothered to turn around and face the right way.

Inside, the two men were TV-side with the football game on. Ron was totally absorbed, Drake looked bored. He and Rusty greeted me like I'd been gone for days. Drake bestowed me with two enormously satisfying kisses, while Rusty thwapped my legs with his tail and led me to his empty food bowl.

"I'm starving," I told him. "Think we can pry Ron away from the game long enough to go to Pedro's?"

"I don't know—it looks pretty serious in there," he said. "But you could get me to go in a wink."

"Okay, then, here's the plan. We tell him we're going.

If he wants to come, fine. If he won't leave, we'll bring him take-out."

Ron opted for the game and take-out, which was just as well with me. I was ready to have Drake to myself again.

"How was the shooting range?" I asked after we'd taken our seats in our usual corner table. Pedro and his wife Concha had fussed over Drake some more. They weren't quite used to seeing me as part of a couple, but I could tell the idea was taking hold fast.

"Well, I could've done better," he said. "But for being as out of practice as I am, I guess it was okay."

"Not a roaring good time?"

"I'd rather you'd been there, too." He looked truly forlorn. "I missed you."

I reached over to stroke the back of his hand. "I missed you, too. I think we're bonding."

"Wow, that's, like, pretty serious isn't it?"

We were in the middle of a kiss when Concha ahummed behind us.

"Now, you little lovebirds," she teased, "you can't be doing that when I'm standing here with hot plates."

She set them down carefully, using potholders.

"Now," she said, hands on hips. "Now you can either eat your food while it's hot or go back to that kissing." She winked at me as she turned to go back to the kitchen.

Steam rose from the plate as I made the first cut into my enchiladas. The combined flavors of tortilla, chicken, onions, cheese, and green chile blended to create heaven in my mouth. Conversation stayed at a minimum for the next few minutes as we both ummmed and rolled our eyes upward.

Initially sated, I told Drake about meeting Larry Sanchez and Rebecca.

"Afraid I didn't learn anything, though."

"What a sad case," he agreed. "I wonder if there's anything we could do for them."

"I don't know what, but I'm thinking I should get over there and see them again. Maybe something will come to mind."

We lingered over the last of our margaritas and shared a small dish of carmelly flan before collecting Ron's styrofoam encased dinner and heading home. The shorter days were catching up with us. The low sun over the volcanoes turned the air golden, the adobe buildings in Old Town to a rose color. I wanted to drink it in and make it last forever.

Ron ate his dinner watching the last two minutes of the game, which took more than fifteen minutes in real time. Drake sat down with him and worked up a little enthusiasm. I made coffee and watched the back garden wall go from gold to gray to charcoal.

It wasn't until after Ron left and I'd showered and put on my terry robe that I remembered the Sandia folder in the car. I'd wanted to try those last couple of phone numbers, but it wasn't worth the effort. We settled onto the couch with a movie on TV and I dozed off before ten.

I woke up just long enough to brush my teeth and drop the robe before falling into bed snuggled into Drake's shoulder.

I was in a warehouse somewhere, walking a high platform that ran, gallery-like around the perimeter of the building. The walkway was narrow and dark and I had to hug the wall to stay on it. My father stood on the same walkway, around the corner from me and out of reach.

"It's all right," he insisted. "Just come toward me. I'll get you down."

I edged along without making any progress. He edged toward the corner but there was some obstacle in the way.

I kept working my way toward him, when my foot bumped something.

"Daddy, it's a man! There's a man lying here!"

"Don't worry, hon. Let me get there and see."

I wanted to step over the man, but Dad kept coming closer, warning me to hold still. His face became clearer in the darkness.

"Just one more minute, Charlie. I'll be right there."

My foot touched the inert man once again and I quickly slipped back. But it was too late—I'd pushed too hard. The man rolled toward the edge and, in slow-motion, tumbled off the platform. As his body fell toward the unseen floor below, he turned face up.

It was Larry Sanchez, smiling thinly and blinking his eyes at me. He mouthed the word "Help," but no sound came out.

I awoke sharply, as though I'd been the one falling.

"What's the matter sweetheart?" Drake asked.

My breathing was shallow and rapid and it took me a moment to figure out that it had been a dream. I felt clammy with sweat. He reached out and put his arm over me.

"Just a dream. I'm fine."

But I didn't fall asleep again until the red digital clock numbers had passed four o'clock.

TWELVE

DARK CIRCLES HUNG under my eyes like death shadows. My hair drooped limply and my mouth tasted like poison. I leaned against the basin for support for a couple of minutes before deciding that I couldn't let a mere dream drag me down like this.

Drake gave my backside a squeeze as he exited the shower, towelling off as he went.

"Your turn," he smiled. "Hon? Are you okay?"

"Yeah, I'll be fine." I squeezed a smile out. "I didn't sleep very well after that dream."

I peeled off my undies and stepped under the hot spray.

"Tell you what," he continued, as I rubbed the bar of soap into a rich lather. "If I may use your car today, I'll take you to breakfast first. Then, you can either come with me to the FAA or I'll be happy to take you to your office."

I let the gentle showerfall rinse lather from my shoulders and breasts. "Well, as tempting as it sounds to spend a morning at the FAA going through aircraft documents, I really should spend a little time at my own office. I'm already feeling guilty for not going in most of last week."

"All right then, office it is. But first things first—what's for breakfast?"

I mumbled something about anything being fine with me, which he asked me to repeat, since I'd had my face under the water at the time.

Thirty minutes later, we were dry, dressed, and on our way to Nouvelle Mexicano, a friend's restaurant downtown, not far from our office. I'd helped my friend, Sharon Ortega, a few months ago when her business partner was killed and it looked like she might lose the restaurant as a result.

Things had been iffy for her for several months afterward, until one day when one of those Hollywood-turned-Santa Fe actors had come to Albuquerque to shoot his newest movie and had publicly declared the place one of the best he'd ever patronized. The newspapers picked up on it and Sharon's place was hopping. The actor still came in often enough to keep the patrons coming back. We all hoped his popularity wouldn't lag, but you know what they say. I guess a restaurant is only as popular as its latest actor.

Even for breakfast, most people needed a reservation, but Sharon did keep that one special table open. As long as you-know-who wasn't there, I got it. So, we walked in past people who'd been in line over twenty minutes to take our special seats.

"I've got a new veggie omelette that's getting rave reviews," Sharon told us as she handed over the menus. She's really getting into this Hollywood talk. "Our chef has figured out a way to make it with absolutely no fat. It comes with hash browns and toast and the whole plate has only 5 grams!"

Thinking back to the enchiladas at Pedro's last night, made the old fashioned way with, I'm sure, lots of lard, I decided Sharon's omelette special sounded good to me. Drake, who can apparently eat anything he wants without second thought, opted for it too.

"Sharon looks happy," I commented after she'd taken our order to the kitchen. "You should have seen her a few months ago. A bad business partnership nearly did her in."

Our omelettes soon arrived, fragrant with onions, peppers

and mushrooms. With an eye toward those at the door still waiting for tables, we ate quickly, paid our check and retrieved the Jeep from the only parking spot we'd found, more than two blocks away. The price of a popular eatery. Rusty waited patiently, expecting a reward for his efforts in guarding the car.

Five minutes later, Drake had dropped me and Rusty at our office, promising to stop back by when he'd finished at the FAA.

"It'll take at least half the day, maybe more," he warned. "Are you sure you won't need the car?"

"I'll be fine. If I'm hungry by noon, I'm sure Ron or Sally can get me something." At that moment I couldn't picture being hungry ever again, but I don't entirely trust those low fat meals to stick with me very long.

Sally had arrived early enough to start coffee, although she claims she really can't drink it much these days. I snagged a mug of it before heading upstairs to face a week's worth of mail and phone messages.

"Ron's not here yet," Sally informed me, sticking her head in my doorway. "He said he had court this morning and then planned to start surveillance on a new case this afternoon."

"Ooh, surveillance, his favorite part of the job."

"Yeah. Right. He won't necessarily be a happy camper when he comes in, especially if it goes through the night." Her shaggy blond hair shook as she chuckled. "Speaking of happy campers, should I duck before you get a chance to start going through that pile of mail?"

I looked at the small mountain on my desk. How *did* it pile up so fast?

"Nah, not really your fault. It's the mailman I want to speak to." I plopped down in my chair and scooped the mess toward me.

Sally disappeared.

Thirty minutes later, everything was sorted into stacks. Aside from the junk mail, which I am ruthless about, the rest of it hadn't dwindled a bit. I'd only rearranged it. I quickly jumped to the important stuff, depositing money in the bank. Then I retrieved Ron's time sheets and billed our regular customers for his services. Since most of our work is done for lawyers and insurance companies, we have very few of those clandestine types who slip you a few hundred-dollar bills. Too bad.

"Charlie, is it safe yet?" Sally's voice came over the intercom.

I chuckled into the microphone at my end of it.

"I'll be leaving in a few minutes," she said. "Do you want any lunch first?"

I thought about the nearly fat-free breakfast I'd had and thought maybe I should stay on a roll with this new healthy living phase.

"Can you order me a sliced turkey on rye, mustard and low-fat mayo?"

"Whoa! No cheeseburger and fries? Gotta keep that body in good shape now that Drake's here, huh."

I stuck my tongue out at the intercom, even though she was right. The phone rang just then and I jumped, like the caller might know I was making a face at him. The blinking red light came on steady as Sally picked up the call downstairs.

"Charlie, Jim Williams with the NTSB on line one," she announced officially.

"Jim, hi, it's Charlie."

"I've found some more stuff for you, Charlie." His voice came through as a raspy whisper.

"That's great. Does it answer my questions?" My stomach tightened as I anticipated his answer.

"I can't say anything now," he whispered. "It's too much to fax and I'm not sure I'd trust the mail with this. Can you meet me somewhere?"

"When? I don't have my car today. Maybe you could come by my office?"

"Uh…I can't get out this afternoon. How about tonight? You know that western nightclub, the Caravan? How about the parking lot there at eight?" He described his car.

"As long as you don't tell me to come alone," I answered, only half joking. "I don't meet men in parking lots unescorted."

"As long as it's someone you absolutely trust who's not any government official."

"Jim, what's going on here?"

"Can't say. Just don't tell anyone about this."

He clicked off without another word. The receiver dangled from my hand as I stared unseeing across the room. What was that all about?

"Charlie?" Sally stood in my doorway, her purse over her shoulder. "You okay? I was just going out to get your sandwich."

I shook myself to attention and slowly replaced the receiver. "Yeah…that was just a weird phone call."

"Government employees making obscene calls?"

"No, it's got something to do with my looking into my parents' deaths. I just wish I knew what."

"I was gonna get your sandwich and then go home for the day. If that's okay?"

"Sure, sure—do it."

She looked at me skeptically.

"Really. It wasn't a threat or anything—just weird."

Sally backed out and I heard the back door open and close, then her four-wheel drive vehicle started up. I turned back to some correspondence that needed answering, but couldn't seem to get my mind back on it. What had Williams unearthed that he had to whisper about in his own office?

When the phone rang again, I almost jumped out of my chair.

"Just checking in," Ron's voice announced. "Any messages?"

I told him about the phone call and asked whether he'd want to go along to meet Williams later in the evening.

"Can't. I'm supposed to be surveilling some deadbeat dad. The ex wants proof in pictures of his extravagant lifestyle so she can go back to court for more money."

"That's okay, Drake can go with me."

"Unless you want to switch places and trail the deadbeat."

"Uh-uh. No way. Besides, I'm not sure Williams would hand over the information to someone he hasn't met. He acted *really* skittish on the phone."

I'd nearly finished paying the bills, around three o'clock, when I heard a car door slam out back.

"It's me," Drake called out.

Rusty leapt up from his post on my oriental carpet and zoomed down the stairs. I could hear Drake teasing him as they came up together.

"Good day?" I asked.

"Ugh, you won't believe the pile of records I have to go through," he said. "I swear, you can trace every nut and bolt on an aircraft back to the year one."

He flopped onto the sofa across the room from me. His face looked pale under his tan.

"You feeling okay?" I asked.

"Yeah, I'll be fine. I ate some kind of ham sandwich from one of those little lunch trucks that came around out there at the FAA. It never quite settled too well."

"You want to go home and lie down? I can quit here any time," I told him.

"Yeah, whatever's convenient." He stretched out the full length of the sofa and dangled one hand to scratch Rusty's ears. "Oh, I came across something interesting for you while I was there," he added as I gathered folders and started backing up my files.

"There's a guy at the FAA who was on the investigation of your parent's plane crash. I've got his card here somewhere..." He scrunched a thumb and forefinger into his jeans pocket digging for it. "Here. Neil Kirkpatrick."

I reached for the card and looked at it closely.

"He's an old timer around the FAA," Drake continued. "Told me he'd worked lots of accidents before he settled into being an office jockey. So, I mentioned that you were trying to find out more about this one and he remembered it. Isn't that amazing? Well, anyway, he couldn't remember keeping any files on it, but said he'd look. And said you could call him any time."

I filled him in on the call from Jim Williams.

"Are you sure you'll feel like going out later?" I asked.

"For you, dear, anything," he replied gallantly. But I could tell he wasn't feeling great.

By seven-thirty, it was clear that Drake wasn't going anywhere. He'd tried to sleep for the rest of the afternoon, but after two trips to the bathroom, he'd only fallen into a restful sleep sometime around six-thirty. No way was I going to make him get up and dressed for what would probably be a thirty minute errand. I wrote him a quick note and left it on the bathroom sink, probably the first place he'd go when he woke up.

Rusty was clearly torn. He knew a man in distress when he saw one, and obviously thought he should stay with Drake. But when he saw me pick up my purse and car keys, the desire to go won out over everything else. Drake's Beretta lay on the dresser, waiting to be cleaned after yesterday's range workout. I picked it up and made sure the magazine was full, then stuffed it in an inside pocket of my jacket.

The night was clear and dark, with a few stars visible from the front yard. Once we emerged onto the city thoroughfares they would disappear into the wash of overwhelming manmade light. The temperature had dropped, probably twenty-five degrees from the afternoon high, common enough here, but something people from more humid climates never seem prepared for. I slipped on the light down jacket I'd brought along.

Although I had to traverse nearly the whole city, traffic was light enough this Monday night that I made good time up Central Avenue. College kids with backpacks casually slung over a shoulder crossed the street anywhere they pleased around the university, all heading somewhere—dorms, the bookstore, or more likely, the Frontier Restaurant.

The usual assortment of hookers strutted their stuff in the midtown area near the old Route 66 motels. I spotted Bubba Mabry's bright red Dodge Ram pickup truck in the parking lot of a 7-11. Bubba's another Albuquerque PI, whose main claim to fame is the fact that he once had Elvis Presley as a client. The only hitch was that Elvis had been dead for years at the time. The fame part came about when some tabloid reporters got involved. I don't care what they said, Bubba really is one of the good guys.

The congestion thinned again as I stayed eastbound past the dark silent fairgrounds and a section of has-been night clubs that change owners every year or two.

The Caravan is one of the few night spots along this stretch with seemingly endless staying power. Even on a

Monday night, the parking lot was at least three-quarters full. I pulled onto the side street to the west, where Williams and I had agreed that it would be easier to find each other.

His pale blue generic government issue mid-size car waited beside the curb, away from the nearest street lamp. I passed it slowly, nodding acknowledgement to him as I found a place to pull over two car lengths ahead of him.

"Stay here, kid, I'll be right back," I told Rusty, who looked like he wanted to jump out and share the adventure. I stuffed my purse behind the front seat, locked the doors, and slipped my keys into my jacket pocket. The night air nipped at me and I zipped the jacket.

A couple who had obviously gotten an early start on happy hour, swaggered around the corner of the building with their arms around each other. A lone man, decked out for a night of dancing and flirting in tight jeans, western boots, and wide-brimmed black felt hat, crossed the side street, heading for the nightclub's entrance. I walked the curb back toward the blue car.

Williams had his eyes on me and he leaned over to unlock the passenger door for me to slip in beside him. I was almost even with the front fender when the windshield exploded in a shower of glass.

THIRTEEN

I HIT THE GROUND unevenly, scuffing my palms on the curb and rolling to land with a thud on the pavement in front of the blue car. My ribs cried out and my lungs wouldn't take in any air. Sparks dangled before my eyes for several seconds. I blinked a couple of times before I realized that I was staring up into the underside of Williams's car bumper. Someone was screaming but I didn't think it was me. My lungs couldn't be working that well just yet.

A car door slammed and it occurred to me that Williams might just decide to take off after whoever had broken his windshield and I was not exactly on safe ground here. I tried to roll over but my right shoulder caught the bumper— damn these low built cars anyway. I had to dig my heels and do an inch-worm kind of maneuver to get out from under it before I could begin to get up.

Rolling over felt like it took forever. My left shoulder had taken the brunt of the fall and didn't want to do anything I asked of it. But that screaming wouldn't stop. A strong urge came over me to find the source and slap it.

I crabbed my way on all fours to the driver's side of the car. A quick recon of the street revealed nothing more than ordinary traffic out on Central. I back-tracked to the curb.

The inebriated couple had sobered up quickly. She, apparently the source of the screams, stood now with her face buried in his shoulder. No one else was in sight. I used the car bumper, then its hood, to pull myself to my feet. Crystalline chunks of windshield littered the hood's surface. Inside, Jim Williams sat strapped into the driver's seat with his shoulder harness in place. He stared at me with the one eye that remained in his half-face. My dinner rose dangerously close to my throat.

Again, I scanned the entire street. No one, except the couple on the sidewalk. I approached them.

"What happened?" I demanded. "Did you see what happened?"

The woman sobbed hiccupping little words into the man's leather jacket. His mouth hung open, emitting a little sound that came out as "huh?" They weren't going to be any help. I turned toward Williams

He wasn't going to be any help either. The bullet had taken out the driver's window, half his face, and a good part of the front windshield. Assuming it was only one bullet. There could have been several, I supposed, with a silencer—I hadn't heard any of them. But then, everything happened so fast I realized now that I hadn't absorbed much of anything.

I gingerly opened the passenger door of Williams's car. The light came on and I scanned the interior thoroughly. No file folder. Hadn't he specifically told me he was bringing me a file? Had I actually seen it in his hands as I cruised past? I couldn't think.

There was a cell phone mounted on a little stand near the floor between the front seats. I picked it up and dialed 911.

Cops in Albuquerque must hang around the east Central area in droves, or gaggles, or herds, or whatever it is you call a big group of them because I'd swear that within two minutes of my 911 call a whole flock of them screeched in. The quiet dark side street blossomed into a riot of color, complete with red, white and blue flashing lights, shouting voices, and what appeared to be the entire population of the Caravan and then some. People must have come from blocks around for the excitement. I hadn't quite scooted my little butt out of Williams's car before the first arrived and the next thing I knew my hands were on the roof, my feet spread apart, and Drake's gun was being snatched out of my jacket.

The now-quite-sober couple, who might have sworn that I hadn't been in a position to do any shooting—if they'd been able to speak—stood now a good half block away, surrounded by three or four officers.

For my part, questions were flying at me so fast I felt like I was babbling. Finally, one voice broke through.

"Charlie?" Kent Taylor, homicide detective and friend of Ron's, pushed past the blue shoulders surrounding me.

"You know her?" One of the officers turned to Kent.

"Yeah. Look, guys, it's fine. Let's back off a little here."

I wasn't sure whether to cry or hug him or both.

"Sir, it looks like we have one of those boyfriend/girlfriend bar scenes here," the other officer said knowingly. "She probably watched him come out of the Caravan here with somebody else, they parted ways, she pulls out this,"—showing Drake's gun—"and blows him away. Her fingerprints are all over the car and the gun."

Where did they get all this? I stared at Kent in amazement.

"You don't seriously believe that, do you?" I asked.

Kent took my elbow and pushed through the group to a quiet spot near one of the tall leafy shrubs that lined the side of the building. "Now, tell me about it," he said, pulling a little notebook from his pocket.

I recounted the story, including a quick summary of the reason for the meeting, right up to the point where I'd crawled out from under the car and dialed 911.

"I have to commend the PD," I said with just a touch of sarcasm. "It wasn't two minutes before they got here and made me assume the position. That's where you came in," I told him.

He'd scrawled constantly in the little notebook while keeping his eyes fixed on my face the whole time. I wondered if that was a skill taught in the police academy.

"Now, the only people you remember seeing were that other couple and a guy in a black hat. Any idea where he got off to?"

I hadn't even thought about him again. But I was sure he was nowhere around when I peeked toward the street from my vantage point under the car.

"Think back, Charlie. Did he have a gun? Did he approach Williams's car?"

"He approached the car...I didn't think much of it at the time because he seemed to be on a direct heading toward the nightclub. He was dressed like anyone else going in there, like he was going dancing. I didn't see any weapon, but come to think of it, his right arm was down at his side." I shrugged. "Anything's possible."

"Could you identify him? Look around. See him anywhere in the crowd?"

We strolled casually down the sidewalk, keeping up the appearance of conversation while I scanned the crowd. The night had become chilly and the people bunched together. Yellow police tape cordoned off the street thirty or forty feet fore and aft of Williams's car. The medical examiner's car had arrived and men in latex gloves crowded around the car gathering evidence. Half of Albuquerque's population were jammed behind the yellow tape, gawking and trying to get a glimpse of some blood and guts.

"I don't know, Kent. Half those guys have on black cowboy hats. I never really looked at his face. He was tall and slim, I know. Had on black jeans and black boots. His shirt was dark—maybe blue or black or red?''

We dipped under the tape and mingled through the crowd, but I didn't see anyone I could pinpoint as being the guy. He'd have to be pretty bold to hang around the scene with three witnesses still here, but then—if he was the shooter—he was pretty bold to fire the shots in front of us too. And there was the strong possibility that Black Hat wasn't the killer at all. He could have just been some guy who'd run like hell when the commotion started.

I looked across the street. There was a small cinderblock building that housed some little businesses, an empty parking area behind it roped off to keep the Caravan's customers out, and the street itself lined with parked cars. A sniper could have been waiting in about a hundred different dark nooks and crannies.

Most of the initial police presence had left to other duties, leaving only two cars with lights flashing, one at either end of the blocked street. The remaining officers attempted to break up the crowd, but the club manager's shouted offer of a free drink if they'd come back inside was what got most of them to vacate the scene.

An ambulance backed in close to the car, the attendants were already placing Jim Williams's body on a gurney. A wrecker had arrived to take the car. Within a few minutes, there'd be no sign that a man had lost his life here tonight. By the time the dancers left the Caravan in a few hours' time, most of them would have forgotten all about it. I wished I could be so lucky.

Who could have possibly known about my meeting with Williams? I couldn't believe this was a random shooting, although Albuquerque certainly had its fair share of those anymore. The file was gone and that told me that the shooter had been close by, he'd known about the meeting, and he'd removed the evidence. Evidence of what? Now I wished desperately that Williams had told me more about the contents of that file.

I thought back to his call this afternoon. His whispered secrecy made me think that he was afraid of someone within his own office. It could also explain how someone may have known about our meeting. But killing Williams was a pretty desperate measure. They could have just stolen the file, but didn't. That meant they had to get rid of Williams. And if they had to get rid of Williams, they might have to get rid of me too. After all, they had no way of knowing how much I already knew.

FOURTEEN

"GUESS THAT WRAPS IT UP here," Kent Taylor said as the wrecker pulled away.

"Can I have my gun back?" I suddenly felt vulnerable.

"Not just yet," Taylor said. "They've taken it to the lab for some ballistics tests."

"You can't seriously be thinking I'm a suspect."

"Unofficially, no I don't think so. But officially, it was a weapon found at the scene of a murder, on a person whose prints were all over the victim's car."

"You'll find the gun's been fired," I told him. "It's Drake's weapon. He and Ron went to the shooting range yesterday and, well, I borrowed it before he had a chance to clean it."

He shrugged again. "Well, you can see how all of it looks. I'm going to put in my report that we questioned you at the scene. I'll want you to come in and sign a statement tomorrow."

Wonderful. A police record.

"You're not under arrest, Charlie," he said, reading my mind. "You can go on home tonight. Just don't forget to give us a statement tomorrow."

Like I should feel lucky about this. I shuffled back to my Jeep where Rusty waited anxiously. Poor thing—I'd forgotten all about him in the craziness. I slipped into the driver's seat and took his big head in my two hands, stroking his ears and sounding a lot more reassuring to him than I did to myself. He licked at my wrists, trying to make everything all better with doggie kisses.

My eyes stayed glued to the rearview mirror all the way home. I used all the diversionary tactics I'd ever read in detective novels and was finally convinced that no one followed me. I pulled into my own driveway feeling jittery as a high tension line.

The living room lamps were on and the porch light spilled a golden puddle down the steps. Leaves had begun to collect in the flower beds and around the sidewalk. A couple more weeks and we'd see the last of our gorgeous fall weather. Rusty bounded for the door while I trailed along more slowly, scanning the street for any sign of strange cars.

"Everything okay, hon?" Drake's voice trailed up over the back of the sofa as we came through the front door.

"What are you doing up? You should be resting." I walked around to the front of the couch so he wouldn't have to get up.

"I thought I'd try a little 7-UP and maybe… What happened to you!"

"What?" I hadn't seen myself in a mirror yet.

He stood up. "Look at this!" He reached out to touch a flapping square of cloth hanging from the shoulder of my jacket. "And sweetheart, your face!"

What had happened to my face? I turned to look in the mirrored back wall of the china cabinet. My reflection came back at me as a series of squares interrupted by goblets and candlesticks.

"Guess I better clean up." I pulled the jacket off and draped it over a hook on the coatrack near the door. My favorite jacket, and now it had a six-inch rip.

"I thought you were going to get a file folder from somebody." Drake followed me into the bathroom like an anxious terrier. "You didn't say anything about this being dangerous."

"Well, I didn't have a clue that it *would* be dangerous," I snapped back. "It started out simple, but got complicated along the way. I thought I'd be fine—I even took protection with me..." I'd also have to explain why the police now had his pistol. "Just let me get cleaned up and I'll tell you all about it." I held my hands up in a "halt" gesture.

"Honey, look at these," he exclaimed, taking my battered hands in his. "You're all scraped up."

My mouth opened to snap back at him again, but he caught the message before a word came. He backed off like he'd been slapped and turned away like a whipped puppy. I felt like a big shit.

In the mirror, my long hair was in tangles and a two-inch swath of road burn crossed my left cheek. My palms were crusty with dried blood and asphalt crumbs. A black streak of oil swiped the heel of my left hand, ending abruptly where the cuff of my jacket had probably picked up the rest of it. I ran the tap water until it was just-bearably hot and shoved my battered hands under the flow.

The pain shot upward to my shoulders, reminding me of that other injury. Luckily the jacket had taken the brunt of the fall, but the shoulder muscle was speaking—loudly. I finished washing out the scrapes, coated them with an antibiotic ointment, and popped three ibuprofen tablets before returning to the living room. Drake stood by the fireplace and I approached him tentatively.

"I'm sorry, Drake..." The apology had not fully come out when I looked down at the coffee table. He'd made me a cup of tea and brought out a plate of my favorite Pepperidge Farm cookies. He came toward me and enveloped me into his bathrobe. I couldn't help it—the tears just gushed.

"Shh, shh," he consoled.

"I don't know…why I…do this," I blubbered. "I was fine…at the time."

He stroked my hair until I began breathing normally again. "Here," he said, "have your tea before it gets cold."

I sank gratefully into the sofa and held the hot mug cautiously, not wanting it to touch my wounded palms. The tea was delicious—he'd put in a shot of amaretto—and the wonderful almondy smell soothed me. Several sips of it and a couple of cookies definitely helped.

"Want some?" I offered the plate.

"No thanks. I'm feeling better now, but I'll just take it easy with this." He held up his 7-UP.

"I really feel like a jerk, getting into this mess with you home sick and all," I told him. "And now I've lost your gun, too, well not really lost but it might take a few days to get it back."

"What? You better start at the beginning, hon. I'm not getting any of this."

I told him how I'd borrowed his pistol for protection and ended up having the police take it away.

"Police? What were the police doing there?"

So then I told him the rest of it, making light of the fact that I'd been within ten feet of Williams when the shot was fired. For the first time all evening, I began to feel the high tension line inside me relax just a little. I didn't tell Drake of my fear that I might also be a target.

No sense in ruining a perfect night.

We snuggled into each other under the covers, each taking comfort from the other's warmth. The painkiller began to take the edge off my aching shoulder and I willed myself to put Jim Williams's face out of my mind. I fell into an uneasy sleep sometime around two.

Gray light began to filter in around the window edges

around six and I finally gave up the attempt to fall back to sleep one more time. Drake's breathing was deep and peaceful. He'd had a better night of it than I had. I rolled groggily from under the covers, taking care to avoid my bruised shoulder while creating minimum disturbance for Drake.

Rusty raised his head from his rug at the foot of our bed then set it back down on his front paws when he saw that I was only heading for the bathroom. I stepped under the steaming hot water, letting it pelt my sore muscles relentlessly while I slicked shampoo over my tussled hair. I treated myself to a full five minutes of scalp massage, the kind you normally only get in a salon where someone takes the time to really pamper you.

Thirty minutes later I emerged from the foggy room, wrapped in my thick terry robe. Feeling a little spacy in the head, but with relaxed muscles and a lot better attitude. Rusty followed me toward the kitchen. I let him out the back door, then dumped coffee grounds into a filter and switched on the machine.

Tuesday. I should spend some time at the office today, but couldn't forget how the quest I'd thought so innocent had now cost a man his life. Because, no matter what else I tried to tell myself, I knew that Williams had been killed for the contents of that file he'd planned to deliver to me.

Rusty scratched at the door, eager now for the breakfast of nuggets I'd dumped into his bowl. He gobbled them down as if he might never eat again. I went to the fridge for some ideas on what Drake and I might gobble down.

Nothing looked too exciting to me, and I doubted he'd want anything very exotic after his bout of upset stomach last night, so I pulled out a couple of choices of cold cereal and the bread and butter. By the time the coffee finished sputtering, I'd toasted one slice of bread and decided that I'd wait and have a real breakfast with Drake.

The morning *Journal* lay in a fat roll on the front porch. What would they have made over Williams's death, I wondered. I carried it inside and took a lot of time pulling off the rubber band that bound it. I ate half my slice of toast and took two good deep sips of coffee before I trusted myself to read.

A triple murder at a convenience store and the indictment of a Santa Fe politician claimed the front page. A single murder just isn't that dramatic any more—Williams merited only about four column inches on page three. I scanned the story, didn't find my name, then went back and read the whole thing.

It was your basic who, what, where, when just-the-facts-ma'am story. Nothing was mentioned about motivation; none was expected anymore, I guess. A dark kernel of anger began to grow in me; this was wrong—why did a man have to die for some papers in a folder? The killer could have demanded the folder at gunpoint and gotten it, surely. But stealing the papers wouldn't erase Jim Williams's memory and that was the whole point.

FIFTEEN

THE OFFICE PHONE rang, pulling Sally's attention away from my recount of the shooting. The scabby place on my face was the only reason I'd starting telling her about it anyway. I went upstairs and turned my attention back to the letters I hadn't finished yesterday.

"Hannah Simmons on line one," Sally announced.

Dad's secretary.

"Hannah, how are you?" I greeted.

"I'm just fine, Charlie. Well, my arthritis has been acting up a bit lately, you know, with the colder nights and all. And then the neighbor's dog barked half the night and I don't guess I slept more than five minutes."

Why did I ask?

"Is there something I can do for you, Hannah?" I tried to sound busy without being rude.

"Oh, yes of course, dear. I didn't call to tell you about my neighbor's dog."

Thank God.

"You remember you were asking me about some of the men your father worked with? Well, you'll never guess who I bumped into yesterday at the grocery store."

A long pause. I suppose she really wanted me to take a guess. "Someone Dad worked with?"

"Heaven's yes, it was Wendel Patterson and his wife. You know she was always the prettiest thing. Kind of snooty around us secretaries, but I guess that could have just been 'cause she was shy.''

Patience, Charlie.

"And you saw them yesterday?" I prompted.

"Yes, at the Smith's over on Montgomery."

"That's great news, Hannah. I couldn't find a listing for him in the phone book. They didn't by any chance say where they live now, did they?"

"Oh yes, they have one of those fancy retirement apartments, with a maid once a week, and all their meals cooked in a big fancy dining room, and the bus picks them up and takes them anyplace they want to go in town."

"Did they mention where the apartment is?"

"Yes. It's up there on Montgomery, pretty close to that store where I saw them. Now, let me think, what did they call the place? Via…something. Via del…something."

I pulled my phone directory out as she struggled with the name. Under retirement apartments I found three starting with either Via or Villa, only one of which was on Montgomery.

"That's okay, Hannah. I think I know the place. You did a great bit of detective work there, you know."

"I told them about you coming by the house here and how you didn't know about your daddy's plane crash until just recently."

"You did?" A bolt of fear shot through me. "Hannah, be careful about this. I…" How could I caution her without scaring her too much? "You know how everything was top secret when you worked at Sandia? Well, I think it would be best if we still treated it that way. Can you swear me an oath?"

"Is something…? You're right, Charlie. If this has to do with the Lab, then it's top secret. I won't tell a soul. And you know I can keep an oath."

"Good. I may soon get to the bottom of this and I'll let you know when it's okay to talk about it. In the meantime, mum's the word." Did people really say that?

"Right, Charlie. And if you need to call me again, let's have a password. Just identify yourself as Sweetpea."

I hung up the phone, chuckling. Sweetpea? Well, I could remember it anyway. It was the nickname my parents used to call me—probably because they hoped it would turn me into a sweet delicate little girl instead of the rowdy, kick-ass little ruffian that I was.

I pulled out a notepad and jotted down the address of Wendel Patterson's apartment complex from the phone book. My pen stopped in mid-air. How many other people from Sandia might remember me as Sweetpea?

Since the Pattersons obviously had an unlisted phone number, I would just have to take my chances at reaching them directly at their place. And if they weren't in, I'd try George Myers's address, which I thought would be within a few blocks of theirs.

Sally sat at her desk, typing letters off the tape recorder. I waved a hand in front of her page to get her attention.

"I'm going out on a couple of errands. If Ron isn't back by the time you leave, just turn on the answering machine. If Drake calls, tell him I'm planning on being home by the time the movers arrive with his stuff this afternoon."

She acknowledged with a little salute and kept on typing.

I walked toward my Jeep into another perfect October day. Leaves on all the surrounding trees fluttered like tissue paper in the slight breeze, attached lightly to their limbs. The next halfway strong wind would send them scattering. I took a deep breath, staring, enjoying the contrast of brilliant yellow against vivid blue.

Rusty had stayed home with Drake this morning, their goal being to clear a large enough space in the living room for the boxes from the moving company. He'd offered to stack them in the garage and put them away later, but I knew how difficult that would be. As long as the cartons were in our way, we'd have to deal with them now. I didn't want Drake to feel that the move was temporary. He should be free to move in and take over as much space as he needed. And a mess in plain sight was much more likely to get put away than a hidden mess.

The late-morning traffic was light as I headed north on Rio Grande Boulevard toward I-40. At rush hour I'd avoid these sections of the freeways altogether, but right now it wasn't bad. Within fifteen minutes, I'd negotiated the interchange to I-25 and made it to the exit at Montgomery. From the address I'd found, I guessed I had two or three miles farther to go.

The building was elegant and modern, a light tan stucco with an attractive portico at the entrance and a brilliant turquoise tile roof. The front parking area contained only a dozen or so cars, while driveways to either side appeared to lead to more parking closer to the individual apartments.

Automatic sliding doors whooshed open for me, with a second set doing the same as I entered. Inside, the lobby was tastefully decorated in shades of tan, turquoise, and burgundy with cozy groupings of couches and chairs, coffee tables with silk flower arrangements, and two fireplaces—one at either end of the long room.

A reception desk just to the right of the front door was the only reminder that this wasn't an exclusive hotel. A discreet sign asked visitors to sign in. In case a visitor decided to sneak by, a woman in a modified nurses's uniform verbally repeated the request.

"I'm here to visit a friend of my father's," I answered to her May-I-help-you, "but I don't know the apartment number."

"The name?"

"Patterson. Wendel Patterson."

She raised the metal cover on a clipboard and ran a shell pink nail down the list. "Number 206. Go to the end of this hall, take the elevator up one floor. It's to your right. Oh, lunch is served in twenty minutes. I'm afraid without a reservation you can't stay for it."

"That's okay. It'll just be a short visit."

I followed her directions, past several side rooms with card tables that had jigsaw puzzles or bridge games in progress. One room contained a small library with comfortable looking wing chairs. The dining room was on my left, just before the elevators. The smell of something meaty wafted out toward me. I pressed the button with the "up" arrow, thinking I could easily get used to this kind of retirement life.

The Patterson apartment was two doors down from a tiny beauty shop and a laundry room. I pressed their buzzer.

The woman who answered looked like she'd just stepped out of the beauty shop across the hall. Her strawberry white hair lay in a bouffant cap covered with little curls that framed her face and set off the pale ivory of her two-piece suit perfectly. Her frosted nails carried through the pearl-colored tones.

"Mrs. Patterson? I'm Charlie Parker. My father used to work with your husband at Sandia. I know it's nearly lunch time, so I won't stay long. May I talk to your husband a few minutes?"

She looked vaguely flustered at having opened the door to a stranger but she graciously stood aside for me. The apartment was an extension of the lady herself, all done in cream and beige, silk flower arrangements, and few personal touches. One framed portrait of a younger family, presumably children and grandchildren, sat atop the TV set. The one out-of-place item in the room was a dark brown recliner covered with a bright multi-colored afghan.

"Wendel, there's somebody here to see you," Mrs. Patterson called out.

Patterson leaned forward slightly in the brown recliner, squinting to get a look at me. I did some quick math in my head. My father would have been sixty-five now—Patterson must have been at least fifteen years older, approaching eighty now. He wore brown slacks and a tan plaid shirt that swallowed his skinny frame.

"Well, who the hell is it?" he asked querulously.

"I don't know, dear. Somebody from work."

I stepped forward. "Mr. Patterson, my name's Charlie Parker. My father was Bill Parker. He worked with you at Sandia years ago."

"Huh? Ol' Bill Parker, you say?" He shifted back into his seat, not offering me one. Mrs. Patterson had melted away into the small kitchen off the entry hall.

I perched on a beige footstool so I could at least be on the same eye level with him. "Yes, Mr. Patterson, I recently learned about the circumstances of my parent's plane crash and I came across an old photo at a company picnic with Dad and you and some other men. So I figured you must have been friends."

"Hmph." His jaw worked his lower denture into place and I couldn't tell whether his noncommittal sound came from that or in reaction to my words.

"Anyway, I'd like to know more about the crash. I understand it wasn't an accident after all, and thought maybe something my father was working on at the time might have been behind it."

"Oh hell, them ol' boys in research always had somethin' goin' on, but it weren't so all fired important as that." He waved a heavily veined hand in dismissal.

"Were you also in research? Working on some of those same projects?"

"Ah hell no," he dismissed. "Course, you know *all* that stuff was real secret. Can't really say what all *I* did. It was all real important to the national security, you know."

"But you didn't work directly with my father?"

"Naw, he was in research, you know."

Mrs. Patterson emerged, her hands making little fluttery motions. "Wendel, lunch is starting in about five minutes," she reminded, looking almost worried that she had to interrupt.

I stood, remembering my manners. "I won't keep you." I pulled my business card from my purse. "If you can think of anything about the crash or anything that was going on around Sandia at the time, please let me know."

Patterson took the card, stood, and shoved his hands into the pockets of his baggy slacks, jiggling loose change. "I sure will, miss." His mouth moved upward at one corner. Was he *flirting?*

I glanced over at his wife, but she was busy draping a cardigan sweater over her shoulders, clipping the top edges together in front with a pearlized gadget.

"Well, have a nice lunch." I left it at that.

The temperature outside had warmed to near summer levels. I peeled off my light jacket and flung it into the back seat, wondering if I'd have time to catch George Myers before getting back home to greet the movers and tackle the stack of boxes that would soon await. Digging my little notebook out of my purse, I found the page where I'd written down addresses. Sure enough, Myers's home was no more than five minutes away.

Taking my life in my hands, I crossed Montgomery Boulevard and navigated my way into the Holiday Park subdivision. The modest homes sat on good-sized lots developed in the days before builders figured out that they could get by with the minimum setbacks allowed by code and jam an extra two houses into every block. In the twenty-five or so years since its inception, the trees and shrubs had matured, giving the neighborhood a well-established feel. Myers's address was two blocks off Montgomery, giving almost enough space to buffer the persistent traffic noise. The driveway boasted two large oil slicks, but no cars. I parked at the curb.

The house was sage green stucco, with turquoise trim around the roofline and a kelly green front door, a color scheme either chosen in the dark or by a design-challenged house painter. The front lawn was neatly trimmed and raked clear of leaves. A gaggle of yellow wooden geese trotted across the lawn, and two bright red hummingbird feeders hung from a sycamore tree in the center of the yard. Two large windows flanked the front door, both heavily decorated with cut-out paper jack-o-lanterns and skeletons, reminding me that we did have a holiday coming up.

I pulled the picnic snapshot from my purse, reminding myself of the faces. Myers was obviously the youngest of the group, probably in his early twenties when the photo was taken. So he'd only be around thirty-five now. Still had young children at home, judging by the window decor. And that probably meant that everyone was either at school or work now. I debated whether to even bother going to the door, then decided that it would be silly not to try after driving out here.

My first ring of the bell brought a cat to the windowsill, a distinctive calico who sat on the other side of the glass checking me out and meowing twice. I smiled at her and rubbed the window pane where her neck was, but no one came to the door. Oh well. It had been worth a try.

Twelve-fifteen. If I could dodge the major streets during

unch hour, I could be home by one. I stepped off the porch, breathing deeply of the spicy autumn air. I'd just inserted my key into the ignition when a vehicle pulled into the Myers's drive.

The woman who emerged from the lime green Plymouth frankly appraised me as she leaned to unbuckle a toddler from his car seat. The child whined and clung to her leg as she proceeded to grab two grocery bags while juggling her purse and keys and hipping the car door shut. Although I was pretty sure I knew the answer, I needed to make one more attempt.

"Mrs. Myers?" I called out to her.

She knew I was a sales person and she knew she didn't want to talk to me, but it's amazing how people can't just walk away when their names are called. She grimaced but nodded at me.

I crossed the drive. "Can I help you with those bags?" I offered.

"No, I'm fine, thanks." Her face remained closed. The toddler remained attached to her leg.

"I'm looking for a George Myers who worked at Sandia Corporation about fifteen years ago," I said.

"Yes?"

"I guess he isn't home now, but is this the right place?" She wasn't sure how much to tell me. "Yes, it is."

"My name's Charlie Parker. My father, Bill Parker, worked with him back then. I'd really like the chance to ask him some questions. Does he still work at Sandia?"

"Yes, he does. Look, I need to get Jeffrey some lunch and put this stuff in the refrigerator."

"Sure. I won't keep you. Would it be easier if I tried to catch Mr. Myers at work?"

"He won't talk about work, you know."

"Really? Even something that happened a long time ago?"

She sighed and her mouth formed a thin line. "If he doesn't even share his work life with his family, what makes you think he'll tell you anything? Unless..."

She grabbed the toddler by the hand and marched toward the front door, effectively ending the strange conversation. I gnawed the inside of my lip, then headed toward my car. What was that all about? Was I emitting some kind of pheromones today, or was it merely my imagination that every person I'd talked with came out with some intensely personal reaction to me?

SIXTEEN

A WHITE MOVING VAN with blue lettering stood in front of my house. Its back doors were open and a ramp angled down to the driveway, which now held about two dozen cardboard cartons of various sizes. Two men with dollies traversed the distance from the ramp to the driveway and back. Drake came out the front door, closely followed by Rusty, picked up a carton and waved at me. I parked in front of Elsa's house and tiptoed around the clutter.

"Hi honey, I'm home," I grinned at him. "Looks like we have our work cut out for us." I brushed a streak of dust from his cheek and accepted a kiss.

"I'm just taking these into whichever rooms they're marked for—kitchen, bathroom, whatever," he said. "Don't worry, they've got almost everything off the truck," he added as I stared at the boxes.

"How about some lunch?" I asked. "Have you eaten yet? I could make us a sandwich while they finish up."

He nodded approval at that idea and turned to carry his load into the house. I followed, with Rusty trailing behind, sniffing at each new parcel he encountered.

I was spreading mayo on bread when the phone rang.

"Ms. Parker?" a strange male voice queried.

"Yes?"

"Hey, you just managed to get my butt chewed royally," he said, with a hint of laughter in his voice.

"What? Who is this?"

"George Myers at Sandia. I don't know what you said to my wife earlier, but she's convinced we're fooling around."

"What! Look, Mr. Myers, I didn't say anything. I told her you used to work with my father years ago."

"Hey, no problem. She gets that way every time some very good looking lady comes along."

I was beginning to get the feeling that she might have good reason. My mind darted back to the picnic picture. George Myers was young then, with a Presley haircut and a Redford smile.

"Look, I don't want to get in the middle of any personal problems here. I wanted to ask if you remembered anything about the work my father was doing right before the plane crash that killed him."

I could hear him thinking over the phone line.

"Let's see, that was when?"

I told him the date.

"I'll have to give that some thought, go back through my records. The '60s and '70s were pretty intense around here. And I was fairly new with the company. I know my first few months I sat on the sidelines a lot, observing but not doing a whole lot of my own research."

"That might be exactly what I need," I told him. "Someone who knew what projects my father was working on."

"Tell you what, Charlie, let me think about this a couple days and give you a call back. Maybe we could meet for a drink and go over it."

Fat chance. "Fine," was all I said. Didn't want to tell him what I really thought of him until I had all the information I could get, but there was no way I'd meet privately with this guy. Bringing Drake along would quench him.

"Oh, George," I remembered, "don't say anything about

this to anyone else. There's already been some...trouble with someone else I talked to."

"Really?"

"I can't elaborate." I got the feeling that trouble was this guy's middle name. I hung up the phone hoping he wouldn't get too daring just now.

Drake and I ate our sandwiches and spent the rest of the afternoon unpacking boxes, me taking the bedroom and office and leaving the kitchen to his expertise. By five o'clock we'd made a sizeable dent and decided to take a dinner break.

I placed a quick call to Neil Kirkpatrick, Drake's contact at the FAA, but he'd gone for the day. I left a message with a secretary who gave me the definite impression that she, too, wanted to go home and would probably forget to tell him I'd called.

Pedro's was crowded for a week night. All six tables were filled, but one couple was getting ready to leave so we nabbed their spot. It felt funny sitting across the small room from our usual corner.

My shoulders ached and my hands burned, even though I'd been careful with my skinned palms. Pedro caught my eye and held up two fingers. I nodded, and the margaritas arrived a couple minutes later. The first one was so good I broke with tradition and ordered a second.

"Those guys with the moving company said the other van, the one with my pickup, should be here in a day or two," Drake said, licking salt off his upper lip. "Then I can get out on my own and not be cramping your style so much."

"You're not cramping..."

"Charlie Parker?"

I stopped in mid-sentence to look up at the stranger addressing me.

"May I?" He pulled out the extra chair at our table and sat down before I could close my gaping mouth.

"George Myers," he introduced, holding his hand out first to me then Drake. "Nasty scrape you have there," he said, nodding toward my cheek.

Drake shot me a puzzled look, while I turned on Myers.

"How on earth did you find me here?" My blood pressure rose, along with my temper.

I turned to Drake. "Mr. Myers used to work with Dad at Sandia. His name was on my list of contacts, but we've never met."

"Unfortunately." Myers wiggled an eyebrow.

What nerve! I noticed that Drake was working as hard as I was not to lash out at the man.

"What are you doing here?" I asked again.

"I found some information for you."

"Does anyone else know about this?" I asked, scanning the crowded room.

"No. I go into the file rooms all the time. Would you believe that about nine-tenths of the work done out there wasn't even computerized in the '70s? Mostly just the scientific research, and even that's stored in some outmoded old program. Everything like travel records, time sheets, minutes of meetings, that was all kept in old fashioned manila files."

"So, what did you find out about my father's work?"

"Well, here's the deal. There was a top secret project just coming into being when I started work there. Like I told you, in the beginning I just sat in on meetings. Didn't do any real research of my own.

"The project was the forerunner of what later became popularly known as the Star Wars defense plan. But this was early on. Around the lab it was simply referred to as SDL-14-X1."

"All that?"

"Well, X1 was what most of us called it. Anyway, Bill Parker headed up the team and ran most of the meetings. So I knew he must have kept a pretty hefty file on it. Figured now, with defense cut way back, and the Soviets no longer our enemies, a lot of that stuff has either been declassified or moved to less secure areas for storage. Figured I could probably find some of it."

"And?"

"And I can't find Bill Parker's name on a single piece of paper in that place."

"That can't be. He worked out there, was deeply involved in all that stuff for nearly twenty years. There's just no way his name wouldn't be all over the place."

"No kidding. I personally saw lots of documents he worked on. He had three file cabinets—twelve drawers full of stuff—in his own office. Now where did all that go?"

Where indeed? "Did you ask anyone?"

"Not yet. You sounded so mysterious this morning. I thought I'd see what I came up with first."

I gnawed at my lip. This whole thing was going beyond strange, venturing into the really weird.

"Tomorrow, I thought I'd go into the computer records. So far, I've only checked the physical files. It could be that Bill's project was considered important enough at the time to be stored on computer. Or even on microfiche. All those files in his office could have been filmed for storage, then the paper files destroyed."

"That's true," I agreed. "Meanwhile, can you think of anyone else I should talk to?" I told him the names I'd already checked out.

"If you've talked to Hannah, you've probably got your best knowledge source right there," he said. "Now Larry Sanchez, he was an inspector. In charge of checking the prototype missiles and guidance systems. He'd probably know if there was anything fishy going on.''

''Maybe he did. He had an accident, not too long after Dad's crash, and he's been paralyzed ever since. I visited, but didn't get anything out of him.''

''I knew Larry pretty well—we were two of the younger members of the team. Maybe I should visit him too,'' George offered. He pushed his chair back. ''Well, I'll leave you folks to your dinner.''

''I don't trust that guy,'' Drake muttered as Myers exited.

''Why? Because he hit on me?'' I teased. ''You know you've got nothing to worry about.''

Pedro rushed up, apologizing for taking so long to get our orders. I broke with tradition and ordered the taco plate, but Drake insisted he still couldn't resist the chicken enchiladas.

''You notice he never did answer your question about how he knew to find you here?'' Drake continued as if there'd been no interruption.

''True. So, how did he?''

''And is he truly so non-busy right now that he dropped everything to go digging through fifteen year old records? Or is there more than idle curiosity at work here?''

''You know, Drake, if this helicopter idea doesn't go through, we could turn you into a pretty decent investigator,'' I hinted.

''Turn me into—excuse me, but I came up with those ideas before you did, my dear.''

He had. I really should be sticking to my financial duties at the office and not poking around wherever I saw trouble. Our food arrived just then so I didn't have to respond. I forked up some refried beans, while a sudden memory of Jim Williams's shattered face and car came rushing back at me.

SEVENTEEN

GRAY LIGHT filtered into the bedroom, giving everything the feel of a badly made black and white movie. Unable to find any position comfortable enough to lull me back into sleep, I rolled off the edge of the bed.

I gently closed the bathroom door before switching on a light to avoid waking Drake. Surely his muscles must be just as achey as mine. I peed, brushed my teeth and popped three Advil. My scraped hands and face were looking somewhat better as I doctored them with more antibiotic cream. Slipping on a robe, I shuffled into the kitchen and started some coffee brewing.

Yesterday's boxes hadn't gone away. We'd gone through about half of them, stashing the empties in the garage until trash day, but the other half still needed attention. Later. I flopped into one of the kitchen chairs.

My mind wouldn't let go of the questions Drake had posed last night. George Myers *did* seem to know a little too much about me and my habits, and he *had* leaped right into the opportunity to dig back into secret records. How involved was he? I wondered if he might also have been involved in the investigation of the crash—and to what extent?

And if he was involved in the investigation, why hadn't he said so? And could there be something in the records that he didn't want me to know? And would he go so far as to cover up or destroy anything he found? Because if he did, it would mean he was definitely a part of the coverup.

And if all this was true, I was playing with fire. And if it wasn't, I was losing my mind.

I lay my head on my folded arms and dozed.

"What are you doing in here, sweetheart?" Drake rubbed at my shoulders as he gently woke me. He wore a fresh blue polo shirt and jeans and smelled like soap and shampoo.

"Oh, do that a little harder, will you?" I winced as he squeezed the muscles. "Yeah, and up the sides of my neck too?"

I became a rag doll as he kneaded my neck, shoulders, and upper arms.

"Now that you're about to drip right off the chair," he said, "let me wake you up again."

He poured two mugs of coffee, dousing them with cream and sugar.

"Are you aching as bad as I am?" I asked. "I feel like I slept on a concrete bleacher."

"I guess I did better than that." He flexed his shoulders and arms a bit. "I'm feeling it, but I slept okay."

He got up and put some whole wheat bread into the toaster while I sipped at my coffee. Rusty stared up at me with that plaintive starving-dog look he's perfected so well, until I finally got up and poured a scoop of nuggets into his bowl.

"What's the plan for today?" Drake asked as he set jars of jam on the table and wafted the heavenly-smelling toast under my nose. "That is, after we've breathed some life back into you."

I grinned. "Well, they say the best way to work out sore muscles is to do the same exercise again, so I guess I'll tackle the rest of the boxes after I've had a hot shower."

"I just about have the office organized in there. I'm taking full advantage of the empty drawers you gave me," he said. "I may have to invest in a filing cabinet once I get the helicopter business going."

"Take all the drawer space you want," I told him. "I can always take some of my stuff to the office. And there's probably lots of it I don't really need, for that matter."

I rinsed the plates and mugs and stuck them in the dishwasher before retreating to the shower. The phone was ringing when I stepped out fifteen minutes later.

"Drake? Are you getting that?" No answer, just the ringing.

I belted my terry robe and picked up the bedroom extension.

"Charlie Parker?" a female voice inquired. "Please hold for Congressman Cudahy's office."

I held.

"Miss Parker? This is Congressman Cudahy's secretary. Please hold for the Congressman."

I held. Did these people forget how to punch telephone numbers after election day?

"Charlie! Hi, Jack Cudahy here," the public voice oiled over the phone line.

"Yes?" Since when were we such buddies?

"Say, Charlie, I've been looking into the records on that plane crash you asked me about? Unfortunately, hon, I can't find anything unusual in the reports. Looks like the weather was just terrible that day and that's probably what brought the plane down."

"Really? Congressman, some of my father's notes indicate that he was feeling under pressure—some kind of 'heat.' What could that have been about?"

"Well, Charlie, I have no recollections about that time. I can assure you that every reasonable means was taken at the time to insure a complete and thorough investigation into the matter.''

Pure politician-speak. Lots of words that don't say anything.

"You actually worked at Sandia during those years, didn't you, Congressman? Did you work with my father on any of his projects?"

"To a limited extent. Oh, excuse me, I've got an overseas call coming in. Well, just wanted to let you know what I found. Please feel free to call on my office any time." Click.

The man was slick. Had the art of appearing concerned, while not doing a damn thing, down pat. He was probably singlehandedly taking credit for the most recent boom in the stock market too.

I toweled my hair and slipped on jeans and a T-shirt. Drake was humming ''Love Me Tender'' from somewhere in the depths of the office that was rapidly becoming his, so I decided to tackle the kitchen cartons.

Jack Cudahy's call still rankled. How did he think he'd get away with such an absolutely blatant lie? The weather caused the crash—bullshit! Jim Williams had told me there was no question about it being an explosion. Even Hannah, hell even Elsa Higgins, knew that. I thought of Jim, and felt a sudden jolt of concern for the two older women. Was I endangering innocent people by asking questions?

By ten o'clock the kitchen stood in pretty good shape, I'd shoved aside things in the linen closet enough to make space for more sheets and towels, and stashed the empty boxes in the garage. Drake was still humming away in the office.

"I think I should go in to Ron's office this afternoon," I interrupted. "It is, after all, supposed to be my full time job. Want to come?"

"Nah, I'm happy here, getting this stuff organized," he answered.

"If you'll want the Jeep for anything, you can drive me down there and then take it."

"Nope. I'll just hang out here. You can leave Rusty with me if you want to." The red-brown lump on the floor raised his head and thumped his tail, but didn't get up.

I slipped on my denim jacket and pulled my purse off the coat rack. It felt like it weighed ten pounds, which it has a tendency to do, being the catch-all for junk and scraps of paper. I flopped it down on the dining table for a minute to rid myself of some of the clutter and weight. Several handfuls of papers came out, along with the contents of my change purse—amazingly heavy—Drake's sunglasses, and a bag of hard candy we'd bought to smuggle into the movie theater but never went.

A brisk breeze whipped through the trees, bringing a first taste of winter chill with it. Disks of yellow scuttled up the street, while a hefty portion of them littered the lawn.

At the office I spent a few minutes getting briefed by Sally about the morning phone calls and mail. She left and I poured myself a Coke before going upstairs to my office. Poking my head in at Ron's doorway, I shot a smile his way as he finalized a phone call.

"Busy morning?" he questioned, raising his eyebrows suggestively.

"Not what you think, unfortunately. Drake's stuff arrived from the movers yesterday afternoon, so we've been merging household stuff—not ourselves. He's still at it, but I thought I better show up for work every now and then."

"Oh, don't worry about it. We've been doing fine," he assured me.

"Ron, do you have a minute to talk?"

"Sure." He followed me into my office and took the small sofa across the room from my desk.

"Remember that I told you I was going to look up some of Dad's old co-workers to see if I could learn anything more about the plane crash?"

"Yeah, did you ever talk to that guy with the NTSB? The one who faxed me the report?"

"Oh, God, Ron. I forgot to tell you—" I filled him in on the horrible night I was supposed to meet Jim Williams.

"What am I getting close to, Ron?"

He shook his head. "Damned if I know. You know how little Dad talked about work. I don't remember ever seeing his office, ever seeing him bring papers home..."

"Then last night George Myers, who *somehow* knew that I'd be eating dinner at Pedro's last night, told me they were working on some pre-Star Wars technology out there. Does any of that ring a bell?"

"Not a bit."

"And then—this morning I had a call from Congressman Jack Cudahy, who *swore,* as much as you can ever get a politician to swear to anything, that the weather caused the plane crash. Ron, we *know* better. We saw the NTSB report. I don't trust either of those men. And Wendel Patterson— I saw him yesterday too. He's pretty old now, but cocky. Sort of swaggers around hinting but not telling what kinds of things he worked on. The only one I can rule out right now is Larry Sanchez because he's bedridden."

His mouth turned grim. "But he wasn't fifteen years ago. Charlie, be careful here. Anyone who would murder a government official just to steal a folder won't think twice about coming after you.

"And whoever killed Williams may have also planted the bomb on the plane. That means they've now killed at least six people."

Suddenly I wanted Drake to hold me.

EIGHTEEN

"SWEETPEA? It's Apple Pie."

"Hannah? What is it?" I dragged myself from a deep sleep and rolled over to see my digital clock. Eight-thirty.

"Sweetpea, I think the story's breaking," Hannah continued.

"Why? What's happening?" I looked over to Drake's side of the bed but it was empty, the covers pulled smoothly up to the pillow. "Hannah? What story?"

"Well, I had a call from George Myers this morning," she whispered.

"Is he there? Or did he just call?"

"Oh, no, he called on the telephone. Guess I don't need to whisper then, do I?" She giggled.

"I don't think so," I told her. "What did he call about?"

"Well, it was real early, probably about seven because the children next door were waiting on the curb for the school bus and it's usually here by seven fifteen, and so I know it was before that."

"And what about George?" I prompted.

"Yes, well George called and asked if I remembered him, and of course I did, but I didn't tell him that I'd just talked to you a few days ago. So I got him to explain who he was and why he was calling. Don't you think that was clever? That way I didn't give away that I already knew why he was calling?"

"Yes, Hannah, that was clever," I worked to keep the sigh out of my voice.

"So anyway, he made out like he'd had the idea to look into that plane crash and he wondered if I had any old papers or documents or clippings or anything like that. Little skunk, he thought he'd take credit for finding them himself, I'll bet.

"Well, I didn't tell him *anything*. Didn't even admit that I'd kept the newspaper clippings about the crash. Let him go to the paper and find that stuff himself, I say."

"That was smart, Hannah. You just keep quiet and play like you don't know anything." I didn't want to tell her that her life probably depended on it. I hung up the phone feeling a heavy weight of responsibility.

I took a fast hot shower, brushed my hair into a ponytail, and pulled on jeans and a T-shirt before scouting around to locate Drake and Rusty. Padding through the house in my socks, I realized there seemed to be a bit of a commotion in the front yard.

A glance out the living room window showed a large truck backed into our driveway. Rusty raced around the lawn in circles and several neighbors stood in a clump on the sidewalk. I stuffed my feet into running shoes and pulled a denim jacket from the coat hook.

Drake greeted me as I emerged into the excitement. "Hey, hon," he said with a kiss for me. "Look—my truck is here!"

Sure enough, the truck driver was in the process of closing the back doors of his rig and Drake's shiny little pickup sat in the driveway.

"I moved your Jeep out to the curb so this guy'd have room to pull in," Drake told me, handing me my keys.

"Looks like this is the big news of the day," I smiled. "The neighborhood sure turned out for it."

I noticed Elsa at the center of the little group, talking animatedly with another couple who lived about three houses up.

"Charlie!" she called.

I walked toward the little cluster, nodding hello to each of the gray heads.

"Oh, Charlie, I just can't believe it," Elsa said. Her white brows pulled together in front. "There's been another break-in right here on our street."

"What! When did this happen?"

The other woman, whom I recognized as Mrs. Fredericks, a quiet retired teacher, spoke up: "It was our house, Charlie! Yesterday afternoon—Oscar and I left for a couple of hours to do our grocery shopping and a few errands—we weren't gone very long at all. Broke in through one of the back bedroom windows, must have carried our stuff out the back door."

"They live on the corner, you know," Elsa chimed in. "The thieves must have parked their car on the side street."

"Did they take much?" I asked.

"Well, the portable TV set that Oscar got me for the bedroom last year. And there was that expensive radio the kids gave us for Christmas."

Drug money. It was so common all over town, but hadn't hit this close to home yet. Most of my neighbors are retired and old enough to be my grandparents. If Elsa's home is any indication, I imagined most of their furnishings were vintage 1950s, and their electronics predated the birth of Bill Gates, making them not exactly hot properties on the hot property market. I wondered how they knew the Fredericks would own a couple of new pieces.

I made some consolatory noises, telling them I hoped they'd reported it to the police on the chance that the items could be recovered, before I turned my attention back to Drake.

He had signed the shipping receipt and sent the truck driver on his way. Now he was busy hooking up the pickup's battery in preparation for giving it a first start-up. I leaned under the open hood beside him.

"Glad to have your baby back?" I teased.

"A man without a truck is only the next saddest creature to a man without a woman," he intoned seriously.

"Well put, helicopter man. If you'd said 'sadder than a man without a woman' you'd have some answering to do." I jabbed him lightly in the ribs and received a kiss in return.

"I'm thinking, if I can get everything put together in the next couple of days, we should drive this baby up to Pueblo and bring us home a helicopter."

"Really? You're that close to being ready?"

He took a deep breath. "Well, I'm not sure one is ever ready to go a half-million dollars in debt, but I'm feeling brave. Or maybe foolhardy."

Whew. I was only glad I didn't have to imagine taking on a project of that size.

"I've got the paperwork from the financing company. The insurance people have given me a quote that, you notice, has turned my hair gray. And the FAA paperwork is in motion."

"Where, exactly, will this new toy sleep at night?" Considering that our garage was full of boxes, our driveway full of cars, and the front lawn not very large. Not to mention the neighbor's wrath and the reams of city ordinances we'd be breaking by landing an aircraft at a residence.

"I can rent hangar space out at the Double Eagle Airport, that new one on the west side—out by the shooting range. It's gonna take some start-up money to do all this, but I've had good news from the Realtor in Hawaii."

"The property has sold already?" I felt a tiny letdown. I'd been hoping for at least one more vacation trip there.

"They got some earnest money, so it looks pretty sure. I should be hearing something within the next few days."

Things were just moving right along, weren't they?

"Meanwhile, let's get some breakfast and make a plan," I suggested. I picked up the newspaper from the porch while he closed the hood and followed me into the house. Rusty stuck close by, trying his starving-dog routine again, but Drake assured me he'd already been fed.

"You—you beggar," I teased the dog. "You'd eat seventeen times a day if you could get away with it." I took his big head in my hands and roughed up his ears. He leaned against me heavily, until I thought he'd fall over.

"How about more waffles for breakfast?" Drake asked. "I'll make them."

He didn't have to make that offer twice. I sat at the table and spread out the newspaper.

"Shit, look at this," I muttered. "Another break-in. This one's just about three blocks over. And did you hear Elsa and the Frederickses telling about it happening to them?"

He hadn't, so I recounted what little I knew about it while he plugged in the waffle iron and began stirring ingredients in a bowl.

"This is beginning to be a pattern here. We've never had burglaries in this neighborhood before. And now there've been two. Maybe we should think about an alarm system."

"Yeah, I could probably install one. And I should probably install one at Gram's house too. I worry about her all alone over there," he added.

"She's got you calling her Gram too, I see."

He blushed. "Yeah, well, she says I'm almost one of the family now."

"It's true, you are," I assured him.

The waffle batter sizzled as it hit the hot iron. He closed the lid on it and began slicing a banana. Rusty's nose twitched toward the countertop. I scanned the remaining headlines, then folded the paper.

Drake, meanwhile, warmed the syrup and put plates and flatware on the table. We again shared the first waffle while the second one cooked.

"I'm going to spend the morning on the phone," he told me between bites. "Try to get all the details put together on this machine."

"Can I help with anything, or would it be better if I just went to the office and got out of your hair?"

"Do you really want to? Help, I mean."

"Sure, as limited as my knowledge is in this area."

"Well, I need to get a business set up, and I'm not really sure how you go about that," he said. "What should we do first?"

"Pick a name for it," I suggested. "Then you'll need to set up a bank account, decide if you're going to incorporate, get a tax ID number... About a million little details."

He stabbed a banana disk and a square of waffle and stuck them both into his mouth.

"This gets to be a major thing, doesn't it?" he mused.

"Pretty major. But it's a matter of doing things one step at a time. None of it's difficult, there's just a lot of it. I'll help with it."

"Charlie, it's a big commitment for you to pitch in and help with my business. Are you sure you want to?" He took my hand.

"Well, if you're asking whether I'll work in your business full time, I'll have to talk that over with Ron too. After all, we're partners in the investigation biz. I'm not putting in full days, as you've noticed, but he does depend on me.

"If you're asking whether I can help with the setting up and the paperwork, sure. Of course I want to help."

"I'd really appreciate it," he said. "We're a great team and I'll take as much of your involvement as you want to give."

I reached for a maple flavored kiss. "Then I guess I better get with it."

I rinsed and put the dishes into the dishwasher while he headed for the telephone. I pulled out some basic business forms that I'd stashed in a file when Ron and I started our venture, and put together a checklist of things that would need to be done and questions that Drake would have to supply the answers to.

"A second phone line is probably going to be a priority, unless you plan to also rent an office at the airport," I told him. "I've already got a list of calls I need to make, and it looks like you do too."

"I'll order one today," he said.

I decided in the meantime to go to Ron's office and make my calls. It would also give me the chance to talk to him about the future, a subject that felt like it was rapidly changing for me.

Yesterday's breezy cool front had brought a dip in temperatures, so I pulled a sweatshirt from the closet. Rusty watched expectantly, wondering whether he'd be better off staying home with Drake or going to the office with me. Finally the lure of staying at home near the dog biscuits won out. I planted a little smooch on the back of Drake's neck as he conversed with an FAA man. He waggled his fingers at me and I left.

The clear blue sky had an edge to it today. The wind was not as strong as yesterday's but had a frigid quality to it. I cruised up Central and traversed the couple of residential streets to the office. Here, the trees were noticeably more bare than two days earlier. It wouldn't be long before ou balmy autumn days were gone. I noticed that the yard ser vice had come by. Our lawn was relatively clear of leaves the grass had received its final trimming of the fall, and bright beds of pansies had been planted for winter. Both Sally's and Ron's vehicles waited in the parking area behind the building.

I called out to Sally that I was here. By the time I reached my desk, she was paging over the intercom.

"Hey sleepy," she teased. "You sure are taking advan tage of the cooler snuggling weather these days."

"Yeah, yeah," I agreed, remembering how I'd awakened this morning to Hannah Simmons's phone call, the delivery of Drake's truck, and the news of my neighbor's burglary.

"You've only had one call so far," she went on, "a woman named Rebecca Sanchez. She sounded real shaky and asked that you call her ASAP." She read the number off to me.

Rebecca Sanchez…Rebecca Sanchez. Larry Sanchez's daughter, who'd so selflessly given up her own life to take care of him. I dialed the number quickly.

"Rebecca? Charlie Parker here. What's happening?"

"Charlie, my father's worse than I've ever seen him. I think he's dying," she wailed. I could tell it was an effort for her not to sob.

"Has the doctor seen him? Is he in the hospital?"

"The ambulance came last night and took him to St. Joe's. It doesn't look good. I called you because he kept talking about Bill Parker. That's your father, right? He keeps saying something about his accident. I don't know what any of it means."

"Can I go see him at the hospital?" I asked.

"I think you should. He really wants to get this off his

chest, and I think you're the only one who's going to know what he's talking about.''

I hung up, wondering what Larry could have remembered after all these years.

"Hey, you're in!" Ron lounged against my doorjamb, peeling the wrapper off a candy bar.

"Yeah...um, Ron, could we have a little office meeting this afternoon? I'd make it right now, but I just got the weirdest call. A dying man wants to talk to me.''

"I'll be here," he answered. "Today looks like phone calls and paperwork. Just check with Sally, though.''

Ten minutes later I was again driving up Central after confirming that Sally would be able to stay late. St. Joseph's Hospital is right off the freeway, but from my vantage point, it was easier to stay on Central until I got close, then cut over to Dr. Martin Luther King Junior Avenue, formerly Grand Avenue. I never have figured out why our city fathers didn't just select a new street to bestow the honor upon, rather than taking simple old Grand and turning it into a huge mouthful. Obviously, I don't have the correct thought processes to ever make it to elected office.

I glanced at my watch as I pulled into the uncrowded visitor's parking lot. Noon. I followed Rebecca's instructions and entered the fourth floor hall just in time to catch the heady smell of scrumptious hospital lunches being delivered to the rooms.

Larry Sanchez didn't have a lunch tray. He was hooked to a number of tubes and bags that I didn't begin to understand, but I assumed he was getting nourishment from some of them. He looked smaller than before—something about hospital beds tends to do that to people. His eyes were about half open when I stepped into the room.

"Larry? Larry, it's Charlie Parker," I called out quietly. His head turned toward me.

"Rebecca told me you wanted to talk to me," I reminded

A slow smile curved his mouth. "Bill Parker's girl?" he said faintly. I sat in the chair at his side.

"Yes, Larry. I'm Bill's girl. I came by your house to see you earlier this week, remember? We talked about my father's plane crash about fifteen years ago. Have you thought of something more about that?"

He lay so still I wanted to check and see if he was breathing. Only his eyes moved and I remembered that Rebecca said he was paralyzed from the chest down. Finally his mouth began to work.

"Bill…Bill was on the…airplane." Took a deep breath. "The plane crashed. A bomb made it crash."

"Yes, the NTSB said they found evidence of a bomb," I told him. "Do you know who put the bomb on the plane?"

"The spy people." His eyelids slowly lowered.

"Spy people? Do you know their names?"

"Some said…Bill Parker was one of the spy people. But I didn't think so. Security…really tight in research. Someone else did it."

"Who? Do you know any names?"

"I fell… One day I fell. The spy people did that too. I…I saw them loading the airplane. And the next day I fell."

"Larry, you've really got to help me here," I pleaded. "Who were they? What were their names?"

He breathed rapidly three or four times. "I…let me think…" His eyes closed again. He had drifted into a light sleep.

I leaned back in the chair, wondering whether he'd wake up again soon. I wanted so badly to learn some names but wasn't sure how much he really knew or whether he'd have the strength to get them out.

"Mmmm…Bill's girl? Are you here?" His eyes remained closed, but his mouth was working.

"I'm here, Larry. Can you talk a little more?"

"Mmm hmm. I wanted to tell you . . ."

"Yes, you'd said something about some spies. Do you know their names?"

"George…"

"George Myers?"

"Mmm hmm. George put the bags into the plane… And there was a mechanic. He's died. He checked the plane first."

"What was his name?"

Larry's brow wrinkled. "He worked for…Southwest Aircraft. They, umm, rented the planes. He was curly. He was bald." Something that might have been a smile played across his mouth.

"Was the mechanic a spy?" I asked.

"I, umm, not sure. Didn't…didn't know him."

NINETEEN

I BLEW OUT a pent-up breath. Couldn't think what else to ask him and he was plainly getting tired.

"Larry, I'll let you rest now. If you think of anything else, will you tell Rebecca about it? Ask her to write down what you say and then to call me."

He nodded almost imperceptibly.

"Especially if you think of any names," I reminded.

His breathing had become regular and slow.

Well, I had one or two clues to follow up on. It was an easy hop to get on I-25 and pay a visit to the airport. If I remembered correctly, Southwest Aircraft was still in business at Albuquerque International and perhaps I could catch Neil Kirkpatrick at the FAA. I steered the Jeep back to DMLKJ Ave. and aimed toward the on-ramp. Even with the noon hour traffic I found the turnoff to the FAA offices less than ten minutes later.

After trying to explain the reason for my visit to the sour-faced woman at the front desk, without giving away any real information, I was guided through a maze of halls and cubicle-sized rooms to Neil Kirkpatrick's office.

Kirkpatrick was in the process of returning his telephone handset to its cradle when we entered his spacious glass-walled office. My guide evaporated, closing the door behind her.

"Mr. Kirkpatrick? I'm Charlie Parker."

He rose from his chair, six feet of slim black man in a charcoal suit with perfectly pressed white shirt and an Armani tie in shades of gray. He looked more like he belonged in the boardroom of a major corporation than buried in the depths of a federal bureaucracy in Albuquerque, New Mexico. His voice only confirmed it—soft, with perhaps a touch of Harvard—when he spoke.

"Ms. Parker. Yes, Drake Langston mentioned you."

I was relieved that the bureaucratic roadblock didn't appear to extend past the front desk. Kirkpatrick offered coffee, which I declined, then suggested that we sit. I outlined briefly the background of the case, leaving out the fact that one government employee had already died trying to get answers for me.

"Call me Neil," he insisted, when I'd finished. "I'm going to be Drake's POI, that's principal operations inspector, when he gets his helicopter company set up." He flashed an orthodontically perfect smile. "We'll probably be seeing more of each other.

"I do remember the air crash you're talking about," he continued, shifting tracks. "I was here in the office. When you mention it happening on Baldy Peak, it rings a bell," he chuckled, "because our supervisor here at the time was bald as a melon and he used to become quite flustered whenever he had to discuss that mountain. As if, somehow it were named for him. And I guess a few of us who were quite a bit younger then, did sort of snicker over it at times."

He rubbed his hand over the thinning spot on the crown of his own head. "Of course now, I can relate to a man's sensitivity on that subject." He grinned again, revealing that he could do it with humor.

"And what happened with the crash case?" I steered him back.

His chocolate eyes reached for a spot on the ceiling. "The only reason this sticks in my mind is because I was so new here at the time. It was the first case with reported fatalities after I started work in this office. I remembered how jarring it was to realize that, even in this labyrinth of a bureaucratic office, I'd be dealing with life and death situations."

"Did you go to the crash site?"

"No, I was a paperwork man, even then. I handled the file at first. Then the NTSB stepped in and took everything we had." He steepled his fingers and tapped them against his pursed lips. "Which I thought was strange, you know. Every other case file we've built since then has stayed in this office, even when the NTSB is involved. We keep our set of documents and they have their own. But not on that one."

"And no one questioned it?" I asked.

"There were a few murmurs from the old-timers, but I didn't know enough to question anything myself. Soon, we were on to other cases."

I couldn't think what else to ask him. Obviously, there wouldn't be any files he could locate for me here. And I didn't want to put him at risk—Jim Williams's death still weighed on me. Neil offered a warm handshake as I stood to leave, as if to apologize that he couldn't offer more answers.

SOUTHWEST AIRCRAFT occupied two large gray hangars with their name in tasteful burgundy letters clearly visible. I parked near the entrance of what I took to be an office and went in.

A part of the hangar had been partitioned off to form a series of small offices, carpeted in dark gray industrial weave, furnished in sturdy metal desks like schoolteachers used to have. My stepping on the doormat triggered a ding-ding sound somewhere in the back and a woman emerged from an adjacent room.

"Hi, how can I help you?" she inquired. Her slim body fit neatly into black size three jeans, which went well with a gray polo shirt decorated with the company logo in burgundy. Her name, Louise, was embroidered on the opposite breast. She was in her mid-forties, with very white caps on her front teeth and a wind-tousled pony tail.

"Hi. I'm sure this is an odd request, but I'm looking for some information about an employee who worked here about fifteen years ago. Is there a manager I should talk to?"

"Well, hon, I'm the owner's wife and we're the only two who've stuck around through everything. So I can probably tell you what you need to know. Sit down." She indicated a chair for me and took the one behind the desk herself.

"This sounds crazy, but I don't know the man's name. And the only description I have is that he was curly and bald."

"Oh, Curly! That was his name." She leaned toward me. "You know how people always call the biggest guy Tiny or the fattest guy Slim? Well, this was a bald guy named Curly. What can I say?"

"I understand he was a mechanic?"

"Yep. Worked here quite a while too—good mechanic. You're not popping up here to say you're his long lost kid or anything, are you?" Louise grinned. "You missed him, 'cause he died some years back."

"Oh, heaven's no." I handed her my business card. "My connection with Curly is much slimmer than that, I'm afraid. I wanted to ask some questions about a plane that your company chartered to Sandia Corporation years ago.

One that he worked on. You see, the plane crashed and my parents were on it.''

Her face closed immediately. She stared at my business card again. ''Private investigators. Y'all hooked up with a bunch of lawyers? 'Cause if you are, you can just get your little ass out of here right now.''

''Oh, no, no, no,'' I assured her. ''This is purely personal. And I know your plane and mechanic weren't to blame in any way. I've already seen the NTSB report. They concluded that a bomb was carried aboard in the pilot's carry-on bag.''

''You got that right. And that pilot was a Sandia employee, not one of ours. If it had been ours, it probably would have been my Rick and he'd be dead now too.'' Her eyes reddened as she stared at the desk top.

It hit me that this is what pilots' wives lived with every day.

''Honey, you just learn to take it in stride,'' she counseled, seeing the stricken look on my face. ''If it ever happens to Rick, at least I'll know he died doing something he loved. He'd rather have it that way than to shrivel up from cancer or something.''

''I...uh, yes I suppose you're right.'' I cleared my throat. ''Do you have any records that go back that far? I mean, I'm trying to find out the names of the pilot and passengers, and I'm getting nowhere with Sandia people.''

''Oh, that bunch. They probably make the directions to the ladies room top-secret. Well, we'd have made a charter sheet out, although Sandia would have done their own flight following. No public flight plans with that bunch.

''We never even knew in advance how long they'd keep the plane or where it was going. Just took the Hobbs clock time before they left and again when they got back. Even then, I always suspected that they'd fly real out-of-the-way routes or circle the airport a couple dozen times or something like that so we'd never be able to plot out where they'd gone. I was required to get some minimum information though, like the pilot's name and how many passengers on board."

"Would there be a record of all that?"

"Hell, I can *tell* you the pilot's name—it sure came up often enough after that crash. It was Joe Smathers. He did most of their charter flights. Like I said, he was a Sandia employee. But Joe purposely carrying a bomb on board? No way. Joe was a careful, careful pilot, and he wasn't out to go killin' himself in an airplane. Had a cute wife and two little kids at home. No, Joe planned on being home for dinner every night."

"Does she still live in town?"

"Pretty sure she does. I think her name was Kathleen," Louise said. "She got a good-sized insurance settlement. Able to put the kids through school without having to go to work or get remarried."

I jotted down the name in my notebook.

"What about Curly?" I asked. "Did he die soon after the crash?"

"Nah," she said. "It was more like three or four years later. It was a tragic accident, though. He walked into a spinning prop. Was over at Sandia doing some maintenance on a rented plane."

"Louise, you seem to know a lot of the inside gossip. What was the word going around about the crash?"

She stopped pushing paper clips around the desk and her eyes found a spot somewhere near the ceiling. "Well, there's always gossip—mostly speculation, 'cause nobody really knew nothin'. I mean, that thing was zipped up so tight so fast. Hardly anything made the newspapers."

"I know. I've seen only two little clippings."

"Yeah, I mean, there were lots of investigators around, and I'll tell you, they went through our maintenance records with a fine tooth comb. You ain't been strip searched until you've had the FAA and the NTSB jump down your neck. But none of that was public, thank God."

"One investigator told me they had a file two or three inches thick," I said.

"At least. Maybe more. They practically wrote down every time I took a piss for a week." She picked up a rubber band and began stretching it between her two index fingers. "Lucky for us they found that bomb evidence. We'd'a been out of business and bankrupt if they'd traced anything to our maintenance records."

The rubber band flew across the room. "I tell ya, hon, this aviation business'll take you by the heart, then it'll take you by the wallet. We get us the best insurance money can buy—work half the year to pay for it—but otherwise those lawyers'd get everything we got. You know, one little slip-up and they're on you like vultures."

My stomach was getting a bit queasy and I tried to tell myself it was because I hadn't eaten any lunch.

TWENTY

IT WAS NEARLY TWO when I got back to the office and I could tell Sally was craving her afternoon nap. Her normally open, freckle sprinkled face looked faded. The hot fudge sundae I'd brought from McDonald's helped a bit.

We were gathered, the three of us, in our conference room opposite the reception area where Sally's desk sits. I'd volunteered to run for the phone if necessary.

"Office meeting, huh," Ron started off. "Well, since both you ladies approached me with the same request today, looks like we better get it over with."

Sally and I glanced at each other, spoons halfway to our mouths.

"Well, I certainly hadn't planned on dropping a double bombshell in one day," I began, "but maybe this way we can get everything worked out at once." I knew what Sally's request would be, or thought I did. I gestured for her to go first.

She rubbed her growing belly. "No surprise here. You both know I've talked about staying home with the baby. I'll work another couple of months, but then probably not want to come back to work for another year or so—unless Ross can work out a schedule where he can stay home half-time. But in construction…I don't think it'll happen."

Ron looked at me. "I'm not pregnant!" I assured him. "Don't plan on it either." He raised an eyebrow.

"Drake's starting his own helicopter business. I'd like to help him as much as I can, but I'm not abandoning ship here, either."

"You won't be much use to him if you're trying to put in full days here," Ron pointed out.

He scraped the bottom of his plastic ice cream cup. His face pulled into its older-and-wiser-brother facade. "Ladies, I knew this was coming," he pronounced.

Sally and I both rolled our eyes.

"Now wait, hear me out," he said, raising a palm toward us. "I'm not saying it's a bad thing. Here's a solution, if you like it. We can solve all this by hiring one full-time person. Ta-da."

"Replace both of us with one person?" Sally questioned, wanting to feel miffed.

"She (or he) will sit at the front desk, performing Sally's tasks. Along with that, Charlie can pass along the grunt-work that she doesn't want anymore and keep the parts she does want. If we hire someone soon, they'll have a couple of months to train with Sally and be ready to take over when she leaves."

"Great plan! So who does the hiring?" I had to ask.

"Whoever you'd like," he answered mellowly. This was just too easy.

Sally wasn't going to argue the point. She tossed her ice cream cup into the trash and said her farewells for the afternoon.

I spent the next thirty minutes on the phone, requesting business start-up forms from just about every government agency in the state. The phone book provided an address and phone number for Kathleen Smathers so I decided to pay a quick visit before going home.

I had to consult the city map to find her street and finally located it, a small cul-de-sac in Tanoan, an exclusive gated community in the north part of town. Smathers's address proved to be a townhouse—two stories of pale tan stucco, narrow windows, and white wrought iron. It was nearly as inviting as the state pen.

I pressed a lighted doorbell and set off a couple of minutes of some Bach fugue deep inside the house. That *must* have been some hefty insurance settlement to afford this lifestyle after fifteen years of joblessness. The chime had not quite finished pealing before a woman in a deep turquoise silk jumpsuit glided to the door. I knew, because I stared unabashedly through the clear glass panel beside it.

She was built like Dolly Parton except that the hair was flame orange. The silk jumpsuit was belted tightly, emphasizing a tiny waist I would have been proud to own, and she carried a portable phone in one hand.

"Oh, it isn't Joey," she said to the phone, "I'll have to call you back, darling." The instrument clicked off with a tiny electronic beep.

"Yes?" she inquired with a you-better-not-be-selling-anything manner.

I handed her my business card. "I'm Charlie Parker. I got your name from your husband's former employer," I said.

"Oh, I'm not..." It took her a minute to remember that she'd once had a husband.

"Oh, you mean Joe's old boss?"

"Could we talk about this inside?" I asked.

She led me to a white silk room just off the wide entry hall. I felt like the hillbilly cousin in my jeans and sweatshirt. I sat up straighter to make up for it.

"The reason his name even came up," I continued, "was because I have some questions about the plane crash that killed him."

She glanced again at the card, apparently thinking many

of the same things Louise had earlier about why private investigators would be looking into a fifteen year old plane crash.

"My parents were on the plane," I explained.

"And what does this have to do with me?"

"I just…" I just suddenly felt hopeless. What *would* she know about any of this? "I just wondered whether Joe seemed nervous that day, or suspicious about anything? Or about any of the flights he did for Sandia?"

She looked like she was having to struggle with remembering Joe, much less anything he'd ever told her.

"Sweetie, I've gotten on with my life these last fifteen years. I suggest you do the same." She stood and began walking toward the front door.

So much for that trip.

I started home feeling drained. I just wanted to hug my man and my dog, in that order.

The rush hour traffic had started early today and was already in full snarl by the time I got to the freeway. The normal slow-down clog at Candelaria Road was at a complete standstill for no apparent reason, as usual. I broke free of it just in time to get entangled in construction on westbound I-40. Forty-five minutes later I dragged myself through the door, ready for a hot shower.

The heavenly smell of roasting meat greeted me at the door. I glanced toward the kitchen. The dining table was set with china and silver, candles and flowers. I tiptoed to the kitchen.

"Hi, honey, I'm home," I said softly.

Drake stood at the oven door, peering inside at a huge standing rib roast. "This will be ready in about ten minutes," he said.

"Wow, I'm impressed. And after the traffic I've fought

nd the people I've talked to all day, I'm ready for a treat. Do I have time for a shower?"

"A quick one." He winked, closed the oven door, and came forward to give me a hug. I let myself relax into it. Then a kiss. I relaxed into that too. Then another kiss.

"Dinner won't wait *this* long, will it?" I questioned.

"Better just opt for the shower—but take as long as you want." He grinned. "Maybe you'll get the rest for dessert."

God, he was wonderful.

I stood under the hot pelting shower without moving for ten minutes. Afterward, I slipped on silk lounging pajamas that may have been my mother's. I honestly couldn't remember where I'd gotten them. A glass of wine waited on the dresser and I took a long cool sip of it. Things were definitely looking up.

We spent the dinner hour playing how-was-your-day-dear. I told Drake about Larry Sanchez's story of "spy people" and we mulled that over for awhile. I didn't tell him of Louise's dire version of being in the aviation business, but did tell him about the new arrangement at the office. He'd handled a number of small details about the helicopter purchase and said he'd be ready to go pick it up in a day or two.

We spent the evening watching an old movie on TV, which put us in a romantic mood and we were in bed by nine. By ten thirty, snuggled into the curve of Drake's shoulder, I was drifting into a luxurious sleep, unbothered by the multitude of thoughts that had plagued me all day.

TWENTY-ONE

"DRAKE, HAVE YOU SEEN my spiral notebook?" I rum
maged through the top desk drawer, the one I'd reserve
for my stuff.

"The little notebook you always carry in your purse?"
he asked from the doorway.

"I just started a new one 'cause the old one was full, an
I put the old one in this drawer. It has a few of my note
from this case."

"I'll admit that I messed up everything in this room
except in that drawer. Haven't touched it."

I muttered some more and shuffled the junk around.
certainly didn't remember leaving the drawer in such dis
array, but the whole house had been a mess this week.
must have put the notebook somewhere else. Maybe in m
desk at the office.

I wandered into the living room and noticed the unrul
stack of papers I'd pulled from my purse yesterday. Amon
them were the picnic photo and Hannah's address that I'
scribbled on a scrap, along with postage receipts, gum wrap
pers, and old grocery lists. I carried the whole mess to th
kitchen counter, where I tossed the junk into the trash an
put the important things back into the purse.

Tomorrow I should go back over to Elsa's and organiz
everything into the boxes from whence they'd come.

"Wanna go buy a helicopter today?" he asked.

His face glowed with the prospect of flying again. In my self-centered cocoon, spending all my time concentrating on the past, I'd put aside the fact that Drake had been away from flying for several weeks now and was really missing it.

"If you'd rather not take a couple of days to do this, I could catch a commercial flight to Pueblo and then fly the new machine home."

"No, I'd really like to be in on the big excitement," I assured him.

"You know, it will take a whole day to drive up there, then you'll have to turn around and drive the truck home, another whole day on the road. Maybe I shouldn't be asking this much of you."

"Actually, it sounds perfect," I said. "My thoughts have become so muddled in the past few days that I could use the time away." Sometimes when I get too deeply involved in a case the questions and people begin to swirl around in my brain. Stepping back from the whole mess lets me look at it again with new perspective.

We jointly packed a small overnight bag, gathered Rusty's food and water, and closed up the house. By noon we decided to pull off the interstate at Las Vegas, north of Santa Fe, for some lunch and a stretch. On one corner of the historic plaza stands an old hotel with a Victorian dining room. We rolled the windows in the truck down to give Rusty some air, then walked the half-block.

Seated in the pale green room with white gingerbread trim, I ordered an elegant-sounding salad and Drake went for Mexican food.

"Are you sure you don't mind my taking over your office at the house to run the new business venture?" he asked, when our iced tea and a basket of rolls sat in front of us.

I smiled at him. "I absolutely don't mind. I'm lookin forward to the change of pace."

I went on to outline for him the steps we'd need to tak to get the business formed. "I'd advise that you incorporate Just adds another layer of liability protection," I told hin "And the first step in any of this will be to choose a busi ness name."

We kicked around names that sounded Southwestern an names that sounded aeronautical. Lunch arrived and we be came distracted by that.

"I'm thinking of a name that relates to you and me as couple," he suggested.

"Yeah, Red Hot Lovers Helicopter Service? That migh attract a strange clientele," I joked.

"How about something combining our names?"

"Langston and Parker? Sounds like a law firm."

"How about CharlDrake Helicopters?"

"You'd put my name first? That's really sweet." mulled the name around my tongue a few times. "I ca envision a logo using enlarged letters for the C and the D— maybe something whimsical yet professional."

"I like it," he said.

We paid our check and retrieved Rusty from the truck Clipping a leash onto his collar, I trotted him across th street to the plaza's park, where he reveled in the variet of strange smells and lifted his leg a couple of times. I another ten minutes we were on the road again.

By late afternoon, the town of Pueblo came into view and Drake headed for High Mountain Helicopter Service Bill Whitaker stood behind the front reception desk, rum maging through some file folders. He and Drake greetec each other while I glanced around the office once again. decided that if Drake ever wanted to rent office space tha customers would see, it would not include grimy Mexican blankets over the furniture or layers of dust on everything.

Whitaker apparently had not organized the paperwork for Drake, and I got the distinct idea that Drake was working to hold back some choice words. I decided to take Rusty out for a run.

The afternoon had turned gray, with clouds building to the west. Would Drake be able to fly out of here tomorrow or would it be storming by then? The weather had suddenly taken on new significance in my life.

I clipped the leash on Rusty once again and we strolled out of the airport's fenced enclosure and began a steady jog up the road. Jogging with a dog isn't easy. He wanted to run, nearly yanking the leash from my wrist a couple of times. Then he decided to sniff at new smells along the way and I took one tumble when I tripped headlong over him. Decided this wasn't a great way to get exercise, so we turned around and kept the pace to a walk all the way back.

"How's it going?" I inquired back at Whitaker's office.

Drake raised an eyebrow toward me, while Whitaker continued digging through a file drawer, coming up with files, papers, and notebooks from time to time. Drake took my elbow and steered me back outside.

"This guy is nowhere near organized to do this," he said in a low voice. "And I'm not leaving here until I know I have everything I need."

I knew how much he hated sloppy work and I felt sorry for him.

"No sense in your hanging around here," he continued. "Why don't you go check into that same motel we stayed at last time. At least you can kick off your shoes and watch TV or something. I'll get him to take me there when we're done. It may be late."

"Want me to bring you some dinner?" I asked.

"Don't worry about it for now. I'll call if we decide to take a break. Otherwise, if you get hungry go ahead and eat."

I wanted to offer some help, but didn't have the faintest idea what needed to be done. Figured I'd be more in the way than anything. Rusty and I hopped back into the truck and headed into town.

We got the same blue and gold shag-carpeted room we'd had on our last visit here. I stocked up on ice and Cokes from vending machines and scooped Rusty's food into his bowl for him. Kicking off my shoes and switching on the television were about the only things left to do, and boredom was setting in fast.

I debated pulling out the book I'd been reading half-heartedly at home. For some reason it just wasn't grabbing my attention—probably because I'd had too many other things tugging for it. I looked through the few notes I'd made in my new spiral notebook, but really didn't want to think about the crash, Sandia, or any of the people involved just now. I let myself become involved in an old *Hart to Hart* episode.

When I woke up it was after eight, I was starving, and there'd been no sign of Drake. Not wanting to phone him at a time when his mood wasn't likely to be the greatest, I walked over to the Burger King next to the motel and came back with a Whopper and fries. Rusty volunteered to help finish them, but I assured him that I could probably manage on my own.

By ten I was feeling drowsy again but didn't want to fall asleep without knowing how things were going with Drake. Just as I was about to dial the number to Whitaker's place, a set of bright truck lights flared behind the drape. I set the receiver down, peeped out and saw Drake emerging with his arms loaded.

I opened the heavy metal door and he dropped his arm-load of folders, books, and papers on the table.

"Wow, no wonder you're so late," I said, reaching to kiss him. "Did you get any dinner?"

"Not yet." He held up a small sack. "I got Whitaker to stop on the way here. Boy, this is frustrating."

"Records not in good shape, huh?"

"Not exactly. The aircraft log book looks okay, but there are several components not shown in the maintenance folder. And this guy has nothing computerized, so it's really tough to figure out what's missing."

"Can I help?"

"Yeah, let's cross check these two lists against each other while I eat my burger."

By one a.m. it began to look as if everything really was here, just not in very good order. I'd already devised a better filing system, using the old folders for now, than Whitaker ever dreamed of. Drake leaned back in his chair rubbing his eyes.

"Well, at least it looks like the deal can go through," he moaned. "I really didn't want to go looking for another aircraft at this point, but I wasn't going to accept this one without a complete set of records."

I had the feeling I was getting a little taste of what the aviation business would be like. We fell into bed to catch a few hours sleep before Drake's nine a.m. meeting to sign the papers.

TWENTY-TWO

THE MILES ROLLED BY for Rusty and me. We'd gotten a bit of a head start—Drake would leave after finalizing his deal, but he'd still get to Albuquerque hours ahead of us. We'd meet up at Double Eagle Airport before going home.

As I'd hoped, the long hours behind the wheel with only the dog for company helped free my mind to think about the case. I ran through the list of people I'd talked to and tried to decide where my suspicions lie.

George Myers still topped my list. Larry Sanchez had told me that George loaded the bags onto the ill-fated plane. And George's sudden interest in my investigation made me wonder if he didn't have something to hide—something that he'd want to know immediately if I stumbled upon it. I hadn't forgotten the creepy feeling a few nights ago when he'd shown up at our favorite restaurant and the way he'd come on to me with Drake sitting right there.

The pilot, Joe Smathers, was a big question mark, too. Louise had sworn he wouldn't have a death wish. But the explosive was in his bag—who put it there? And the adoring wife he'd left behind had all but forgotten him now. So, were they really that close in their marriage?

Wendel Patterson was either a nobody who wanted to appear more important than he was—or he was a cagey one, able to cover his motives and actions with a lot of swagger.

And Larry Sanchez. Such a tragic figure. I just couldn't

believe he had an evil spot in him. *If* he'd been one of the "spy people" way back then, they would have finished him off at the time, because he'd certainly have implicated those involved after his accident—assuming he had reason to believe they'd caused the accident. My own theory was that he knew something and they'd tried to kill him for it, but botched the job. Either the bad guys had not had access to him after that, or they figured no one would believe his "spy people" story anyway.

And the mysterious man in black at the Caravan—I felt virtually certain that he'd shot Jim Williams, but no one I'd talked to resembled him physically. A hired hit man?

The motive was still the tough part. I could only surmise that my father had figured out that someone planned to sell defense secrets to the Soviets and he was about to blow the whistle. The other five people on the plane had merely been in the wrong place at the wrong time.

Including my mother.

My eyes brimmed at the thought that my brothers and I had lost both parents over something we'd had nothing to do with.

I pulled off the interstate in Raton for lunch and a break from thinking. Twenty minutes later, I'd consumed a Big Mac and Coke and Rusty'd had a small cheeseburger and cup of water. We both felt better.

Once again as the white lines darted by, my brain kicked into gear. I tried to think back over the notebook entries my father kept, but remembered nothing of relevance. I'd have to review them again soon, in light of the names I'd come across. Maybe something would stand out this time.

My mind whirled and I finally tuned in to a talk radio station so I could listen to someone else's problems for a change.

We hit the outskirts of Albuquerque before the nastiest

of the rush hour traffic began and, amazingly, the construction zone on I-40 westbound wasn't nearly as clogged up as before. I cheated a little on the speed limit as we left the western edge of town behind and we arrived at Double Eagle Airport about twenty minutes later. I had the feeling I'd soon get to know this route well.

Drake stood there, showing off his new toy to the other pilots and mechanics in the hangar. The ship really was gorgeous and they were all grinning like kids at Christmas. Louise had told me that aviation really takes you by the heart.

I pulled up to the open hangar door and a border collie ran out to greet us. I closed my car door quickly, not knowing how the two canines would mix.

"It's okay to let him out," a man shouted toward me. "Sparky's used to sharing her space with other hangar dogs."

I opened the door again, gradually, and the two dogs sniffed noses. Sparky bounded into the building where she ran three rapid circles around the perimeter. Rusty followed suit and a solid friendship came to life. Rusty proceeded to sniff every corner of the place, including two airplanes and several red tool boxes, before finally plopping at Drake's side.

Darkness began to settle in and the air took on a chill as we transferred gear from the helicopter to the truck. Drake gave a wistful look as the large hangar doors closed on his baby and we backed out of our parking slot.

"Want to spend the night here?" I teased.

He squeezed my leg. "Much as I love helicopters," he said, "you're a lot more fun to snuggle at night."

I edged over next to him to prove it was true.

"Let's stop by the office on the way home," I suggested. "If I check my phone messages and mail tonight, I won't have to go in tomorrow and I can get started on filing your corporate paperwork and getting some of those details done.''

He exited I-40 at Rio Grande, east on Central, and turned in at our quiet side street. The office was completely dark, the two reception lamps we keep on timers at night apparently burned out. We pulled into the driveway that flanks the left side of the building leading to the parking area at the back. The kitchen light, which we don't normally leave on, was on. What was Ron doing, messing with the whole system?

"You can wait out here if you'd like," I told Drake. "I'll just be a minute."

I fished into my purse for keys. When I reached the back door, key aimed toward the lock, I realized that the door stood open just a crack. My hand froze.

Ron's car wasn't here and this wasn't right.

"Drake, maybe you better come here," I called out to him. "Something's wrong," I whispered when he stood beside me.

"Wait a second," he cautioned. "Let me get us a weapon." He returned to the truck and pulled a tire iron from under the seat.

I edged the door open with my toe and he slid past me with the weapon ready. Rusty tried to shove his way in but I gripped his collar. The kitchen was clear and normal-looking. I flipped the light switch in the hallway leading toward the front. The conference room and reception area were dark and I flipped on overhead lights there too. Sally's desk had been ransacked.

I rushed to it, while Drake quickly scanned both rooms, found no one, and worked his way upstairs, followed by Rusty.

Sally's drawers had been pulled out, rummaged roughly,

and left gaping. I couldn't tell that anything was missing, but she'd have to verify that.

"We're alone," Drake said. "But you're not going to like what you find up there."

I raced up the stairs to my office. Sally's desk was frisked—mine had been raped.

"Oh my God, what is this?" I cried out.

Books lay in scattered heaps on the floor, swept from the bookcases with angry swipes. My desk drawers rested upside down, the contents strewn over the floor like someone had dumped them then sifted through the wreckage. File folders spilled papers everywhere. Rusty circled the room, frantically sniffing.

Drake came up behind me and placed his hands on my shoulders.

"We better call the police," I said dully.

I stabbed 911 on my telephone, using a pencil eraser to touch the keypad. It really would be the final insult if the intruders had run up the phone bill while they were here.

"What about Ron's office, hon?" I called to Drake after I'd given all the particulars to a bored-sounding operator who probably handled fifty break-in calls every shift.

Drake reappeared in my doorway. "I can't tell whether Ron's office was hit or not," he grinned.

I rolled my eyes. "Geez, we might never know either." I'd told Ron his sloppy housekeeping ways would catch up some day.

"Guess I better call him, too," I sighed.

Again my trusty pencil-dialer went to work and I interrupted Ron's dinner to brief him. He said he'd be there right away.

I had no idea how long it would take the police to arrive. Calls that don't involve bleeding, dying, or thefts of big money from federally insured institutions have to take second seat to all the ones that do. I was itching to clean up the mess but knew that I shouldn't. After all, there was that one-in-a-million chance that they'd actually get an identifiable print out of the clutter.

I slumped downstairs to the kitchen where I brewed a pot of coffee and rummaged through the fridge until I came up with one three-day old cheese sandwich, a package of Twinkies, and four saltine crackers. We called it dinner.

We'd just polished off the last of our scrumptious fare when Ron showed up. I wanted to rehash all the questions— who had done this? how did they get in? what did they take? was it part of the recent crime spree in the area?— but since Drake and I had already done all that, I just didn't have the energy. I pointed a finger upward and let Ron go up to view the situation himself.

He clumped down a few minutes later. "You called the police?" he asked.

I nodded.

He sat heavily in his chair. "It looks like they mostly targeted you," he said. "My office shows minimal disturbance."

"Sally's desk isn't too bad either."

"And," Drake pointed out, "they didn't really take anything they could have easily sold. The microwave, computers, phone equipment—that all seems to be here."

He was right. As far as I knew, the neighborhood break-ins all involved the theft of electronics. My mind immediately flew to the Sandia case. Had one of my suspects broken into the office, thinking it would be the logical place I'd keep any files?

I struggled to think back over the past few days. How many people had I given a business card to? It was the only logical way I could think of that any of them would connect me with this address. And it would explain why my office had been hit hardest.

Anyone scoping out the place could figure out, from the small personal memorabilia, which were the two desks occupied by females here. Sally's desk had probably been checked first, yielding nothing. By the time they got to mine, they were angry enough to trash the room—perhaps to send me a message as much as anything.

A sharp rapping at the front door grabbed our attention. Ron and Drake went to answer it, admitting an officer that looked like he'd just graduated high school. Rusty greeted him like he'd found a kid to play with. I swear, authority figures are getting younger every day.

I halfheartedly showed him Sally's desk and told him the real mess was upstairs.

"There've been a lot of break-ins in this neighborhood recently, ma'am," he told me.

Ma'am. Oh, God, they weren't getting younger, I was getting older.

"I know. But I don't think this is one of those." I shared our reasons for that conclusion.

"I'll radio for a fingerprint team," he said. "We can at least get some prints on file that way."

"Don't bother. I really think this is related to a case I'm working on right now, which narrows it down to about a half-dozen people. At a glance, I don't think they took anything, which means they didn't find what they wanted." I paused. What *did* they want, anyway?

I could guess that they'd want any evidence I'd found on the plane crash. Or perhaps my father's notes and files.

My small spiral notebook.

I looked over at Drake. He hadn't put it together yet.

Oh, shit—what if they decided to wreak this kind of havoc

on the house? But if someone had broken in and taken the spiral, wouldn't they have already wreaked?

"Charlie?"

I snapped to. Ron looked at me quizzically.

"The officer asked whether you wanted him to list any missing items on his report."

"I better check a little more closely. It's okay to start touching things, isn't it?"

"Unless you want that fingerprint team to come in, ma'am."

I shook my head. The thought of cleaning black powder off every surface in the office wasn't an appealing one. "Let me just check my files and I'll let you know. I can always call and add something to the report later, can't I?"

We'd trailed the nice young officer through the building, showing him the ravaged areas. As the men showed him out, I stayed in my office, inserting the upturned drawers back into the desk, gathering files and replacing them. Drake joined me and reshelved the books.

The seven hour drive, the excitement of the new helicopter, capped by this mess had really sapped my strength. I stuck the files back into the drawers most any old way, knowing that I'd soon be sorting carefully through them to pass along some of my duties to the new employee. I performed a similar once-over on Sally's desk and left her a note explaining.

I leaned against his shoulder as Drake drove us home, with Rusty curled on the narrow jump seat in back. At this moment I only wanted a hot bath and my own bed. But the closer we got to home, the more I feared finding another destructive mess there.

TWENTY-THREE

I AWOKE FROM a deep sleep, snuggled against Drake's back, where I was tempted to stay for hours, but knew I couldn't. We'd enjoyed a thoroughly lazy Sunday yesterday, driving out to the airport and taking the new machine for a short spin around the west side of town, then going to the shooting range for a little target practice.

Today I needed to get serious about getting Drake's corporation set up and ready to go, at least in the paperwork department. I nuzzled his back and kissed his bare shoulder a couple of times to get his attention. He rolled over to face me, returning the kisses and enveloping me in his warmth.

"Mmmm, I could do this all day," he murmured.

"Hah. I doubt that," I laughed. "You're anxious to get out there and play with your new toy."

"And what are you anxious to do? I get the feeling that, now you're rested, you aren't about to lounge around all day either."

I outlined my plan to drive to Santa Fe, visit the corporation commission, and set the new company in motion.

"I have a couple of things to do here first, typing up a form or two, then how about if we have a nice hearty breakfast out somewhere before I go?"

"Good suggestion," he agreed. "Then I'll be sufficiently fed that I can go out to the hangar and work most of the day without taking a break."

While he showered, I filled out the corporate paperwork for the new CharlDrake Helicopters, Incorporated, then I took over the shower. Thirty minutes later we were seated in a booth at Denny's waiting for the omelettes and toast we'd just ordered.

"I'm really feeling stumped on this plane crash," I told Drake. "I feel like I'm close to something important. I mean, I'm virtually certain there's a guilty person or two walking around out there—and the scary thing is that they know about me but I don't know who they are."

"Yeah, that break-in at the office sure looks like it points that way. Like someone desperately wants to get their hands on something you've found. Something pretty incriminating."

We paused while our waitress set warm plates down for us. The omelettes looked fluffy and hot. Mine was loaded with ham and veggies. I stuck my fork in and cut out a wedge before I spoke.

"I'm just stymied as to what evidence they think I have. I've been through nearly all Dad's boxes and files and haven't come up with much. His references to the heat being on is still a mystery to me, even though it does somehow tie in with Larry Sanchez's telling me about 'spy people'."

Drake spread grape jelly on a toast triangle. "And we sure didn't find any physical evidence at the crash scene, did we?"

"I guess the scariest part so far is the fact that Jim Williams was murdered for that file he was bringing me. And when I was in his office he told me that the investigation file was, at one time, two or three inches thick. And yet, what he had then was only a few sheets of paper.

"So, what did he find in the meantime that he planned to bring me? And how on earth did someone know he was meeting me and arrange to have him killed before he could do it?'' I chewed slowly while I mulled it over.

"Seems to me that someone in Williams's own office would have had to know that he'd taken a second look at the case. And either that person was somehow involved from the start or they are close to one of the guilty and alerted them,'' Drake said.

My mind flew again over the possibilities. Who indeed? I just couldn't seem to get the puzzle pieces to slip into place. I changed the subject.

"I'll leave for Santa Fe now,'' I told him. "Hope to get into the Corporation Commission offices before they close for lunch, and with any luck that whole procedure won't take long. When I get back, I'll stop in at Ron's office so I can use the fax machine for a couple of things. If you need me during the day you can call there and Sally will leave me a message. I might also try to pop in at the State Aviation Division while I'm in Santa Fe to see if they keep any records about plane crashes.''

"Okay, hon, you know where I'll be.'' He pulled a card from his wallet and read off a phone number. "That's the operator who owns the hangar. If you need to get in touch with me, I'm sure they can find me. The mechanic's name is Bobby McNeil—nice guy—and I'll probably be working with him quite a bit. I'm listing his company in my FAA documents as my authorized maintenance facility.''

We left money on the table and parted ways in the parking lot. Rusty, who'd ridden over with me, opted to go to the hangar with Drake.

I stopped at the north edge of town to top off the Jeep's gas tank and run her quickly through the car wash. Although the temperature had once again dropped, we'd lucked out with another clear blue day. I hit the outskirts of Santa Fe less than an hour later and followed the circuitous Paseo de

Peralta to the PERA Building that houses the Corporation Commission.

Stepping into the molasses-paced world of state government, I waited my turn to be greeted, then waited my turn to be waited on, then waited while they typed up some more forms and added a gold sticker and signature to the forms I'd submitted. I sat in a stiff upright chair facing several rows of cubicles that I couldn't see into and occupied myself with memorizing the southwestern art prints on the walls.

Finally, my newly formed corporation in hand, I exited the building, practically in time to be stampeded in the lunch hour rush to get out. I located a phone directory and looked up the State Aviation Division, only to get a recorded message informing me that the offices were closed from twelve to one-thirty. So much for that idea.

With no desire to hang around Santa Fe two more hours on the chance that they could or would actually provide me with useful information, I headed out Cerrillos Road where I got a Coke from the first fast food place I came to, then headed south.

An hour later, I stepped into the kitchen of Ron's and my office and found him munching down on a Quarter Pounder and fries.

"Sally gone already?" I asked.

He nodded, his mouth too full for a real answer.

"Was she upset about the vandalism? I didn't put her desk back in the greatest shape."

He swallowed deeply. "She dove right in like a little bird nesting," he smiled. "Had that sucker put right back in order."

"Good. I need to send some faxes. Where are we in the hiring process? Should I be getting my stuff organized for that too?"

"Let's wait a week or so," he said. "Sally's not leaving right away. I don't mind doing the interviews if you'll help me screen them. But my calendar's really filled up this week. I've got two depositions that could take anywhere from a couple of hours to several days."

I left him to the Quarter Pounder and proceeded with my own projects. Over the next hour, I managed to secure CharlDrake Helicopters a federal tax ID number, a state tax ID number, and a City of Albuquerque business license. I then drew up bylaws for the corporation, naming Drake to all the offices except myself as secretary, since the law for some reason required it that way.

By five o'clock I'd thoroughly had it with government forms and my breakfast omelette had long since worn off. I wondered what Drake and Rusty were up to. I called the house and checked the messages on the answering machine. There was only one.

"Sweetpea, call me," Hannah Simmons's voice said. She sounded like she was crying.

TWENTY-FOUR

I DIALED HANNAH'S number and allowed it to ring twelve times before deciding that she wasn't going to answer and didn't have a machine. Should I drive up there? I really didn't want to, not in the rush hour traffic, but something wasn't right.

A male voice answered the hangar number Drake had given me. "Is this Bobby?" I asked. I introduced myself, apologized for the interruption, and asked if Drake were there. Bobby put him on the line.

"Hi, I'm back from Santa Fe and got your paperwork mostly done," I told him. "I also had a really strange phone call from Hannah Simmons and, although the machine recorded that she only called about ten minutes ago, she didn't answer when I called back. I'm thinking maybe I should drive up there and see if she's okay. What time were you planning on coming home?"

He said he'd be at least another hour and with the driving time to get home, I figured I wouldn't see him much before seven. "I'll go on up there then. See you later."

I had to look Hannah's address up again in the phone book since I'd written it in the spiral that was now missing. Rush hour traffic was in full swing and it took me nearly forty-five minutes to get there.

Her car sat in the driveway of the blond brick home, drapes stood open, the place looked as occupied as any house on the street. I glanced around the yard and approached the front door. Reached out to ring the bell. The front door stood open a few inches. I opened the screen and nudged the wooden door gently. It swung inward without a sound. The house was quiet as a tomb. My senses went on full-alert.

"Hannah?" I called out softly.

Silence hung thick in the air. I called her name twice more, then stepped into the living room.

"Oh, God," I moaned. Just as in my office, the room was a shambles. I scanned for a sign of Hannah. Her knick-knacks lay scattered on the floor, swept from their shelves ruthlessly. From the shelves below them, her photo albums had been tipped out onto the floor and spread open. Pillows and cushions from the sofa were upended and scattered. In the kitchen, drawers hung open, an address book and telephone directory had been riffled and flung down on the table.

"Hannah?" I called again.

This time I thought I caught a faint noise from deep inside the house. I followed a hallway that apparently led to bedrooms. The first one I peeked into was a spare bedroom that also served as Hannah's sewing room. Her sewing machine, scissors, multiple spools of thread, a red tomato pincushion, and a partially finished garment seemed undisturbed. The twin beds in the room were made up and, although they were the catch-all spots for miscellaneous stuff, appeared untouched by the vandals.

The next bedroom was obviously the one Hannah used. Her dresser drawers stood open and had been hastily rummaged. The bed coverings were pulled loose and strewn out. Her bathroom received the same treatment.

Thump, thump. I caught the faint sound again.

"Hannah? Where are you?" I called louder.

The thump responded louder. I traced it to a storage closet off the hall. I snatched the door open and there sat Hannah on the floor, her wrists, ankles and mouth bound with duct tape.

"Oh, Hannah! Here, let me get you out of there."

I retrieved her scissors from the sewing room and carefully clipped the tape off in a straight cut, trying to touch it as little as possible. It would be the perfect surface to contain fingerprints of the attackers.

She gingerly struggled to her feet, bracing herself against the doorjamb and leaning heavily on me.

"I'll be okay," she assured me, limping on numbed legs.

"Here, let's go in the kitchen and I'll make us a cup of tea," I suggested. I took her elbow and steered her that direction.

"Hannah, do you have any idea who did this?"

"Well, I didn't know their faces," she said, watching me fill the kettle with water. "But it had to do with your investigation."

My stomach dropped. I'd dreaded this.

"Tell me about it," I suggested.

"Well, I was working on my sewing. Had been in there all afternoon. I'm making jumpers for my grand-nieces for Christmas. They'll be red velvet with white lace trim..."

"And someone came in—" I prompted.

"Well, yes, I heard this little noise near the front here. Sounded like the front door opening. And I tell you, my heart just started racing." She put her hand to her chest. "And then a man's voice—one of them—whispered something to the other one.

"I just couldn't think! I heard them come into the kitchen and by then they were making some noise—not much, but I knew they were going through things. And I ran into my bedroom and picked up the phone and was going to call the police. You know with all the burglaries we have in Albuquerque these days, I just knew they were some kind of drug addicts coming in to steal something they could sell."

The kettle whistled and I located cups and tea bags.

"So why did you call me instead?"

"Well, I could hear them in the hall by then and I got so scared. Then one of them said your name."

My stomach did another plunge. I set the two cups of tea on the table and sank into the chair next to Hannah's.

"Yes, I mean they were talking about you and the questions you've been asking. So I just dialed your number—your card was right there on my nightstand, and it was the only thing I could think to do right then. And you weren't home so I talked to your machine, and by then my voice was shaking and I didn't know what to do next.

"And then they walked right into my bedroom!"

"Oh lord, what did you do?"

She shuddered. "I guess I just froze. I remember hanging up the phone and wondering if they'd heard me talking. One guy pointed a gun at me and he told the other one to find something to tie me up. I just stood there in the corner, acting like a scared little baby, but thinking to myself that at least if they were going to tie me up, maybe they didn't plan to kill me. I mean, otherwise wouldn't they have just shot me right then?"

I sipped my hot tea and reached out to hold her hand. Her fingers were like ice.

"And they wrapped tape around you?" I asked.

"Yes, did my hands first, then that strip across my mouth. That stuff tastes terrible! Then they didn't seem to know what to do next. I got the idea they didn't want me in the room with them—like I'd be able to remember their faces better, or maybe they didn't want me to watch them searching the house. So they found that closet, put me in there and taped up my ankles.''

"Oh, Hannah, I feel so bad about this. I've put you in danger. I hope they haven't stolen anything from you." I thought back to the break-in at the office. We still hadn't noticed anything missing, which told me they were looking for something very specific and hadn't found it yet.

"Hannah, do you feel up to checking the house, finding out if there's anything missing?"

"Do you think I should call the police, Charlie?"

"It's up to you. It would be a good idea to file a report, but truthfully, I don't think they'll solve it. I glanced into the living room and here in the kitchen. Things commonly stolen in robberies, like television sets and microwave ovens, aren't missing here. And since we know it's connected to my investigation, I tend to think they were after notes, papers, anything that might incriminate the guilty people." I shrugged. "The police aren't going to be able to do much with that."

She finished her tea. "Let's check the house," she said. "If there's anything valuable missing, we'll call them. If not, maybe I'll just try to forget about it."

That wouldn't be easy.

I glanced at my watch and noticed it was already after six-thirty. "I'll stay and help you clean this up," I told her. "But I better let Drake know what's happened." I called home, left a quick message on the machine where he'd find it when he got home.

Hannah's color looked much better until she surveyed the damage. Her eyes welled.

"Why did they do this, Charlie?" she cried.

I put my arm around her thin shoulders. "I don't know. It's sick, isn't it. This is all my fault." I suddenly wished I'd never started poking around—what was I going to learn?

The outcome wouldn't change and innocent people were getting hurt along the way.

She began replacing her treasured travel mementos on their shelves, arranging them precisely as they'd been before. I tackled the rest of it—righted the sofa cushions, straightened magazines on the coffee table. Went into the kitchen and neatened the items in the drawers. The mess actually involved little damage. Nothing was broken, slashed, or smashed. These guys had been very specific in their wish list. Whether they'd found anything, I didn't know.

Hannah was still sorting and placing little items on shelves so I went into her bedroom, remade the bed with fresh sheets I found in the linen closet and closed her dresser drawers without getting too personal as to their contents. I also went around the house, switching on lights and checking doors and windows.

"Hannah, you really should get deadbolt locks put on your doors." I demonstrated just how easily the men had probably broken in using a flexible plastic card. "I don't mean to scare you, but even when you think you're safely locked in, they can get past these things."

Her face went white again.

"For tonight, we'll rig up some protection. But promise me you'll call a locksmith tomorrow."

She agreed, as we shoved a stiff chairback under the knob on the back door and set up a pyramid of tin cans that should wake the dead if the door knocked them over.

"Now, after I leave, you do the same thing to the front door," I said.

I showed her my handiwork in the bedroom and kitchen and told her I'd checked all the windows.

"Did you notice anything missing?" I asked her.

"No. You know my scrapbook that had the Sandia clippings in it? Well, they must have only flipped through a few pages that had family photos, 'cause they didn't take anything out.''

''I'm glad to know that,'' I smiled, giving her a hug before leaving. ''You keep my number handy and call me if you get another scare. I don't think they'll bother you again, though. At this point, they know you don't have any evidence that'll hurt them.''

''But *you* might, Charlie,'' she cautioned. ''You better be extra careful.''

I drove home wondering what the hell I was doing.

TWENTY-FIVE

DRAKE LEFT EARLY the next morning, looking chipper and pleased about something.

"I think I have a job lined up for Thursday," he said, glowing with enthusiasm. "It's a scouting trip for a film crew. They want to fly up around Farmington and check out locations for a couple of days. If they find what they like, I may get to do the camera work later, and that could involve quite a bit of flying."

"Cool." I made him stay for a prolonged kiss. "Good luck with it."

"The catch is that my FAA inspectors are coming out today. Gotta pass all that before I'm legal. Oh, I better take my office paperwork with me," he added. "I'm sure they'll want to get a look at all that too."

I helped him gather the recently acquired incorporation papers and his other documents.

Rusty stared at Drake with ears cocked and head tilted, waiting to receive word on whether he'd get to go.

"Not today, kid," Drake informed him. "FAA probably doesn't see a dog as necessary to the operation."

"You can go with me," I told him. "We'll be investigators today."

"You realize all he got out of that was 'Blah, Blah, GO, Blah, Blah, Blah'," Drake laughed.

"Hey, he understands everything I tell him," I asserted.

"Yeah, yeah. Kiss me, you beautiful woman."

I did.

The house turned quiet after Drake left. I reached for my new spiral notebook and decided to go back over my suspect list. There was still one of the men in Dad's circle that I hadn't reached—Harvey Taylor—and I meant to give that another try.

First, I dialed Rebecca Sanchez's number. It rang five times and I was just about to hang up.

"Hello?" The voice was breathless.

"Rebecca? It's Charlie Parker. Did I catch you in the middle of something?"

"I just walked in." I could tell she was doing other things as she spoke, as she instructed her son to hang up his jacket and wash his hands.

"I just wanted to check and see how your father's doing," I told her.

"He's gone into a coma," she sighed. "It doesn't look very hopeful at all."

"I'm so sorry to hear that."

"Yeah."

"Rebecca, I don't mean to come across as self-centered, but did he say anything more about Sandia or my father? It could be important."

"He mumbled a lot of things, but most of it didn't make sense and wasn't even understandable," she said. Her voice was extremely weary.

"Thanks, Rebecca. Is there anything I can do to help?"

"I don't think so. I'm spending almost all my time at the hospital, on the chance he'll wake up. My best friend watches J.J. for me. We're doing okay."

"Well, call me if you think of anything." I gave her my number again.

Next, I called the office and asked Sally if Ron was in.

"Hey, kiddo," he greeted.

"Ron, I'm trying to locate an old co-worker of Dad's, a man named Harvey Taylor. The last address I got was an apartment on Carlisle, but that was really old. The sleazeball manager said he'd been there for several years but never heard of Taylor. He's not in the phone book. So do you have anything in your investigator's arsenal that might give me an address?"

"Only assuming that he's still in Albuquerque. If he's moved away, I'd need some information and more time."

"Do what you can that's easy, and I'll follow up on that," I told him before hanging up.

I pulled the picnic photo out of my purse and gave it another look. The faces were familiar to me by now. In light of the visits I'd made and the personalities involved, I tried to analyze the body language of those in the picture.

Dad stood at the far right in the photo, next to Larry Sanchez, his arm draped over Larry's shoulder. They both wore straight neutral faces. Next to Larry, in the center position, stood Harvey Taylor, tall and lanky with bushy sideburns down to his chin and blond hair that dipped in a thick wave to his eyebrows. His polyester shirt was open two buttons down and a gold chain with a big gold bear claw dangling from it made him a real middle-aged '70s fashion plate. He smiled a camera-smile, like most people do. Without having met the man, I didn't know how to read his expression.

Wendel Patterson, the oldest of the group, came next. His swagger and crooked smile came through clearly in the photo. Both he and George Myers grinned at the camera in a way that made me think the photographer was probably the prettiest girl in the office. They had their arms over each other's shoulders in a good-ol'-buddy kind of posture.

Were George and Wendel really that carefree, or were

they indeed flirting with someone behind the camera? Were Dad and Larry worried about something, or were they simply more serious about life? And, of everyone in the picture, why were they the two who'd suffered? I couldn't believe that was merely a coincidence.

The phone rang, startling me.

"Charlie, I've got a Harvey Taylor for you," Ron's voice began. "Can't say for sure it's the one from Sandia, but it's a current address and phone."

I wrote down the information and thanked him.

Taylor lived in Rio Rancho, the westside community that had burst into rapid growth in just the last few years. I consulted the phone directory map and figured I could locate it. Rusty was thrilled to join me in the Jeep for the trek.

We headed north on Rio Grande and got on I-40. I vaguely knew that taking Rio Grande all the way to where it T'd at Alameda would also get us there, but had the feeling that the freeway would be quicker. I'd no sooner exited at Coors to head toward Rio Rancho than I quickly became disoriented.

Things change so quickly in Albuquerque. The miles of Coors Boulevard that used to be long and empty with no traffic lights now felt like it was smack in the middle of the city. Fast food places, new shopping centers, car dealerships, and heavy traffic had sprouted in a surprisingly short time. I stayed in the center lane, hoping that I wouldn't have trouble spotting my turn-off.

Luckily, the Chevron station that had always marked the intersection of 528 and Southern Boulevard was still there. I glanced at my map and made a couple of turns. The Taylor address was in the Country Club area, developed in the '60s and one of the few areas of Rio Rancho that has fully-developed trees and gives the feeling that it's been there longer than a few weeks. I pulled up in front of a little box that sported sparkling white vinyl siding and a brick-red shingle roof.

Pyracantha bushes sprouted thick clusters of fat orange berries, disguising the fact that they also harbored inch-long deadly spikes that would make your finger ache for several days if you pricked yourself with one. The shrubs had not been trimmed so the laden branches arched gracefully in every direction, including over the narrow walkway that led to the front door. The rest of the spacious front yard was landscaped in a mixture of gray river rock and red lava rock, with generous quantities of weeds and grass growing up through them.

The single garage door began to crank upward as I started up the walkway, so I paused. A red convertible shot backward, its driver not giving a glance to where he was going. When he did turn my direction, he jumped visibly and the car squeaked to a stop. The set of golf clubs in the back seat rattled noisily.

"Whoa, I didn't see you there," he called.

Still the fashion plate, his now-white hair was trimmed short at the sides and back, with a modified dip at the front that somehow floated rigidly above his forehead like the bill of a ballcap. Somehow, I had the feeling it would be just as perfect after the convertible ride.

"Are you Harvey Taylor? Hi, I'm Charlie Parker," I said, approaching the side of the car. "I think you worked with my father, Bill Parker, at Sandia Labs years ago?"

His gradated sunglasses gave the impression that I could see his eyes, without actually allowing me to do so. Squint-wrinkles formed in the leathery tan skin around them.

"Yeah, hon. Bill Parker was your dad?"

I got the feeling that he couldn't believe any colleague of his could possibly have a grown daughter. Despite the white hair, he clearly still thought of himself as being in his studly prime.

"Do you have a minute?" I asked. "I wanted to chat for a bit."

He looked at the sporty plastic watch on his wrist. "Five minutes," he said. "I got an important tee-time at eleven." He switched off the ignition.

I walked around to his side of the car and stood near his side-mirror. When I briefly explained that I was looking into the plane crash, he shook his head.

"I don't think you're going to get many people who worked at Sandia to tell about any of the top secret projects that were going on at the time, even if most of it is old technology by now. That 'oath of secrecy' stuff was pretty ingrained."

"I don't want to know any government secrets," I reiterated. "I'd just like to know *if* my father was working on something at the time that might have gotten him killed. Among his papers there are some notes that appear to be in a kind of code. But I can't figure it out. He said something like 'the heat is on.' What kind of heat would that be?"

Taylor scratched a spot on his head with his index finger. The cap of perfect hair moved back and forth, no strand escaping from the heavy spray-job. His face screwed up in deep thought.

"I vaguely remember there being some pressure from the top. Some supervisor was giving Bill a hard time, wanting to get Bill's research notes. But Bill didn't want to turn in his work yet because he wasn't finished. Said he had a few more tests to conduct before he felt like he had something to show them."

"Who was the supervisor?"

His head wagged back and forth. "You know, I just don't remember. Don't remember Bill ever saying—he may have, but I can't recall the exact conversation now. Look, I gotta go..." He turned the key in the ignition.

I fished in my purse for a card. "Could you call me if it comes to you? If you remember anything at all?"

He stuck the card into the breast pocket of his polo shirt, nodding distractedly as he backed out the driveway. I'd just about bet money that the next time he thought about the card would be when it came out of the washing machine as a glob of white mush.

I walked slowly back to my car where Rusty greeted me with a welcoming doggy kiss, like I'd been gone for hours. What to do next? I felt like every lead ended up as a dead end—nobody seemed to have any real information for me and I was seriously beginning to question why I was even doing this. The only reasons I kept going were the break-in at our office, which *could* have been standard B&E and the break-in at Hannah's. That one couldn't be easily sluffed off, since she'd heard the intruders say my name. I turned the car around and headed for home.

Harvey Taylor's words about a supervisor putting on the heat nagged at me but I couldn't fit it into place. I decided to spend the rest of the day finishing my search through Dad's boxes of stuff. I'd go through everything again to see if any of it made sense in light of the scanty information I'd gotten from his fellow workers. I was beginning to get impatient with the whole thing, wanting to wrap it up as soon as I could.

When I pulled into the driveway at home, Drake's truck was still gone. I hoped all was going well with the FAA inspectors.

Rusty bounded out of the Jeep and nosed his way through the front door as soon as I unlocked it. I walked through to the kitchen to let him out back and noticed that the message light was blinking on the answering machine. I tapped the playback button as I set my purse on the counter and reached for the nearby notepad and pen.

"Charlie, this is Rebecca Sanchez," a tearful voice said. "I, uh, well, my father died this morning." She sniffed loudly. "I wanted to call you before I forgot to. He woke up for a short time last night and talked a little. He said 'tell Charlie that Bill was spy people.' I'm sorry Charlie, I don't even know what that means." The electronic beep signalled the end of her message.

Bill was spy people? My father a spy? Is that what Larry was saying? I felt the breath go out of me.

TWENTY-SIX

RUSTY ZOOMED AROUND the back yard, while I stared blankly through the window at the plants that were slowly phasing into winter brown. I felt a rush of anger at the dead man. Larry had no right to accuse my father of spying. He wasn't! I wanted to shout at Larry, to grab him by his frail shoulders and shake it into him. And now he was dead and there was no way to take it out on him, or to get anything more from him. Tears stung my eyes as I realized the futility of it.

I poured a can of Coke over ice in a glass and swigged it until the gasses welled up in my throat. The cold caffeine cleared my head. Standing here in my own kitchen, railing at a dead man wasn't going to solve anything. I had to think.

None of this top-secret business that was going on fifteen years ago should even matter today. So why did it? Why had my asking a few questions warranted one man's violent death and break-ins at our office and Hannah's house? For that matter, had our house actually been broken into as well? My desk drawer had been messed up and my spiral notebook was missing—I'd attributed it to our moving day mess, but maybe I was off track. Perhaps that had actually been the first break-in.

And what about Larry Sanchez's death? Had that some-how been engineered too? My brain went into overdrive. Larry'd been in bad health for a long time, but why, just now, did he take this sudden downturn and die? Who had access to him in the hospital? I should ask Rebecca who his other visitors had been. Could someone have put something into one of those many tubes hooked up to him? I felt myself going crazy.

Deep breath.

All this was getting me nowhere. I needed evidence, not speculation.

I walked through the break in the hedge to Elsa's. She was raking leaves in her back yard.

"You shouldn't be working this hard," I told her. "Why don't I ask my yard service to come over and do this for you?"

"It doesn't hurt me to do a bit of work," she said. "Keeps me young."

She was probably right.

"Do you mind if I go back and work on those boxes of papers I left in your guest room?" I asked. "I need to finish with them and store them away again soon."

"They're not in my way," she assured me. "Take as long as you want."

I whistled for Rusty and he trotted over, following at my heels as I went inside. Elsa's kitchen showed the remains of breakfast, a plate and bowl in the sink and toast crumbs on the countertop. I peeked into the cookie jar and swiped two ginger snaps.

My cartons were stacked just as I'd left them in the guest room. The two I hadn't investigated yet waited in one corner. That looked like the best place to start.

The first one appeared to be more of what I'd already found in the previous cartons—personal memorabilia, photos, a few interoffice memos, but nothing that could remotely be considered secret. I lifted out a couple of inches worth, fanned the pages with my thumbnail, and set them aside. I'd spent so much time reading details on the earlier finds, and I didn't want to get bogged down again. Another two-inch stack, same procedure. Still nothing that looked important.

By the time I reached the bottom of the carton, I'd just about decided not to bother with the last box. I set aside a pile of what appeared to be some of my own first grade work, thinking it might be fun to go through that later. A bluish-white corner of something lay in the bottom of the carton and I tugged at it, thinking it was a scrap ripped off something.

It wouldn't come loose. I realized that a large folded document had somehow become wedged under the bottom flap of the cardboard box. Lifting the cardboard, I pulled the paper out. It was a large sheet of paper, folded in quarters, with some faded words rubber-stamped on one corner. Initials and the date, 3-18-78, had been handwritten over the stamped words.

"Charlie, would you like some lunch?" Elsa's voice startled me. She stood in the doorway, picking dried leaf particles off her polyester slacks.

"Oh, no thanks. I think I'll try to finish up here so I can take all this stuff back and store it away."

"Whatever you think, dear. I'm heating up a can of tomato soup and you're certainly welcome to some."

"You go ahead," I told her.

She shuffled away, mumbling something, and I wavered between finishing the job at hand and taking the time to be more sociable. I unfolded the paper in my hands.

It was a blueprint of some kind. Two sheets. The weight of all the other junk in the box had flattened these. I stared back into the empty box, lifted the flap again to check under it, and carefully spread the pages out on the carpet. Obviously, my father had gone to some trouble to hide these plans, tucking them under the box bottom and filling it with family memorabilia.

Why?

I stared at the plan, trying in my very unscientific mind to figure out what I was seeing. Wording at the bottom of the page told me it was something to do with the SDL-14-X1, the pre-Star Wars project George Myers had told me about. These two sheets couldn't possibly be all of it, but perhaps it was a very strategic part. And in that case, why would it be hidden away in our attic? My heart rate quickened.

Larry Sanchez's dying words came back to me. Spy people. He accused my father of being a spy and I refused to believe it. But I also had a real bad feeling about the piece of paper spread out in front of me. I refolded the sheets, took a deep breath and stood up. Paced the room a couple of times.

Okay, I told myself, what is the real meaning of this? My father had no way of knowing he'd be in a plane crash. He'd brought this home and hidden it away sometime within the couple of months before he died. Had he planned to deliver it to someone? An enemy agent? I plopped heavily to the bed.

No. If, and I refused to even think of my father in this capacity, *if* a person planned to deliver top secret information to someone, he would have arranged a meeting and taken it there immediately. He would have never hidden something so potentially deadly in our home.

I stood up, itching to move, and paced across the room again. No, I kept telling myself. There had to be a good reason something like this would end up in our house. Dad must have been trying to keep it away from someone at Sandia. Prevent it from getting into the hands of the real spies. It was the only answer that made sense.

Or was I only deluding myself?

I laid the blueprint on the bed and opened the other box. It yielded only kid schoolwork, some mine and some my brothers'. I slowly laid everything back inside, taking my time in an effort to stall having to think about those plans. What should I do?

My first thought was to tell Drake, but he was busy and I thought about Ron. Maybe he'd have some idea of what I should do next. I stacked all the boxes against one wall and picked up the plans. I'd go by the office and show them to Ron, then come back later to carry the boxes back to the attic.

Elsa dozed in her rocking chair, the television playing her favorite soap opera. Rusty and I tiptoed by, locking the back door behind us.

"Come on, kid, let's go to the office."

His ears perked at the magic words. He bounded for the Jeep. I patted my pockets for my keys, realizing I'd have to go in the house for them. I opened the car door and made sure Rusty hopped in. He watched me through the front windshield with head cocked. I reached for the front doorknob, then remembered I'd locked it before going out the back to Elsa's. I circled the house and pushed the back door open.

Smoke billowed out.

TWENTY-SEVEN

I STUMBLED BACKWARD off the back porch and landed on my butt. Pain jolted through my hip, but all that registered was the thick black smoke pouring out the door. I pulled myself up and tried to look into the kitchen. I couldn't see five feet into the room.

Help. All I could think about was getting help. I raced crookedly with my sore hip through the hedge to Elsa's. Pounded on the door, hoping I'd wake her up.

"Gram! Wake up!" I shouted. "Unlock the door!"

Through the door's window panels I could see her shuffling into the kitchen, clearly just waking from her nap.

"Quick, Gram, the house is on fire!"

I pushed past her as soon as the door was unlocked, dashing for the phone. I dialed 911 on the incredibly slow old rotary dialer. In a few words, I gave the address and told what I'd found.

"Gram, stay here. I'm going to bring Rusty over. Keep him in the house with you so he won't get in the way." I knew I sounded like a drill sergeant, but couldn't take the time to nicen it up any.

Once Rusty was safely delivered, I glanced around trying to decide what to do next. The garden hose lay in a coil beside the house, waiting for the final watering I'd planned to give the yard before winter set in. I grabbed it up, screwed on the sprayer attachment, and turned it on full blast. In the distance I could hear sirens.

I aimed the spray in through the kitchen door. It made no difference. I couldn't see flames, only the treacherous black smoke. I pulled the hose to the north side of the house. Could see flames behind the bedroom window. My brain struggled to think. Was it smart to break out the glass and aim water in, or would that only fan the fire even more? I couldn't remember.

The sirens became louder.

I watched the bedroom drapes turn into shreds of dripping flame. I thought of our bed, the puffy comforter that I loved so much, all our clothes. My arms turned shaky.

The sirens quit abruptly.

"Back here!" I screamed. "The fire's in the back bedroom!"

I raced around to the front. A fire truck was parked at the curb, lights flashing in the deepening twilight. Three firemen were climbing out, looking around, unsure whether they'd come to the right place.

"Back here!" I shouted again. "The fire's in back!"

They snapped to attention.

"Quick, it's already engulfed the bedroom," I yelled. With a jerk, I came to the end of the garden hose. I'd forgotten I was still holding it with a death grip. I dropped it and waved toward the firemen, ready to lead the charge.

"Okay, ma'am," said one of the men. He was so encased in bright yellow rubberized gear that I couldn't get a sense of his size and build, but he took me by the elbow and led me toward the sidewalk.

"Is there anyone else in the house, ma'am?" he asked.

"Uh, no. No, my fiancé's gone and I've taken the dog next door. Just hurry up and put it out."

"Can you go next door, too, ma'am?" he asked. "You look like you're freezing."

I hugged my upper arms. The skin was cool, but my fingers were positively frigid.

"I want to help," I cried. "I can't just go inside."

"Ma'am—what's your name, anyway?"

"Charlie Parker. That's my house!"

"Okay, Ms. Parker. Why don't we just have you go to your neighbor's place now. I can't let you help. You're gonna have to stand back so the men can get to it."

I looked over and saw the men stretching a hose across the yard. Someone had attached the other end to the fire hydrant across the street. Neighbors were standing on their front porches. Elsa stood on hers, waving me toward her. The fireman gently took me by the shoulders and led me to her.

It wasn't until I reached her front porch that I realized I was shaking. My head suddenly felt weird and black dots danced before my eyes. I sank down to Elsa's front step and put my head between my knees.

"Charlie? Dear, are you all right?" she asked.

"Ummm, hmmm. I just feel kind of strange."

I felt her slip a thick wool sweater around my shoulders. For some reason, I couldn't stop shaking. I rested my forehead on my knees and tried to keep up with the action by listening to the jumble of shouts and orders coming from across the lawn. The daylight had completely gone and the eerie red flashing lit the neighborhood garishly. From a hollow tunnel, I heard Rusty barking.

"Charlie! What's happening?" Strong male arms lifted me up and wrapped around me.

"Ron? How did you know...?"

"I caught the call on the scanner. Just about shit when they gave your address."

He rubbed my arms, while I leaned my head against his shoulder.

"I called Drake," he said. "Remembered you said he'd be at the hangar today. He's on his way in."

"I…" I couldn't think what to say. My earlier clear-headedness had completely gone.

"What happened?" Ron asked again. "No, it's okay. Just wait until Drake gets here and you can tell us both. Did you get Rusty out of the house?"

"Yeah, we were both at Gram's when it started. I don't know what happened. I was just about to come to the office and I was going inside for my keys. But smoke came out the door…and the bedroom…I couldn't make the water spray. I—"

"It's okay. It's gonna be okay," he soothed.

"Charlie!" Drake's voice came out of the confusion from a distance.

My head snapped up, eyes searching for him. Ron turned around. "Over here," he shouted.

My numb body got shifted from one hug to the other. "Oh, God, Charlie, are you okay, babe?" His voice shook as he practically squeezed the breath out of me.

"Mmmff," I said from the depth of his chest.

"Sorry."

He held me at arm's length, watching my face intently. I assured myself that he was all right, but my attention was quickly drawn to the house.

Flames had begun to rise from the roof at the back corner, above our bedroom. A second truck had arrived and the men were in the process of raising the ladder to take aim over the top of the house. The original team stretched their hoses around to the back yard and were working on it from that angle. I didn't want to look but couldn't manage to tear my eyes away from the action. I became dimly aware that Ron had taken Gram inside.

We sank down to sit on Elsa's front porch to watch our home go up in flames.

TWENTY-EIGHT

I AWOKE BESIDE Drake in a strange room and the night's terror came back. The firemen finally declaring the fire out sometime around eleven, their stern instructions that we were not to try to enter until the investigators came tomorrow, and Gram practically dead from exhaustion, insisting that we sleep in her guest room that night. I moaned and Drake reached an arm around my waist.

Part of me wanted to roll back over and go to sleep again, and part of me wanted to run home and confirm that none of it had really happened. I couldn't make either scenario happen. My eyes stayed wide open.

I could only imagine what lay ahead. I already knew that many of the shrubs and flowerbeds had been damaged by trampling boots and heavy hoses. But the house—I only knew that the outside walls still stood. Beyond that, the inside could be anything. And my active mind could envision only the worst. My childhood home, all my mother's lovely furniture, china, and keepsakes… Hot tears stung my eyes.

"Sweetheart?" Drake's sleepy voice queried. "What are you doing awake so early?"

I sniffed loudly.

"Hey, it's gonna be okay," he soothed. "Want to go over there now? Look around?"

I nodded. Not knowing what we'd find was far worse than just getting it over with.

"Okay, then," he said, "let's put our clothes back on and just go see."

We each rolled to our edges of the bed. We'd come over with literally the clothes on our backs, so there'd be no choosing of wardrobe today and no brushing of teeth. We'd have to work out that part *real* soon.

Rusty stood with his nose pasted to the crack in the door, his tail slowly waving back and forth. His ears perked up and he turned his head to one side then the other, making me think that Elsa must be up and making little sounds around the house.

I pulled on my T-shirt and jeans, yesterday's socks and shoes, and the wool sweater Gram had placed around my shoulders last night. Grabbed Rusty's collar so he wouldn't charge through the house until I could be certain Gram was up. He lunged when I opened the bedroom door and, seeing that hers was open already, I let him go.

"C'mon, kid," I said softly. "Let's go out back."

He paused a moment on the back porch, realizing that his own territory waited next door. As the dog raced through the hedge to find his own sacred places, I followed slowly.

My kitchen door gaped open, the frame smeared smoky black. The bedroom windows were broken out, revealing nothing but charred black and the roof was gone over that corner of the house. Under the kitchen window, the last of the autumn chrysanthemums lay trampled and broken, smashed by heavy boots. I bent to retrieve one purple blossom that struggled on a crooked stem. A tear slipped heavily to my cheek.

"It's gonna be okay, sweetheart," Drake said, slipping an arm around my shoulders.

I leaned into him. "Why?" I wailed. "How and why did this happen?"

He stroked my hair. "I don't know, hon. I just don't know."

I took a deep breath and tucked the purple flower into his shirt pocket. "I want to go inside and look around. Maybe it's not as bad as we think."

"The fireman told you not to," he cautioned.

I headed for the back door, pulling out of his grasp.

"Charlie, what if the floor caves in? What if the ceiling gives way?" He followed me to the porch. "Don't touch anything," he said resignedly. "They'll be coming to investigate, you know."

I spun around. "I just want to see if there's anything left."

A little sigh escaped him. "Okay. But I'm coming with you."

Mud coated the kitchen floor and the walls were gray with a filmy haze. I wanted to reach for the light switch, but realized that would be futile. They would have cut the power to the house to prevent a spark.

"This doesn't look too bad," Drake said. "A good cleanup will do wonders here." He sounded like he was working hard to be optimistic.

The dining room hardwood floors were in worse shape than the kitchen tile. Puddles of water stood in places and muddy tracks crossed back and forth across the room. The table and chairs had been shoved roughly against the front wall, clearing a path from the kitchen to the living room. Mother's china cabinet was still intact and the dishes appeared unharmed, although the glass fronted doors were hazy with gray. Then it began to get worse.

Heavy fire hoses had been dragged through the front door, which had been hacked open with axes. My white linen sofa showed wide tracks where hoses were dragged over the back of it on the way to the bedrooms. The hallway was charred and the three bedrooms and two baths were gone.

"Looks like the fire started back here, probably in our bedroom," Drake said. "It's in the worst shape." We stopped at the entrance to the hall, not trusting the floor beyond that point.

The walls that once defined the master bedroom, master bath, and guest room were gone. Charred studs were all that remained of the guest bath off the hallway, and the third bedroom which had served as our office was only a shell. All the windows on the north side of the house had burst or been broken out. Frigid water dripped from the remaining rafters and the entire place smelled like damp charcoal.

"What a mess," I moaned, rubbing my temples. The fanatically orderly person inside me screamed at me to do something. But the carnage at this end of the house was too much to contemplate.

Drake took my hand. "Don't you get any ideas about cleaning this up just yet," he teased. "I know you want to."

My mouth tried a little smile—he was trying to lighten up the situation after all—but I couldn't quite manage it.

"I'm sure an investigator will come out soon. They won't be happy if you go moving things around."

"I know," I grudged. "And I better call the insurance company. Maybe some of the forty years worth of premiums that have been paid on this place will finally pay off."

"C'mon," he said, "let's get some breakfast."

I tried to close the front door, which hung crookedly now, but it wouldn't have made any difference. The door frame was nothing but splinters anyway. I did retrieve my purse from the coatrack by the front door. Flipped through my wallet, which still had cash and credit cards intact. I had a feeling we'd be needing those real soon.

We retraced our steps through the kitchen, where we found Rusty waiting at the porch, whining softly.

"Oh, you poor guy," I said. I sat down and slipped my arms around his neck. "You're upset about this too."

He squiggled out of my grasp, slurped his pink tongue up the side of my face, and scampered toward the hedge. It doesn't take too long to make everything all better for a dog.

Ron's car sat at the curb; he was just making his way up the front walk.

"We're over here," I called out.

He crossed the battered lawn and took me into a giant bear hug, released me, and shook hands with Drake. He looked like he'd probably awakened as early as we did. His shirt wasn't tucked in and his hair stuck out in little tufts around the edge of his hat, like he'd stuck the Stetson on without combing his hair first.

"Have you been inside yet?" he asked.

We briefed him on what we'd found.

"I'd like to take a look before the other investigators get here," he said. "You have any ideas on what started it?"

Truthfully, I hadn't even gotten that far.

"The blueprints! Oh, God, what happened to them?" My mind searched frantically. I'd come from Elsa's with them in hand, put Rusty in the Jeep, then went to get my car keys. Where were the plans?

Drake and Ron were staring at me like I'd started speaking Japanese.

"There were some blueprints," I explained. "I found them among Dad's papers and I was about to come to the office and show them to you, Ron." My eyes darted around, trying to get my brain to engage. "I never made it into the house—that's when I discovered the fire."

I retraced my steps from the previous afternoon, looking

on the ground around trees and shrubs. When I got to the Jeep, where I'd put Rusty when the fire broke out, I spotted them on the dash. I must've tossed them there when I opened the car door and completely forgotten them all night. I hugged them to my chest.

What if someone had set the fire, hoping to destroy these? The thought overtook me like an avalanche.

TWENTY-NINE

NUMBNESS CAN ONLY last so long and then a person has to move into action. The four of us sat around Elsa's kitchen table, where she'd fixed us a breakfast of scrambled eggs and toast, while Rusty waited expectantly to catch whatever morsels might fall his way.

"So, what do you think they mean?" I asked. I'd briefed Ron and Drake on my find, and we now had the plans spread out on the table.

"Well, it's obviously part of the plan for that fancy missile system they were working on at the time," Ron observed. "But it certainly isn't all of it."

"I'd guess that this is a portion of the guidance system," Drake offered. "From what I remember of my Navy experience in ordnance, it looks like this first page shows the guidance system for the missile, then the second page is the detailed schematic for one of the phases. See how this section," he indicated the plan on page two, "would fit right here." He flipped the large pages back to page one and indicated where the other section would go.

We all stretched to see what he meant. Ron nodded, "I think you're right."

"Well, it really doesn't matter *what* it is at this point, does it?" I said. "I mean, whatever it is, the real question is why did Dad hide these in the bottom of a box of personal stuff, and why are they important enough to someone today to kill for?''

''Yeah,'' Ron agreed, ''it has been fifteen years since the plane crash. The cold war is over. The Soviets are no more.''

''It makes sense that someone within Sandia might have wanted to sell the technology to the enemy, but that reason certainly isn't valid today. And why would Dad have these?'' I asked.

Unless Larry Sanchez's dying words were literally true. That my father was a spy. I told the group that I'd only picked up that little tidbit yesterday.

''No way!'' Ron exploded. ''I can't remember meeting anyone, anyplace, who was more straight-forward and honest than Dad. I mean, I was twenty-one at the time he died and I can remember him getting after me for fudging a job application. I'd come by the house here on my way to an interview and he saw the application laying on the table. Chewed my butt for listing my job experience as more than what I really had.

''Does that sound to you like the same guy would then turn around and sell his country's secrets? No way.''

''Well, maybe Larry meant to say that Dad knew who the spy people were,'' I suggested. For some reason I felt defensive of Larry Sanchez too.

''Whatever.'' Ron said it grudgingly. ''Either way, like you said earlier, how can all this matter now?''

''Right. There's someone around today who very much wants all this to stay buried. Someone who thought they were safe once that plane went down in the mountains.''

''Probably thought the plans were on board with Dad,'' Ron added. ''And his little notebook—normally it would have been with him.''

''And the trouble started when I found the notebook and

began asking questions about the notes in there.'' I thought of the little leather-bound book, which I'd already verified was still tucked safely away in my purse. If an arsonist truly had come into the house yesterday and set the fire, he was within a few feet of the notebook. If he'd only taken the time to look. A chill crept up my arms.

Pieces of the puzzle were beginning to slip into place. Whoever had broken into the house the first time had taken my little spiral notebook. Maybe they knew it was mine and were hoping I'd made notes about my investigation. Then again, maybe they'd been told to look for a little notebook and they thought they were getting Dad's. If the thief was not a Sandia employee, but had been hired by one, he wouldn't know exactly what he was looking for. He may have decided the fire was the way to wipe out all the evidence at once, without having to come back and search for little pieces here and there. My mind spun with the implications and variations.

''Well, on to more practical matters,'' Drake interrupted. ''We have to figure out where we'll be living for awhile now, and unless we plan to wear these same clothes forever, I'd say we have some shopping to do.''

I rested my forehead on the palm of my hand. I didn't even want to think about it.

''Remember, I have that film job lined up for tomorrow and I may be out late,'' Drake said, ''so it seems like we're going to have to address this pretty soon.''

He was right. All the talking and speculating wasn't solving the case and it wasn't getting our personal situation resolved either.

''Let me put in a call to the insurance company. And I wish I knew when the fire investigator will come. I'd like to be here to see what they find out,'' I said.

''You can plan on staying here,'' Elsa piped up. She'd

been so quiet, I'd practically forgotten her presence. I hoped we weren't endangering her by saying too much.

"Oh, Gram, that's a wonderful offer," I said, "but it could be months. I have no idea how long it will be before we can be back in our house."

"That's all right," she said readily. "You know I can stand a lot of you."

It was true that she'd taken me in for three years after my parent's deaths, but that stay hadn't included a large dog and my lover. Having three of us around for several months might be pushing the envelope. And our love life might not include much spark when staying in the room next to my almost-grandmother. Not to mention that our mere presence might put her life on the line.

"Let's all think about it," I suggested. "There might be a way that would be less disruptive to your life."

Twenty minutes later, I'd secured an appointment with the insurance adjuster for three p.m., a locksmith and a carpenter would be there sometime during the day to board up and make the place secure, and I'd attempted to brush through my long hair with the pocket-sized hairbrush from my purse. If I didn't get hold of a toothbrush soon, things would become desperate.

We opted to leave my Jeep in the driveway and take Drake's truck for a shopping trip. Rusty would stay at Elsa's, although the look he gave me clearly indicated that he didn't want to be left behind.

A quick stop at Osco netted us basic toiletries and I made use of the toothbrush and toothpaste in their ladies' room before I even paid for them. At the mall, we went our separate ways for wardrobes. Looking through the racks, I came upon items that would remind me of a favorite sweater or blouse that were now gone and a flash of sadness would hit me. However, fashion slave that I'm not, two hours later

I had enough basic items of clothing to get through a few days. I met Drake, as planned, at the fountain in the center of the mall and we settled in at Chelsea Street Pub for a late lunch.

A margarita helped lighten my mood, and things were going well until we pulled into our driveway to find two vehicles parked out front with the fire department's logo and the words Arson Investigation Unit.

THIRTY

WE'D NO SOONER stepped out of the truck than a third car cruised slowly by, U-turning at the end of the block, and coming to a stop behind us, blocking our driveway.

"I'll go check out the guys inside," Drake volunteered. "This new one must be your insurance adjuster."

I waited beside the truck while the man gathered his tools—a metal clipboard with a cover and a stack of forms. He had red-blonde hair generously sprinkled with gray, sparse on top, and a matching beard. His gray pinstripe suit had seen a long day, with wrinkles in the pants, light smudges at the knees, and a tomatoey-looking food stain on the pale yellow tie. He introduced himself as Don Cannon.

His handshake was firm but distracted, like he just wanted to get this over with so he could settle into his sweats and a ball game. Much the same way I was feeling right about now.

His handy clipboard already appeared to contain my policy information, so we didn't have to cover any of the basics. I led him through the front door and he began rapidly making notes, starting with the notation that the front door and frame would have to be replaced.

"Let's start with the little stuff and move on to the worst of it later," he suggested.

I took him to the kitchen and dining room, where the costs involved would be mainly for cleanup.

"The worst damage is to the bedrooms and baths," I told him. "They're pretty much destroyed."

"How did the fire start?" he queried.

"I don't know. I wasn't home at the time."

He raised a reddish eyebrow and wrote that down.

"Since the damage was in the bedroom areas, I'm assuming there were some valuables destroyed," he said. "I'll need receipts and appraisals for any jewelry, furs, guns, computers, etcetera."

Receipts? Those little scraps of paper that were probably in the drawers of the desk that was now burned to a crisp? Great. I could see my life becoming instantly complicated.

"Hon?" Drake interrupted my thoughts. "The investigator wants to talk to you a minute."

"Go ahead," Cannon said. "I'll get my camera and take some pictures. I can make a list of all the obvious losses."

Yeah, like my memories? Like the days of work we'd put into setting up Drake's home office? Like the cards and love notes Drake had sent me while we were apart, tucked into my bottom dresser drawer?

I swallowed and gave my head a quick shake to clear it. I'd have to schedule time later to break down.

"Ms. Parker?"

I turned to face the arson man.

"Inspector Wilson. Albuquerque Fire Department." He was a man of large build, built even larger by the extra fifty pounds he carried in the gut that hung over his belt. At six-three, well over two hundred pounds, he filled the doorway. He wore rubber boots and surgical gloves. A sooty streak ran down the side of his face, like he'd gotten caught under one of the dripping eaves.

"Can you come with me a moment, ma'am?" he requested. All business.

I trotted behind like an obedient puppy. He crunched his

way over fallen debris in the hallway, then cautioned me to follow exactly in his footsteps as we entered the bedroom, lest the floor give way and send us crashing into the crawl space under the house. My throat constricted as I surveyed my former bedroom.

The outer wall was completely burned away, leaving a wide view into the back yard, and the attached bathroom now consisted only of a few charred upright timbers and blackened ceramic fixtures. The bed's metal frame was the only indication of where Drake and I had spent pleasurable hours in each other's arms. Across the room, the dresser stood like a giant chunk of charcoal, blackened and solid. Flames had burned through the wall to the adjoining guest room, which appeared in only slightly better shape. My mind went numb.

Wilson turned to me. "Did you always have your morning coffee in bed?" he questioned.

"What?" My brain couldn't grasp the question.

"How large a policy did you carry on the house?" Again, that accusatory tone of voice, with questions that I couldn't quite fathom.

"What are you talking about?" I finally managed.

"Wait here," he ordered.

I stayed near the charred doorway, while he picked his way through the rubble to the edge of the metal bedframe. Poking a gloved index finger through the debris, he came up with a small metal part and a few strings of black spaghetti, which he held up to me.

"This, ma'am. We've seen a lot of these faulty coffeemakers go up in flames, but not usually in the bedroom, and we *usually* find that the wiring's bad."

I struggled to think what, exactly, he was telling me.

"Coffeemaker?" The words came out sounding like I wasn't quite sure what a coffeemaker was.

Wilson dropped the conglomeration of parts into a plastic baggie. "The lab will analyze these," he informed me. "But my own twenty-odd years in the business make me think this was tampered with." He stared closely at my face, and I tried to imagine what he might be reading there.

He zipped the baggie closed and started toward me, with an air of okay-we're-done-here. I stepped aside, let him pass me, then followed him into the smoky living room. My internal fog was beginning to clear a little.

"What were you saying about coffeemakers?" I queried.

"Surely you've seen the warnings and the TV specials about this. Well, some of these coffeemakers are notorious for catching fire. The plastic parts don't just melt, they'll actually sustain a flame for several minutes, and that usually means that whatever else is nearby catches fire too. Thing gets too hot, bad wire causes a spark, something like that...you got yourself a fire. The thing is," his eyes turned accusatory again, "there's always evidence left behind."

"What does *that* mean?" I demanded.

"You and your old man getting along okay? One of you decide to set up a little romantic atmosphere by having the breakfast coffee in bed?"

"What are you saying?" My voice was coming back to me.

"I'm saying, *ma'am,* until the lab results come back on this, I don't want either of you leaving town." He turned on his heel and stomped out through the chopped up front doorway.

My mind reeled.

I paced the gritty living room. I hadn't taken the coffeemaker into the bedroom. I tried to remember back to this morning. Had Drake brought it in there to make coffee in bed for me? No. It had been in the kitchen. Always.

So, who *did* put the coffeemaker in the bedroom? And

why? My pacing picked up speed. Why? Okay, if someone did want to burn down our house—and the list of suspects was certainly getting longer—why not just rig the coffeemaker in the kitchen? Why put it in the bedroom where we'd surely notice that it was out of place? My mind zipped through the possibilities—everything from their hoping to kill us in our bed, to their wanting to destroy a certain part of the house because it's where I might have stashed evidence in the case.

Elsa. Oh, God. Thankfully, they didn't know I'd taken all my father's records to her house. Or did they?

"Hon?" Drake came in just as I was coming to the most dreadful of conclusions.

"Drake, what are we going to do?" I wailed. It was all getting to be too much. I sank down in a chair at the kitchen table and rested my head on my forearms on the grimy surface. I finally let loose with the tears that had hovered near the surface all day.

Drake rubbed my shoulders gently. I heard him let out a huge sigh. I turned in my chair and pressed my face to his stomach. He was hurting too. All his things had been lost in the fire too, all the files we'd so meticulously set up for his business. I raised my head to look at his face. He was managing to be brave—staying tough and comforting me—but I could see that his emotions were very near the surface too. I stood and faced him. We wrapped together into a tight embrace and there in the dark, both of us let the tears flow.

THIRTY-ONE

CCCLLAAANNNNGGG! The old-fashioned alarm clock Gram had loaned us sent me reeling toward the side of the bed. My heart pounded as I reached to make it shut up. No wonder people's life expectancy used to be so much shorter, if they woke up to one of these things every day.

Drake groaned and rolled toward his edge. I managed to aim a quick kiss at his shoulder before he sat up.

"Five-thirty already?" he mumbled. "My, how time flies."

"Mmmm." I couldn't manage much more than that.

"You don't have to get up, you know," he said. "I can find a piece of toast or something and head for the airport." We'd decided that, rather than give up a flying job, I'd cover for him if the fire investigator asked where he'd gone.

"No, I'm sure that alarm woke Gram too, so I shouldn't be the only one to lie around in bed. Plus, I have lots to do today. It won't hurt me to get an early start."

I gave him first shot at the shower. In our own house, I probably would have shared it with him. Already, living in someone else's home was cramping our style. I dressed (another thing I wouldn't have had to do at home) and went into the kitchen. Let Rusty out back where he conveniently lifted his leg on Elsa's side of the hedge. I should have gone out with him and pointed out that he could still use his own yard.

I opened a package of blueberry muffins I'd bought yesterday to contribute to the food supply, poured juice, and brewed a pot of coffee with Elsa's little stove-top percolator with the glass bubble in the lid.

Drake came in a few minutes later, neatly dressed in khakis and a knit shirt, with his leather bomber jacket, which had luckily been with him during the fire, slung over his shoulder. His hair was still damp and he smelled of that sexy aftershave he wears that always makes me want to jump him. We shared a long, hot kiss until I heard Gram shuffling around in the living room.

"How long will your job take you away, Drake?" she asked as the three of us sat down to breakfast.

"Probably just today," he answered, after washing down a muffin with some juice. "The customer wants to recon a film location, which should only take two or three hours. I should be back at the hangar by dark. Then, with any luck, if they do find a site, maybe they'll hire me later to do the actual filming. I'll have to locate a Tyler Mount for the camera. It's gonna be too expensive to buy one for the occasional job, but maybe someplace around here rents them." He turned to me. "What's your big plan for the day, hon?"

We'd talked about it a little last night, so this was mainly for Gram's benefit.

"I'm thinking that we should find a place of our own. The repairs on the house are going to take awhile, and we're really going to be in your way."

"Now don't you even think of spending money on an apartment or anything," Gram began. "You really won't be in my way here, you know."

She really wanted the company, I realized, and my selfishness nagged at me.

"Well…" I felt myself waffling.

Drake shot me a look as he reached for his jacket.

"Let me just see what I can work out. Chances are, I'
be over here a lot anyway while they do repairs on th
house, so it's not like you're really going to get the chanc
to miss us very much."

I walked Drake out to his truck.

"Hon…"

"I know. We can't have sex in the bedroom right nex
to hers, and we *sure* can't go without sex for months. I'v
got an idea that I'll check out today."

He reached an arm around my waist. "It's only been tw
days and I'm going crazy. See if you can get us moved b
tonight."

I gave him another teaser kiss.

"Oh." He remembered something. "Are you going to b
near the phone all day? I need someone to do my fligl
following."

"I'll be here another hour or so, then probably back her
by late afternoon."

"Okay. Give me the number and I'll call you just befor
I take off. Here's a list of emergency numbers. If I'm mor
than an hour late, you've got to report me as an overdu
aircraft." He climbed into the small pickup and gave m
another kiss. "Love you."

A weak smile played across my lips as I waved goodby
Overdue aircraft? Oh, please don't throw another obstac
at me, I begged. I slumped back to our blackened abode.
desperately wanted to sit on the floor and have another goo
cry, but didn't dare start. There was too much to do.

An hour later, knowing that Drake was safely on hi
flight, and having made a To Do list, I called Rusty to actio
and we headed for the office.

"Oh, Charlie," Sally cried, taking me into a strong hu

with the lump of her big belly between us. "I'm so sorry about the house. Is everything gone?"

I poured a mug of coffee and recapped the previous day's events, leaving out the part where Inspector Wilson had practically accused me of setting the fire myself. Instead, I ended the story with my idea for solving our housing plight.

"Move here? Into the office?" she said.

"Sure, why not? It used to be a house. I'm going to do some measuring in my office to be sure we could fit a bed in there. I think we can manage if I move my desk over. We can cook in the kitchen. Rusty's familiar with the place and the yard."

The canine subject thumped his tail against the kitchen floor, but otherwise lay perfectly still with his head on his front paws.

I carried my mug up to my office, peeking in at Ron's door to say hello. With the phone pasted to his ear, he grinned and nodded at me while telling someone on the other end that if they didn't show up for their bail hearing he'd personally kick their ass. I just shook my head.

Okay, I thought, with a little rearranging I think we can make this work. I set my mug on the desk and looked in the supply closet for a tape measure. Chewing on my lower lip, I looked around. If we moved my little sofa downstairs to the reception area...pushed the desk into the corner facing the door...put a bed so that it faced the sunny bay window... I could see it coming together. A TV set could sit on top of the bookcase, a chest of drawers might fit in the hallway. Or we could keep clothes in suitcases. I was beginning to feel a spark of enthusiasm for the idea.

The phone rang, startling me.

"Hi hon." Drake's voice came through over the loud background of rotor noise. "I'm in Farmington, safe and sound."

"Good! What do I do next?"

"Nothing. I'll call you when I'm leaving here, probably sometime between two and three o'clock."

I told him about my idea of moving into the office, but the details became lost in trying to communicate over the noise. He said he liked the plan and to just do whatever I wanted to.

Since shopping isn't something I revel in, I headed for American Furniture, figuring its many departments could take care of our every need with just one stop. By noon, I'd ordered a bed and dresser to be delivered that afternoon. The electronics department netted me a portable TV with built-in VCR, and the linen department supplied us with sheets, blankets, and towels. I hoped Drake would agree with my color choices, but figured if he absolutely hated any of this it could end up in the guest room later. The main thing was that we'd soon have a place of our own.

When Sally left the office at one o'clock, Ron and I proceeded to move the furniture. The phone rang as we were rearranging a tangle of computer cords.

"RJP Investigations," I answered.

"I'm still gonna get that file," a deep voice rasped.

"What? Who is this?"

The phone had gone dead. I stared at the handset, my heart fluttering.

"Who on earth was that?" Ron asked, staring at me with concern.

"Wait." I put my hand up to silence him. The voice replayed through my head a dozen times, my brain searching for some connection, some vague hint of recognition.

The caller had clearly been working to disguise his voice, but I felt sure it was male. I also had the nagging sensation that I'd talked with this person. There was something…

perhaps just a bit of an accent? Then, like a wisp of smoke, the connection vanished.

"I don't know." I shook my head, clearing it.

"Well, if you want my help getting this sofa downstairs, you better take me while you can," he said. "Remember, I have a deposition to give at three."

We struggled with the furniture while my mind struggled with the puzzle. The killer obviously believed there was another file out there somewhere, some evidence not contained in Jim Williams's stolen papers, and something as yet uncovered in the searches of Hannah's home, my home, and my office.

The blueprints were in Ron's office and I had the sense that they provided a real clue. I just couldn't figure out what it was.

THIRTY-TWO

By FOUR O'CLOCK, the big orange-yellow American Furniture truck pulled away, our new belongings neatly arranged in my office upstairs. Ron had gone to give his deposition and Drake had called to say he was on the way back from Farmington.

Rusty and I headed west on Central toward what was left of home.

The sun was already dropping toward the horizon and dark gray clouds streaked across the sky, giving the impression that twilight was nearing. Brown leaves huddled against the curbs, awaiting either the next hefty breeze or the whir of the street sweeper's brushes. I thought of Drake flying into the escalating weather.

Elsa's windows glowed with golden lamplight, while our house stood dark and abandoned. I pulled into our driveway and walked around the house to check the carpenter's work. The front door had been secured with a hasp and padlock and plywood boards covered the broken-out windows. Satisfied that the house was as secure as possible, I trekked over to Elsa's.

The phone was ringing as I walked in the door.

"Charlie, it's for you," Elsa said, holding out the receiver to me.

"Hi, hon, I'm back at the airport here," Drake said.

I felt a knot of anxiety relax inside me.

"I'll be out here another hour or so, then I could meet you somewhere for dinner," he suggested.

"Sounds good to me. I'll be eager to hear about your flight."

We agreed to meet at Pedro's at six. I turned to Elsa after hanging up.

"Would you like to come to dinner with us?" I asked.

"Oh, no thanks. I don't eat much at night." She said it tentatively and I felt another stab of guilt at leaving her behind.

"If you won't come with us tonight, then I want to take you to lunch tomorrow."

"Thanks, but that's okay. I have lunch tomorrow with my ladies group from church."

I laughed. "You're such a social butterfly," I teased.

Briefly, I told her about our plan to move into the office until our repairs were done. I may have imagined it, but I thought she almost looked relieved.

"Meanwhile, before I meet Drake for dinner, I'm going to get those boxes stacked out of your way. I can take them back home tomorrow and stack them in my own kitchen, since we won't be using it for awhile."

I scanned Elsa's guest room for our personal belongings, tucking the few items into a plastic grocery bag. The cardboard cartons I'd carefully searched were arrayed in front of the closet door, so I picked them up and moved them to a corner beside the 1920s chest of drawers. Stacking the boxes atop each other, I realized there was still one carton I hadn't looked into. Yesterday, I'd had two cartons to go, and had stopped when I found the blueprints at the bottom of the first one.

Surely this one would contain more personal mementos and kid's schoolwork. I'd already found the important clue.

But I couldn't just assume it. I stacked all the other boxes and carried this one over to the bed.

My shoulders ached and I really didn't have the patience or enthusiasm for reading every scrap of paper, like I'd done in the beginning. I began pulling papers out in handfuls, flipping the edges of them as I went. This carton, like the previous one, contained lots of my own report cards and school papers. Some day I might get a kick out of reading them, but not tonight. I glanced at my watch. Five-thirty.

In the third handful, about halfway into the carton, I realized I had something other than paper in my hand. I set the papers aside and separated out the odd item.

It was a round metal box about eight inches in diameter and three-quarters of an inch thick, like a film container. The gray can was not labeled in any way, but was sealed with blue electrical tape that ran around the edge. I picked at the end of the sticky old strip.

Finally getting a grip on the tape, I pulled it off in one long piece. It came away with a whining sound. The lid was stubborn and the edges were sticky with tape residue. I tugged and wrestled with it until it finally lifted.

A yellowed newspaper clipping fell into my lap. I carefully unfolded it. A photo. The caption noted that Jack Cudahy, Special Defense Project Coordinator for Sandia Labs, was receiving a Congressional Commendation for his work. Shaking his hand in the photo was the Speaker of the House. But that wasn't the interesting part. Beaming up at Cudahy like an admiring groupie was a younger but still voluptuous Kathleen Smathers.

Inside the can was a reel that wasn't film. I could only guess that it was an old computer disk. I knew it wasn't going to be readable on any computer that I'd ever seen. Now what?

DRAKE WAS ALREADY seated at our special table when Rusty and I entered Pedro's. Two margaritas waited, along with a basket of tortilla chips and a small bowl of Pedro's fiery salsa. Rusty assumed his position in the corner behind the table, ready to catch chips in mid-air.

"Look what I found!" I glanced around the room to be sure no one was paying attention to us, then pulled the large disk out of my purse and showed it to Drake.

He grinned. "Guess I don't have to ask how *your* day was. You're practically glowing."

"I am? Well, maybe, compared to how I felt twenty-four hours ago."

We kissed and toasted each other with our margaritas. I slurped a section of salt off the rim of my glass and mingled it with the tart lime drink on my tongue.

"How do you suppose we could find out what's on this thing?" I asked, opening the metal can to show Drake the disk.

"Boy, that's an oldie," he commented. "And pretty specialized. Probably only used in government offices twenty years ago."

I told him about the phone call, the whispering voice that had tracked me down at the office. "Maybe this is 'that file' that he mentioned.

"It has to be someone from Sandia," I said. "Someone who knew about the existence of this disk...or maybe they don't know it's on a disk. Maybe they think there's still a paper file somewhere. And if it's the same person who set the fire, how do they know they didn't get everything already?"

Drake scooped salsa onto a chip and held it out to me. "Well, the thing that worries me is that he seems to be watching your movements so closely. How did he know

you'd be at the office this afternoon? How did he know tha
you weren't home yesterday afternoon?''

I chomped on the chip and helped myself to another
There didn't seem to be an answer to his questions.

''Please be careful, Charlie,'' he said. ''I couldn't stand
it if anything happened to you, hon.''

''I'll be on alert at all times, sir!''

He swigged the rest of his drink and signaled Pedro to
bring two more.

''I didn't mean to be flippant, Drake. I really will be
careful.''

Pedro brought the second round and I suggested that we
better have some dinner. Forgetting lunch was probably the
reason my margarita was suddenly going to my head.

''So, I wonder how I'm going to find out what's on this
disk,'' I mused.

''My thought would be to contact the most computer
geekiest person you know. Ask their advice.''

''The computer-geekiest people I know probably weren'
even born when this disk was made.'' My skepticism
showed through.

''Well, it was just a thought. You could always go out
to Sandia, walk right into the department where your father
used to work, and ask them to plug it in.''

And alert someone there as to the disk's existence
Hmmm. The chicken enchiladas arrived just then, saving
me from making a decision. We dug into the wonderful
concoction of tortillas, chicken, cheese, and green chile
sauce. I belatedly remembered to ask Drake about his day
and was pleased for him that the prospect of further work
from the customer looked good.

We finished our dinner, visited briefly with Pedro and
Concha, then headed toward our new sleeping quarters at
the office. While Drake made the bed with the new linens

I placed a couple of phone calls to computer freaks I knew. No answer either place, so I left messages on voice-mails. Drake had headed toward the bathroom to shower in the ancient claw-footed tub while I rummaged for the combination to Ron's small safe. I locked the computer disk, the two pages of blueprints, and Dad's small leather notebook safely away before joining him under the hot spray.

Twenty minutes later, the hot water was well on its way to lukewarm and would soon become downright cold. And we were just getting started. Drake had just suggested christening the new bed when the phone rang.

"I'm ignoring that," I mumbled into his lips.

The answering machine on my desk clicked on. My voice, sounding stilted, came on to inform the caller of our office hours.

"Uh, Charlie...I'd hoped to reach you tonight. I'm leaving at five in the morning for a hiking trip in Mexico. If you want me to look at that computer disk, it'll have to be tonight or else after I get back. I think I know what kind of disk you're talking about, and I could probably convert it...uh—"

I groaned but leapt up to grab the phone.

"Todd? Is that you? I'm here," I called out.

"Oh, Charlie! Glad you're there. Did you—"

"Yeah I heard what you were saying. Do you think you can read that disk?"

"I can sure try. A buddy of mine rigged up a contraption for me, a..."

"Never mind, I wouldn't understand it anyway," I interrupted. "I just need to know what information is on this disk."

"Can you bring it over tonight? Like I said, I'm leaving real early in the morning."

Tonight? I looked over at Drake and the inviting new bed.

"Will it take long?" I asked Todd.

"You never know with this stuff. Could take minutes, could take hours."

Drake rolled his eyes, but nodded to me. "Go ahead," he whispered.

It was still only nine o'clock. Maybe with any luck I'd be home and back in his arms by eleven. After a day at the stick though, I had a feeling his arms would be snuggled around a pillow by then.

I covered the receiver with my hand. "Are you sure?" I asked.

"Yeah, this might be your only chance to get your answers. I'm sleepy anyway. May just go ahead and doze off." He switched on the new TV set with the remote. "Or maybe I'll still be glued to this thing when you get back."

"Okay, Todd, I'll be there right away. Tell me again how to get to your place," I said, reaching for a notepad.

Todd's little duplex in the university area was only about ten minutes away. I'd grabbed my denim jacket, the warmest thing I'd moved to the office yet, and brought Rusty along for security. He waited in the car, ears cocked in concern, as I walked up the sidewalk.

Compared with our quiet neighborhood, the university area was hopping like Times Square. Kids this age didn't sleep, at least not at the same hours we did. Rock music blared from the apartment next to Todd's. I pounded on his door in hopes he'd hear me, but he was apparently waiting because he opened it after just one knock.

A huge backpack leaned against a Goodwill sofa just inside the front door, its zippered compartments gaping open, nearly filled with rolls of socks and bunched up T-shirts, along with packets of freeze-dried camp food. A giant-screened TV set played a cartoon show with foul-mouthed little characters mouthing obscenities at their equally foul-mouthed parent characters. I could picture myself as a cartoon girl splatted against the wall if I'd talked to my parents in that tone.

"Hey, Charlie, howsit?"

"Great, Todd. Here's the disk." I pulled out the round can and handed it to him.

"You wanna watch the process? It won't look like much."

"Sure." I followed him into what would have been the duplex's dining area, but looked more like the command center at NASA. Todd's chin-length blond hair swung in front of his face as he bent forward to open the metal box. At fifteen, the nephew of my doctor friend, Linda Casper, was the kind of kid most parents would love to have—too involved with computers and hiking in the mountains to get into drugs, gangs, or crime. Unfortunately, his parents were into those things and he'd ended up in the custody of an uncle who was a university professor at thirty-one. Todd was already talking like the next Bill Gates.

He pulled the old-fashioned disk from its container, murmured something including the word "relic," and pulled the cover off a machine at the far right end of his work table. The thing resembled an old reel-to-reel tape player with a clear hinged plastic cover over the reels. Todd snapped some kind of small adapter onto the disk and tested to see if it would fit the machine. It clicked into place and he pressed a couple of buttons, which set it spinning.

Meanwhile, he pulled out a sliding keyboard drawer connected to his own modern computer setup. He tapped the keys so quickly I couldn't make any sense of the result, but soon his monitor screen was filled with zeros and ones.

"Uh, oh," I said. "That doesn't look like anything."

"Oh, no, it's just what we wanted. It means the new computer is reading the text on the old disk."

"Really?"

"Well, we can't read it, but this baby can." He lovingly patted the CPU on the floor beside his feet. "Just give it a few minutes."

The rows of print on the monitor began to scroll so fast I couldn't look at it without getting woozy, so I stared around the room instead. Todd's uncle had indulged him with every conceivable piece of computer equipment. Besides the state of the art CPU and monitor, he had the latest in both color ink jet and laser printers, a top quality scanner, and several other pieces I didn't even recognize. It was all wired together with about twelve miles of cable, plugged into the old house's probably overloaded electrical circuits.

"All done," he announced, like he was accustomed to doing this every day of the week. He popped a standard sized diskette out of his computer and handed it to me.

"This is it?" I asked.

"Yep, converted to ASCII text. You should be able to read it on any computer now."

"Wow, I imagined it would be a lot more difficult than this."

"It's all code. Just a matter of converting it to a new readable format."

"What do I owe you, Todd?"

"Well, at my usual consulting fee of four thousand dollars an hour…" he grinned. "How about a hot fudge sundae after I get back from my trip?"

"It's a deal," I said, pulling two twenties from my purse. "Meanwhile, you might need some extra food during your travels. Take this. And you still get the sundae."

He disconnected my old disk from the fancy contraption,

placed it back in the can, and handed it back to me. I stuffed it, along with the new disk, down into my purse.

Outside, the wind had picked up, taking on a wintery chill, signalling the end of our warm October days. Rusty greeted me through the car window, pawing at the door handle from the inside. I unlocked the door and had to shove at his chest to get him to move to his own seat. Finally, convinced that I hadn't brought food, he moved over. According to the dashboard clock, it was only a little past ten. Maybe I could get home before Drake was too sound asleep.

I pulled into the well-lit heavily trafficked Central Avenue. Gradually the boom-box traffic noise dimmed as I traveled west and made the turn toward the old Victorian.

THIRTY-THREE

THE OLD HOUSE was dark except for the night lamp burning on Sally's desk downstairs, and quiet except for the low murmur of the television in our new bedroom accompanied by Drake's rhythmic soft snore. I held Rusty's collar so he wouldn't disturb Drake and pulled the bedroom door closed.

Knowing that I wouldn't sleep now anyway, I made a mug of hot tea and carried it to Sally's desk. Turning on her computer, I sipped the soothing brew and leaned back in her chair. As soon as the computer had booted, I slipped the new diskette into the drive and looked at it. Todd had named the file TOPSECRET. Interesting.

I started up the word processing program and retrieved the file.

Here we go, I thought.

The file began with some scientific notes. I read the words but didn't know what they were saying. A couple of the strange words that I'd encountered on the blueprints showed up, and I decided later I would retrieve the blueprints from the safe and compare the two.

About ten pages down, there was a letter, addressed to the FBI. It was dated five days before my father's death.

I read eagerly, skimming the paragraphs, until a sentence jumped out at me: "A supervisor in our sector, Jack Cudahy, is involved in the sellout scheme."

Jack Cudahy. The senator who'd so smoothly tried to

blow off my questions. The creep—all along he'd known exactly what I would find. And he was certainly in a position of power, in which he could manage to arrange all the disasters that had happened. Jim Williams's death, my house burning, maybe even Larry Sanchez's sudden downturn and death. I suddenly became aware that all the window blinds on the first floor were open and I felt highly visible sitting there in the small pool of light.

I quickly skimmed the rest of the document, which went back into techno-speak, then went around and closed all the blinds. There wasn't anything I could do with the information tonight, I decided, so I shut down the computer and locked the old and new disks back in Ron's safe.

Upstairs, I brushed my teeth in the old-fashioned bathroom, locked the bedroom door from the inside, then slipped out of my clothes and under the covers next to Drake's warm body. Rusty quickly adopted my Oriental rug as his new bed and was soon snoring away. I lay under the smooth new sheets with my eyes wide open.

The names and faces kept racing through my mind. If Jack Cudahy was behind the plane crash, why? What did he get out of it? And who helped him, because certainly one man would have a hard time pulling off the crash, covering up the investigation, and then following all my movements over the past days and weeks. I pictured George Myers with his arrogant attitude, Harvey Taylor with his polished good looks, or Wendel Patterson—retired now and seemingly harmless, but what had he been doing fifteen years ago?

Gradually, I drifted into a light sleep, but the new bed was harder than the old comfy one, and I kept being aware of tinking sounds in the radiator pipes and creaking noises in the old house. A digital clock on the front of the new television set told me it was now after midnight. At two I awoke, sure that I'd heard creaking on the old stairs leading up from the reception area. By three I'd become convinced that it was my imagination, and at five I awoke to the sounds of tree branches scraping in the wind against the window panes. Groaning, I rolled over into Drake's arms and we managed to keep each other occupied for the next hour.

"Why don't you snuggle in and sleep a couple more hours?" he mumbled into my hair.

"Ummm, tempting. But I'm too wide awake. I think I'll make some coffee and read the rest of that disk." I kissed him soundly. "But you stay in if you'd like. Make some noise when you want me to bring you coffee."

The hardwood floor was icy when my bare feet touched it. I pulled on my socks from yesterday and reminded myself that a pair of slippers might be a good purchase. I pulled on sweat pants and shirt and ran a brush through my hair. Rusty followed me downstairs and I opened the back door for him.

The kitchen linoleum was even colder than the wood floors so, after putting the coffee brewer to work, I searched out the automatic thermostat we'd installed a few years ago. It was fine to keep the place minimally heated at night when we didn't come in until nine o'clock, but living here, the situation was different. I located the gadget and reset it so the old heater in the basement would fire up earlier in the mornings.

Back at Sally's desk, coffee and a roll at my side, I re-inserted the TOPSECRET diskette. Again, my father's words filled the screen. After the letter to the FBI director, there were pages of notes. Evidence that he'd gathered proving Cudahy's culpability. Evidence that showed how Jack Cudahy, as department supervisor, had taken the research done by his co-workers and subversively channeled it to our enemies.

Dad had, as always been meticulous in his own research. He'd named Cudahy's contacts and outlined the chain of espionage, showing just how the documents had moved from one person to another within the spy ring. All this was spelled out in the ten-page letter to the FBI.

My stomach rose to my throat as I read the names. Some were unknown to me, at least by their Russian names, but many were household names here in New Mexico. Wasn't this one a city councilor about ten years back? Killed in a car accident, as I remembered. And there was the prominent Santa Fe family that regularly made headlines with its charitable contributions. One of their daughters had been kidnapped and murdered in the early '70s I thought. A sharp pain twisted at my gut.

Conspiracy? Those things really only happen in the movies, don't they?

My mind raced back over the events of the past few weeks. Jim Williams's murder. The break-ins at Hannah's house, our house, this office. The fire that nearly destroyed our home. It all pointed toward this disk. Cudahy knew he'd never be absolutely safe until this evidence was gone. But how did he know he hadn't already gotten it? How did he know it didn't burn up in the fire? A crawling feeling crept up my legs. I rubbed my hands vigorously over my thighs to make it go away.

I glanced over at the closed miniblinds at the windows. Was someone watching my every move? I thought of the others who might be in danger now—Elsa, Todd...Drake! Oh my God, they'd already sabotaged one aircraft. I couldn't lose the most important person in my life to this...this... *plot*.

Rusty! I dashed back to the kitchen and flung open the

back door, relief flooding over me as my red-brown buddy pushed his way in and headed straight for his food bowl.

Unable to sit still, I poured another cup of coffee. I held its warmth between my frigid hands and paced the hallway. What to do? Think, Charlie. Obviously, my scrawny neck and the people I cared about meant nothing to these guys.

Think. Think.

I'm still gonna get that file, the telephone voice had said.

Okay, that means he knows there's a file out here. Probably thinks there's a printed version of what's on this disk. Probably thought he'd destroyed the evidence, along with a planeload of people, fifteen years ago, and it was only when Jim Williams began poking around again that he realized that some evidence still exists.

My mind reeled with the implications—connections in the NTSB offices (still today), connections in the FBI (back then, and possibly still today), a U.S. Congressman at the heart of it, able to pull any strings he wanted to. Who would I turn the disk over to? Who could be trusted?

THIRTY-FOUR

A WAVE OF NAUSEA washed over me. My head felt light and my stomach rolled. Too much caffeine, too many emotions, and too little food. I sat gingerly in Sally's chair and reached for the untouched danish roll. It tasted like cardboard but I made myself eat it. My stomach settled almost immediately. I shook my hands to make them calm down.

I wanted to wake Drake and talk this over. We needed to make a plan. Paranoia rolled in, reminding me of my childhood nightmare where a steam roller is after me and I'm running and running but can't outdistance it. I took a deep swig of the hot coffee and stood up.

Okay. There's safety in numbers, I thought. How could I get this information out to the greatest number of people as quickly as possible. Once I was no longer the keeper of the secret, at least there'd be no benefit in coming after me, my friends, or my family. If I could just make the contents of the disk public, then Cudahy and his cohorts would have to answer for it.

I sat down at Sally's computer and began typing. I told it all, from the suspicious nature of the plane crash to Jim Williams's death and the disappearance of his files, to the arson at my home. At the end of my own letter, I appended my father's file, creating one document of twenty-five pages.

Now, what to do with it? I thought about calling the news

departments of the two Albuquerque papers, but discarded the idea. The names involved were too locally prominent. Local news people would either not believe me and dump my story in the trash, or they'd call the people involved to verify it, which would have the combined effect of having the whole thing emphatically denied and putting a death warrant out on me. I wasn't happy with either of those scenarios.

At one time, Ron had taken a case for a public relations firm, doing a background check on one of their clients. One of the publicists there was a woman who'd single-handedly made the career of a local author when she planted the story of the author's exposé book on one of the hottest fad diets in the country. The publicist, Stephanie Claridge, and I had hit it off instantly, probably because I'd gushed over her perception in getting the timing of this particular story just right.

Would she remember me now? Would she have the right contacts in the right places to get this story out? Could I trust her?

It was still only seven o'clock. No, she wouldn't be in the office this early. Think, Charlie.

I called her office number and got a machine. Looked in the phone book, but didn't find her listed. Somehow, I seemed to remember that she was married and her husband's last name was different. Damn!

I called the office again and spoke to the machine.

"Stephanie, this is Charlie Parker from RJP Investigations. I hope you remember me." How much information should I give over the phone? The paranoia crept closer. "Listen, Stephanie, I've got a very important story that needs to get out nationally. I mean, *really* important. I know you can do this. I'm going to e-mail it to you. It's a fairly long document and I hope it'll come through okay. Please don't tell anyone about this until you're able to get it out nationally. *Don't* just take it to the local papers. Uh, maybe you should just call me when you get this message and I can explain better. But if you can't reach me, break the story anyway. Something may have happened to me.''

My voice rose shakily at the end and I hung up wondering if I'd just made a big mistake. She didn't know me that well and I probably just came across sounding like a nut case. I took a deep breath.

Now if I could just remember how to attach a document to an e-mail message. I logged onto Sally's e-mail program and composed a short note to let Stephanie know that this was the document I'd referred to in my phone message. I repeated the need to get it out urgently, just in case someone in her office was in on the plot and erased her voice mail messages. Oh, God, I really was becoming a nut case.

The modem whirred and squawked and I clicked a series of commands. At last, fairly confident that the message was in the competent hands of cyberspace, I shut down Sally's computer and locked the disks back in Ron's safe.

Still no sound from Drake, but I felt antsy. I needed to get out of here for awhile. The sun had not quite cleared Sandia Peak yet, but the sky was pearly gray. I looked around and spotted my running shoes where I'd kicked them off the night before, under the kitchen table. A quick walk around the block would help clear my head and then I'd see what I could rustle up for a real breakfast after Drake woke up.

Rusty watched as I tied my shoe laces, not missing a clue in the preparations for the walk.

"Yeah, you get to go," I assured him. I jammed my keyring down into the pocket of my sweats and locked the kitchen door behind me. Rusty raced ahead down the st into the back yard. I'd just reached the bottom step when two men stepped out in front of me.

THIRTY-FIVE

THEY WORE DARK SUITS and ties and wraparound sunglasses, even though the sun wasn't out yet. Proverbial bad guys. I froze.

"Good morning, Charlie." A third man stepped around the corner of the building. Jack Cudahy.

Even paranoids have enemies. For some reason, the stupid phrase was the first thing that popped into my head.

"I hear you've been a very busy lady," Cudahy crooned in his oily voice.

Rusty stood at my side, the hair on the back of his neck bristling.

One of the clichés in black spoke first. "Hey, boy," he addressed the dog. "Wanna go for a ride?" His voice was upbeat and friendly. "Yeah, hey, let's go."

Magic words to a dog. He waved his tail back and forth.

"No—" I started. But he kept up the friendly chatter, drowning out my voice. I reached for Rusty's collar but the other man displayed a gun, aimed at my midsection. I stepped back.

"Come on boy, let's go for a ride," the man wheedled. He headed toward my Jeep, his step light and bouncy. "Okay, here we go," he called as he opened the car door.

Rusty followed gladly and hopped into the back seat. The man slammed the door, leaving the dog wondering when the ride would happen.

"Okay, Charlie, now *we're* going for a ride," Cudahy said conversationally.

The man who'd trapped Rusty in the Jeep grabbed my right arm roughly. Rusty began to bark, muffled through the vehicle's closed windows.

"Drake!" I screamed.

Everything went black.

MY HEAD HAD NEVER hurt so bad. I floated up through layers of consciousness and back down again.

Pounding, pounding.

Rocking, rocking.

My stomach lurched and I heaved but couldn't throw up. I couldn't get my mouth open. My eyelids felt stuck together but I couldn't seem to coordinate my arms well enough to reach up to rub them.

Air—I needed air. My mouth was sealed shut and my nose felt crusted over. I snorted, trying to clear it. Finally drew a trickle of oxygen. My eyes worked again at opening. It didn't help. All I could see was darkness with an eerie red glow that dimmed and brightened. My head felt like someone was repeatedly smacking it with something hard and metal. I gave in and drifted back to sleep.

When I opened my eyes again, the rocking had stopped. It occurred to me that I was in the trunk of a car. We'd been moving but now we weren't.

Three men. Two of them had grabbed me. The other was someone too important to do the rough work. My brain hurt too much to figure it out.

The world wavered, up, down, still.

"So, you're awake!" A loud male voice hit me at the same time a blinding light filled the world. My eyes slammed shut.

"Poke her! See if she's still alive," a second voice commanded. It was the oily voice, but it wasn't bothering to be polite-sounding now.

"She's alive," the other man snarled. "Too bad."

"What are you gonna do now?" a third voice whined.

The blinding light left my face and I dared a peek through my lashes. The trunk of the car stood open with the three men outlined against a night sky. No city lights nearby.

Night? How much time had passed? I wanted to ask questions, but my mouth still wouldn't work. I realized it was covered with duct tape. I tried stretching my arms and legs but they too were tightly bound. I decided my best defense for the moment was to lay quietly, trying to appear unconscious.

"Shit, I don't know," the Congressman said. "You two were supposed to get rid of her during the day, not drive around with her until you got *me* back into it. Can't you fuck-ups do anything right?"

"Hey, I wanted to off her this morning," the mean voice growled again. "Wimpy here wouldn't go along with it. Said you wouldn't like it, sir."

"Okay, okay," Cudahy said. "He's right. I didn't want to kill her unless we needed to. But you guys never did come up with those documents. How do we know exactly what she found unless we can question her?"

"Oh, boss, I'd like to *question* her," the mean one said. I tightened up at the thought of what he meant by that.

"Okay, look. We know she found some kind of computer disk. We know she had that geeky kid copy it for her. You take care of him?" He waved away the answer. "The question is, who else did she share it with? She came right home last night, didn't see anyone else but the boyfriend, then got up this morning and started out for a walk. Didn't have the disk on her, so it's gotta be somewhere in that office."

"We tossed the office before," the whiney one said. "There wadn't nothing there."

"Well, it's the only place she's been," Cudahy explained, as if to a six-year-old, "so it has to be there. Now, tonight I want you to go back there and look again."

"What about the boyfriend? He'll be there."

"Well, you know what to do about *that*." Smooth, oily.

Think, Charlie. I had to figure out how to get myself out of a mile or two of duct tape, overpower three large men who had at least one gun, get back into the city, and be sure Drake was safe. And I'd forgotten to take my vitamins this morning. Shit!

I tuned back into their conversation.

"I say first we dump her, boss," the mean voice was saying. "What's gonna happen if we get stopped driving around and she makes a noise?"

"With Congressional plates on the car?" Cudahy sneered, "Not a damn thing. The cops would probably wink and nudge, and think we're into some kind of cute sex games. Might even want to join in."

Now I really wanted to throw up. Partly from the thought of sex games with a slime like Jack Cudahy and partly because the cops overlooking it was probably true.

The men were still chuckling over Cudahy's little scenario when he slapped one of them hard across the face.

"You jerks! Get her out of the car. I'm not having my reputation smeared at this stage of the game. It's cost me a lot to get this far."

My teeth clenched behind the duct tape barrier. *Cost you a lot?* How about all the people whose lives you've taken, whose homes you've taken?

"Look, she's awake now."

Yeah, my eyes must have been flashing fire.

"Okay, get her to the edge of the trunk here, then cut

her legs loose so she can walk. Take her out into the desert and do it, then get your tails back here quick," Cudahy ordered. "I'm gonna be in the car, and I'm seeing none of this."

Rough hands pulled my legs toward the opening. The second man leaned over and reached for my shoulders. I saw the flash of a knife blade. In an instant I knew what I had to do.

The moment the duct tape at my ankles was free, I kicked out, going first for the man who had the gun in one hand the knife in the other. Both weapons flew, but I couldn't tell how far.

"Hey!" Mean Voice clenched his two hands together, rubbing the bruised knuckles.

I went for Cudahy next. Both feet right to the gut, but he was quick. I barely grazed him before he leaped out of reach.

The effort of kicking outward threw me off balance and I toppled back into the trunk, landing on my shoulder blades and whacking my head against the spare tire.

Whiney Voice looked like he didn't quite know what to do next and I took advantage of the moment by rolling sideways and kneeing him in the chin. His head smacked the trunk's hinge and his eyes rolled back. I got myself up on one elbow and managed to shift my weight again so my legs were free and kicking wildly.

I could see Mean Voice grappling on the ground for his weapons, but so far he hadn't come up with one. I threw myself forward and came out of the trunk, landing on my knees in the dirt. I was on my feet in a split second.

Cudahy was doing the manly thing, trying to dial his cell phone. What was he going to do, call 911? I kicked him in the balls. He dropped the phone and went down on his knees.

I spun and looked around me for the first time. The lights of Albuquerque glowed in the distance, with the Sandia Mountains behind them. We were on the west mesa, beyond the newest housing developments, but apparently near enough to a road that the Lincoln Towncar hadn't had any trouble getting here.

The previous evening's changing weather had moved in full force. A bitter winter wind whipped across the open mesa, driving dust and particles of trash against the luxury car. We weren't *that* far from civilization. Low gray clouds blocked the stars, allowing the moon to peek out occasionally, but quickly hiding it again. The glow of the city bounced off the light clouds, casting an orange aura over the area and providing the only illumination out here in the far reaches.

Cudahy's flashlight, which had blinded me so badly when they first opened the trunk, lay on the car's back bumper, aimed toward the city, fortunately of no help to the goon who was still scrambling on the ground for a weapon.

All I could think was, Run!

So I did.

I put the car between the men and myself, running toward the city as efficiently as one possibly can over sand and sagebrush, on legs that have been bound for more than twelve hours, with arms tied in back with duct tape and gasping for air through one semi-clear nostril.

I made it about twenty yards before I heard the distinctive click of a gun being cocked.

I almost stopped, having seen far too many TV movies, but clear thinking took over and I realized that was sure death. Instead, I doubled my speed. I tripped on a clump of cactus and rolled to the ground just as something sizzled past my left shoulder.

It would be a matter of seconds before he'd catch up with me and finish me off. I struggled desperately for a plan, when the ground gave way beneath me and I began tumbling downward into hell.

THIRTY-SIX

I CAME TO A STOP abruptly with a whoosh as I bounced off a huge fluffy chamisa bush and landed in a mound of soft sand. Stars twinkled in front of my eyes, but they were not the celestial kind.

Somehow, during the tumble, my arms had done a shoulder-wrenching inside-out with my legs, and I now had my hands in front of me. I grabbed at the duct tape on my face and ripped it from my mouth, hogging huge lungfuls of air at the same time.

My head pounded and my ears rang, but I was alive.

Maybe not for long. I looked to the edge of the arroyo into which I'd just fallen and there stood the goon who'd shot at me, outlined against a curiously light place in the sky. He hadn't spotted me yet. His body twisted from one side to the other, looking for a spot to aim the gun. With my light gray sweat clothes it wouldn't take long.

I raised my wrists to my mouth, working to find the end of the duct tape with my teeth. The pounding, throbbing sound in my head grew louder. The tape tasted awful. I closed my eyes and worked at it by feel. Was just finding an edge I could bite onto when it occurred to me what the throbbing was.

I looked again at the arroyo's edge, just in time to see a bright spotlight trained on the goon.

Tears sprung to my eyes as I recognized the blue and white JetRanger overhead.

Another helicopter, APD's OH-58, hovered into view. A voice over a loudspeaker yelled, "Put down that weapon!"

The man in black aimed his gun toward the JetRanger, but realized the futility of it. Slumping and dropping the weapon, he raised his hands in the air. The APD machine took over with its spotlight and Drake hovered over the arroyo until his spot found me dancing and waving madly with my two arms still tied together.

He edged eastward, illuminating the wide dry riverbed, landing in the center of it. I waited a moment for the upwash of dust to clear, then ran toward him. I reached the pilot's door just as he yanked his headset off and swung his leg over the cyclic to jump to the ground. I buried my head in his shoulder and let my sobs of joy merge with his.

"Could we hurry it up a little?" a voice shouted from the back seat.

I raised my head and noticed that Drake had three passengers.

Drake nodded his chin toward the man who had shouted. "In a second!" he shouted back. To me, he said, "Vic Ratcliffe, from the *Journal*. He caught up with me at the hangar—said some big story was breaking over the wire services...I didn't know what he was talking about, but let him hitch a ride. Guess I better get him up there to the action."

Ron occupied the front passenger seat, and he hopped out as I approached, enveloped me in a big hug, and offered me the seat. But the other backseat passenger was quite anxious that I join him, so I told Ron to keep his spot.

Rusty licked my face as I threw my arms around his furry neck. The *Journal* man snapped our picture. I edged Rusty to the middle seat and I latched my door and pulled my shoulder and lap belts into place. Pulling a headset from the compartment behind my right shoulder, I put it on and adjusted the microphone.

"All set?" Drake asked.

Three heads nodded. Rusty was too busy burrowing his muzzle against my leg. The turbine picked up speed and we lifted gently above the rim of the arroyo. Air traffic had picked up considerably as all three TV stations' helicopters were now on scene. The APD ship had kept the black limo in its spotlight until three squad cars arrived, and it was preparing to depart the area.

Drake radioed the police and got clearance to land a short distance from the scene, which, in the glare of three helicopter spotlights and headlamps from three squad cars, showed Congressman Jack Cudahy in that most undignified "spread 'em" position. This was going to look really good on the ten o'clock news.

Our onboard newsman was out the door before the skids had quite touched down. I could tell Drake wanted to say something, but he let the guy go.

"You guys doing okay back there?" he asked over the intercom, grinning at Rusty and me.

I just nodded.

"They're gonna want to talk to you, Charlie," he advised. "Are you up to it?"

"Can I fake a fainting spell or something?" I joked.

"You can do anything you want."

"Let's get out of here."

We lifted off before the uniformed officers quite figured out that their material witness was getting away.

THIRTY-SEVEN

THREE NIGHTS LATER, Mr. and Mrs. Drake Langston raise
new crystal champagne flutes to each other.

We were sitting cross-legged on our new bed in my up
stairs office of the old Victorian. Not exactly where I'd pic
tured spending my wedding night, but after one day of grill
ing about my kidnap ordeal by the police and another da
of dodging and fielding questions by reporters, I didn't hav
the energy to drive even to Santa Fe for a real weddin
night in a real hotel so here we were.

Jack Cudahy and George Myers would face arraignmer
tomorrow. Turns out Myers was feeding the Congressma
even more inside information from Sandia for years vi
Kathleen Smathers who shared her favors equally betwee
the two, in return for her lavish lifestyle at Tanoan. An
she'd been the one who packed the gift-wrapped explosiv
package in Joe Smathers's bag. They'd all been an *à tro*
item for years.

Already Cudahy's PR people were appealing to the voter
in their best roundabout-dodge'em political-speak to cor
vince people that he'd really done nothing wrong. Betwee
the evidence on the disk, which Stephanie Claridge ha
beautifully printed out and faxed to every major new
source in the country, and the irrefutable news coverage c
his honor spread-eagled over the hood of his limo at th
kidnap scene, I didn't think he had a snowball's chance c

getting away with this one. But you just never know with voters. The sex scandal aspect of it probably assured he *would* be reelected. Here in New Mexico I've seen some pretty incredible stuff. I wondered if a person could actually serve in the U.S. Congress at the same time they're serving behind bars...I'd have to look it up someday.

The arson investigation met a swift end when Whiney Voice confessed to the deed, and the arson investigator himself called me to apologize for even *thinking* I was involved. A small consolation, considering we still didn't have a house.

And Kent Taylor informed me that Mean Voice had admitted hiring the tall man in the black Stetson to blow away Jim Williams. Kent was only too happy to return Drake's gun to me at the wedding and to forgive the fact that I'd never gone by to give a statement after the shooting.

The wedding? Oh, yeah. Well, we discovered that you can get a marriage license at the courthouse right across from the police station, and that judges are sometimes still in their offices after six p.m.

Ron's longtime contention that a P.I.'s work is mostly done on the telephone was proven out when he managed to get Elsa Higgins, Sally and her husband Ross, Hannah Simmons, Kent Taylor, Pedro and Concha, Linda Casper and Todd the computer whiz (who had indeed escaped the killers—the two thugs had been bragging to please the boss—although his trip to Mexico had been cut short by a case of Montezuma's revenge), and of course Ron himself and his three kids downtown and into the judge's chambers for the ceremony, all with less than an hour's notice. Elsa bustled in carrying a tissue-wrapped package for me that contained the ivory lace dress my mother had worn as her travel outfit after her own wedding. I slipped into it in the ladies room. Sally and Ross brought the crystal champagne flutes, and

Pedro and Concha's restaurant contributed a bottle of Asti Spumanti.

Being a media darling has its benefits. Having my face splashed all over the news—including my kidnapping, the fact that I solved a fifteen year old plane crash, a murder, an arson, and several burglaries, not to mention putting a crooked politician out of office—has led to certain privileges being granted. For instance, Rusty was allowed in the judge's chambers to attend the wedding. And our wedding photos were taken gratis by the staffs of both Albuquerque newspapers. Of course, they may turn out to look more like mug shots, but that too will be a happy memory someday.

All in all, it was a perfect wedding.

We're thinking about a honeymoon trip, but maybe later. Christmas time might be nice.

For now, we're just happy to be together, realizing that having each other, having a life together and a home that we'll go back to someday—these are things we very nearly might have lost forever.

Lost in Austin

A Tony Kozol Mystery

When a broken arm sidelines the guitarist for a popular country band, struggling musician Tony Kozol gets a gig as the temporary replacement. But when the band arrives in Austin for a week at the Southwest Music Conference—murder takes center stage.

The victim was a roadie with the group, and Tony soon spots an unsettling connection to the band—especially when the body of a pretty young groupie is found next. Sounds to Tony like a song in the making: a tale full of heartbreak and woe, longing and desire. It could be a hit. That is, if he lives long enough to write it.

J. R. Ripley

"J. R. Ripley continues to delight."
—*Midwest Book Review*

Available April 2002
at your favorite retail outlet.

 **W❂RLDWIDE LIBRARY®**

WJRR417

FASHION
Victims

SOPHIE DUNBAR

Hollywood's beautiful people turn out for the launch party for a trendy new line of Japanese-inspired ready-to-wear. Husband-and-wife production team Ava and Frank Bernstein hope to get a commercial deal out of the swanky soiree. But the party turns out to be murder when the body of a model is found stabbed and strangled.

Yet the real drama unfolds in a torrid soap opera of broken hearts, dirty secrets and big money. As the bodies pile up faster than film on the cutting-room floor, Ava races to find the killer. Because "dying" can mean many things in Hollywood. And Ava doesn't care to experience any of them.

Available April 2002 at your favorite retail outlet.

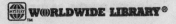

WORLDWIDE LIBRARY®

WSD418